MAGISTERIUM

THE IRON TRIAL

www.magisteriumtrials.com

MAGISTERIUM

THE IRON TRIAL

HOLLY BLACK ✕ CASSANDRA CLARE

DOUBLEDAY

MAGISTERIUM: THE IRON TRIAL
A DOUBLEDAY BOOK 978 085 753249 7
TRADE PAPERBACK 978 085 753250 3

First published in the United States by Scholastic Press.

Published in Great Britain by Doubleday,
an imprint of Random House Children's Publishers UK
A Random House Group Company

This edition published 2014

1 3 5 7 9 10 8 6 4 2

The Random House Group Limited supports the Forest Stewardship Council® (FSC®),
the leading international forest-certification organisation. Our books carrying the
FSC label are printed on FSC®-certified paper. FSC is the only forest-certification
scheme supported by the leading environmental organisations, including Greenpeace.
Our paper procurement policy can be found at www.randomhouse.co.uk/environment

Set in Adobe Caslon

Doubleday Books are published by Random House Children's Publishers UK,
61–63 Uxbridge Road, London W5 5SA

www.randomhousechildrens.co.uk
www.totallyrandombooks.co.uk
www.randomhouse.co.uk

Addresses for companies within The Random House Group Limited
can be found at: www.randomhouse.co.uk/offices.htm

THE RANDOM HOUSE GROUP Limited Reg. No. 954009

A CIP catalogue record for this book is available from the British Library.

Printed and bound in Great Britain by Clays Ltd, St Ives plc

For Sebastian Fox Black,
about whom no one has written any
threatening messages in ice.

↑ ≈ △ ○ @

PROLOGUE

FROM A DISTANCE, the man struggling up the white face of the glacier might have looked like an ant crawling slowly up the side of a dinner plate. The shantytown of La Rinconada was a collection of scattered specks far below him, the wind increasing as his elevation did, blowing powdery gusts of snow into his face and freezing the damp tendrils of his black hair. Despite his amber goggles, he winced at the brightness of the reflected sunset.

Still, the man was not afraid of falling, although he was using no ropes or belay lines, only crampons and a single ice axe. His name was Alastair Hunt and he was a mage. He shaped and molded the frozen substance of the glacier under his hands as he climbed. Handholds and footholds appeared as he inched his way upward.

By the time he reached the cave, midway up the glacier, he was half frozen and fully exhausted from bending his will to tame the worst of the elements. It sapped his energy to exert his magic so continuously, but he hadn't dared slow down.

The cave itself opened like a mouth in the side of the mountain, impossible to see from above or below. He pulled himself over its edge and took a deep, jagged breath, cursing himself for not getting there sooner, for allowing himself to be tricked. In La Rinconada, the people had seen the explosion and whispered under their breaths about what it meant, the fire inside the ice.

Fire inside the ice. It had to be a distress signal . . . or an attack. The cave was full of mages too old to fight or too young, the injured and the sick, mothers of very young children who could not be left — like Alastair's own wife and son. They had been hidden away here, in one of the most remote places on the earth.

Master Rufus had insisted that otherwise they would be vulnerable, hostages to fortune, and Alastair had trusted him. Then, when the Enemy of Death hadn't shown up on the field to face the mages' champion, the Makar girl upon whom they'd pinned all their hopes, Alastair had realized his mistake. He'd gotten to La Rinconada as fast as he could, flying most of his way on the back of an air elemental. From there, he'd made his way on foot, since the Enemy's control of elementals was unpredictable and strong. The higher he'd climbed, the more frightened he'd become.

Let them be all right, he thought to himself as he stepped inside the cave. *Please let them be all right.*

There should have been the sound of children wailing. There should have been the low buzz of nervous conversation and the hum of subdued magic. Instead, there was only the howl of the wind as it swept over the desolate peak of the mountain. The cave walls were white ice, pocked with red and brown where blood had splattered and melted in patches. Alastair pulled off his goggles and dropped them on the ground, pushing farther into the passage, drawing on the dregs of his power to steady himself.

The walls of the cave gave off an eerie phosphorescent glow. Away from the entrance, it was the only light he had to see by, which probably explained why he stumbled over the first body and nearly fell to his knees. Alastair jerked away with a yell, then winced as he heard his own shout echo back to him. The fallen mage was burned beyond recognition, but she wore the leather wristband with the large hammered piece of copper that marked her as a second-year Magisterium student. She couldn't have been older than thirteen.

You should be used to death by now, he told himself. They'd been at war with the Enemy for a decade that sometimes felt like a century. At first, it had seemed impossible — one young man, even one of the Makaris, planning to conquer death itself. But as the Enemy increased in power, and his army of the Chaos-ridden grew, the threat had become inescapably dire . . . culminating in this pitiless slaughter of the most helpless, the most innocent.

Alastair got to his feet and pushed deeper into the cave, desperately looking for one face above all. He forced his way past the bodies of elderly Masters from the Magisterium and Collegium, children of friends and acquaintances, and mages who had been wounded in earlier battles. Among them lay the broken bodies of the Chaos-ridden, their swirling eyes darkened forever. Though the mages had been unprepared, they must have put up quite a fight to have slain so many of the Enemy's forces. Horror churning in his gut, his fingers and toes numb, Alastair staggered through it all . . . until he saw her.

Sarah.

He found her lying in the very back, against a cloudy wall of ice. Her eyes were open, staring at nothing. The irises looked murky and her lashes were clotted with ice. Leaning down, he brushed his fingers over her cooling cheek. He drew in his breath sharply, his sob cutting through the air.

But where was their son? Where was Callum?

A dagger was clutched in Sarah's right hand. She had excelled at shaping ore summoned deep from the ground. She'd made the dagger herself in their last year at the Magisterium. It had a name: Semiramis. Alastair knew how Sarah had treasured that blade. *If I have to die, I want to die holding my own weapon*, she'd always told him. But he hadn't wanted her to die at all.

His fingers grazed her cold cheek.

A cry made him whip around. In this cave full of death and silence, a cry.

A child.

He turned, searching frantically for the source of the thready wail. It seemed to be coming from closer to the cave entrance. He plunged back the way he had come, stumbling over bodies, some frozen stiff as statues — until suddenly, another familiar face stared up at him from the carnage.

Declan. Sarah's brother, wounded in the last battle. He appeared to have been choked to death by a particularly cruel use of air magic; his face was blue, his eyes shot with broken blood vessels. One of his arms was outflung, and just underneath it, protected from the icy cave floor by a woven blanket, was Alastair's infant son. As he stared in amazement, the boy opened his mouth and gave another thin, mewling cry.

As if in trance, shaking with relief, Alastair bent and lifted his child. The boy looked up at him with wide gray eyes and opened his mouth to scream again. When the blanket fell aside, Alastair could see why. The baby's left leg hung at a terrible angle, like a snapped tree branch.

Alastair tried to call up earth magic to heal the boy but had only enough power left to take away some of the pain. Heart racing, he rewrapped his son tightly in the blanket and wound his way back through the cave to where Sarah lay. Holding the baby as if she could see him, he knelt down beside her body.

"Sarah," he whispered, tears thick in his throat. "I'll tell him how you died protecting him. I will raise him to remember how brave you were."

Her eyes stared at him, blank and pale. He held the child more closely to his side and reached to take Semiramis from her hand. When he did, he saw that the ice near the blade was strangely marked, as if she had clawed at it while dying. But the marks were too deliberate for that. As he bent closer, he realized they were words — words his wife had carved into the cave ice with the last of her dying strength.

As he read them, he felt them like three hard blows to the stomach.

KILL THE CHILD

CHAPTER ONE

CALLUM HUNT WAS a legend in his little North Carolina town, but not in a good way. Famous for driving off substitute teachers with sarcastic remarks, he also specialized in annoying principals, hall monitors, and lunch ladies. Guidance counselors, who always started out wanting to help him (the poor boy's mother had died, after all) wound up hoping he'd never darken the doors of their offices again. There was nothing more embarrassing than not being able to come up with a snappy comeback to an angry twelve-year-old.

Call's perpetual scowl, messy black hair, and suspicious gray eyes were well known to his neighbors. He liked to skateboard, although it had taken him a while to get the hang of it; several cars still bore dings from some of his earlier attempts. He was often seen lurking outside the windows of the comic book store, the arcade, and the video game store. Even the mayor knew him. It would have been hard to forget him after he'd snuck past the clerk at the local pet store during the May Day Parade and taken a naked mole rat destined to be fed to a boa constrictor. He'd felt sorry for the blind and wrinkly creature that seemed unable to help itself — and, in the name of fairness, he'd also released all the white mice who would have been next on the snake's dinner menu.

He'd never expected the mice to run amok under the feet of the paraders, but mice aren't very smart. He also hadn't expected the onlookers to run from the mice, but people aren't too smart either, as Call's father had explained after it was all over. It wasn't Call's fault that the parade had been ruined, but everyone — especially the mayor — acted like it was. On top of that, his father had made Call give back the mole rat.

Call's father didn't approve of stealing.

As far as he was concerned, it was almost as bad as magic.

↑ ≈ △ ○ @

Callum fidgeted in the stiff chair in front of the principal's office, wondering if he'd be back at school tomorrow and if anyone would miss him if he wasn't. Again and again, he went over all the various ways he was supposed to mess up on the mage's test — ideally, as spectacularly as possible. His dad had listed the options for failure again and again: *Make your mind totally blank. Or concentrate on something that's the opposite of what those monsters want. Or focus your mind on someone else's test instead of your own.* Call rubbed his calf, which had been stiff and painful in class that morning; it was that way sometimes. The taller he grew, the more it seemed to hurt. At least the physical part of the mage's test — whatever it was — would be easy to fail.

Just down the hall, he could hear other kids in gym class, their sneakers squeaking on the shining wood of the floor, their voices raised as they shouted taunts to one another. He wished just once that he got to play. He might not have been as fast as other kids or as able to keep his balance, but he was full of restless energy. He was exempt from a gym requirement because of his leg; even in elementary school, when he'd tried to run or jump or climb at recess, one of the monitors would come over and remind him that he needed to slow down before he hurt himself. If he kept at it, they would make him come inside.

As though a couple of bruises were the most awful thing that could happen to someone. As though his leg was going to get worse.

Call sighed and stared out through the glass doors of the school to where his father would be pulling up soon. He owned the kind of car you couldn't miss, a 1937 Rolls-Royce Phantom, painted bright silver. Nobody else in town had anything like it. Call's father ran an antique store on Main Street called Now and Again; there was nothing he liked more than taking old broken things and making them look shiny and new. To keep the car running, he had to tinker with it almost every weekend. And he was constantly asking Call to wash it and put some kind of weird old car wax on it, to keep it from rusting.

The Rolls-Royce worked perfectly . . . unlike Call. He looked down at his sneakers as he tapped his feet against the floor. When he was wearing jeans like this, you couldn't tell there was anything wrong with his leg, but you could sure tell the minute he stood up and started walking. He'd had surgery after surgery since he was a baby, and all sorts of physical therapy, but nothing had really helped. He still walked with a sliding limp, like he was trying to get his footing on a boat that was rolling from side to side.

When he was younger, he'd sometimes played that he was a pirate, or even just a brave sailor with a peg leg, going down with a sinking ship after a long cannon fight. He'd played pirates and ninjas, cowboys and alien explorers.

But not ever any game that involved magic.

Never that.

He heard the rumble of an engine and began to rise to his feet — only to return to the bench in annoyance. It wasn't his dad, just an ordinary red Toyota. A moment later, Kylie Myles, one of the other students in his grade, hurried past him, a teacher beside her.

"Good luck at your ballet tryouts," Ms. Kemal told her, and started back to her classroom.

"Right, thanks," Kylie said, then looked over at Call oddly, as though she were evaluating him. Kylie *never* looked at Call. That was one of her defining characteristics, along with her shining blond hair and unicorn backpack. When they were in the halls together, her gaze slid past him like he was invisible.

With an even weirder and more surprising half wave, she headed out to the Toyota. He could see both her parents in the front seats, looking anxious.

She couldn't be going where he was, could she? She couldn't be going to the Iron Trial. But if she was . . .

He pushed himself off the chair. If she was going, someone should warn her.

Lots of kids think it's about being special, Call's father had said, the disgust in his voice evident. *Their parents do, too. Especially in families where magical ability dates back generations. And some families where the magic has mostly died out see a magical child as hope for a return to power. But it's the children with no magical relatives you should pity most. They're the ones who think it's going to be like it is in the movies.*

It's nothing like the movies.

At that moment, Call's dad pulled up to the school curb with a squeal of brakes, effectively cutting off Call's view of Kylie. Call limped toward the doors and outside, but by the time he made it to the Rolls, the Myles's Toyota was swerving around the corner and out of sight.

So much for warning her.

"Call." His father had gotten out of the car and was leaning against the passenger-side door. His mop of black hair — the same tangly black hair Call had — was going gray at the sides, and he wore a tweed jacket with leather elbow patches, despite the heat. Call often thought that his father looked like Sherlock Holmes in the old BBC show; sometimes people seemed surprised he didn't speak with a British accent. "Are you ready?"

Call shrugged. How could you be ready for something that had the potential to mess up your whole life if you got it wrong? Or right, in this case. "I guess so."

His father pulled the door open. "Good. Get in."

The inside of the Rolls was as spotless as the outside. Call was surprised to find his old pair of crutches thrown into the backseat. He hadn't needed them in years, not since he'd fallen off a jungle gym and twisted his ankle — the ankle on his *good* leg. As Call's father slid into the car and started the engine, Call pointed to them and asked, "What's with those?"

"The worse off you look, the likelier they are to reject you," his father said grimly, glancing behind him as they pulled out of the parking lot.

"That seems like cheating," Call objected.

"Call, people cheat to *win*. You can't cheat to lose."

Call rolled his eyes, letting his dad believe what he wanted. All Call knew for sure was that there was no way he was going to use those crutches if he didn't have to. He didn't want to argue about it, though, not today, when Call's father had already uncharacteristically burned the toast at breakfast and snapped at

Call when he complained about having to go to school just to be removed a couple hours later.

Now his father crouched over the wheel, jaw set and the fingers of his right hand wrapped tightly around the gearshift, changing gears with ineffectual violence.

Call tried to focus his gaze on the trees outside, their leaves just starting to yellow, and to remember everything he knew about the Magisterium. The first time his father had said anything about the Masters and how they chose their apprentices, he'd sat Call down in one of the big leather chairs in his study. Call's elbow had been bandaged and his lip was split from a fight at school, and he'd been in no mood for listening. Besides, his father had looked so serious that Call had gotten scared. And that's the way his father spoke, too, as though he was going to tell Call he had a terrible disease. It turned out the sickness was a potential for magic.

Call had scrunched up in the chair while his father talked. He was used to getting picked on; other kids thought his leg made him an easy target. Usually, he was able to convince them he wasn't. That time, however, there had been a bunch of older boys who'd cornered him behind the shed near the jungle gym on his way home from school. They'd pushed him around and come at him with the usual insults. Callum had learned most people backed down when he put up a fight, so he'd tried to hit the tallest boy. That had been his first mistake. Pretty soon, they had him on the ground, one of them sitting on his knees while another punched him in the face, trying to get him to apologize and admit to being a gimpy clown.

"Sorry for being awesome, losers," Call had said, right before he blacked out.

He must have only been out for a minute, because when he opened his eyes, he could just see the retreating figures of the boys in the distance. They were running away. Call couldn't believe his rejoinder had worked so well.

"That's right," he'd said, sitting up. "You better run!"

Then he'd looked around and seen that the concrete of the playground had cracked open. A long fissure ran from the swings all the way to the shed wall, splitting the small building in half.

He was lying directly in the path of what looked like a mini earthquake.

He'd thought it was the most awesome thing that had ever happened. His father disagreed.

"Magic runs in families," Call's father said. "Not everyone in a family will necessarily have it, but it looks like you might. Unfortunately. I am so sorry, Call."

"So the split in the ground — you're saying I did that?" Call had felt torn between giddy glee and extreme horror, but the glee was winning out. He could feel the corners of his mouth turn up and tried to force them back down. "Is that what mages do?"

"Mages draw on the elements — earth, air, water, fire, and even the void, which is the source of the most powerful and terrible magic of all, chaos magic. They can use magic for many things, including ripping apart the very earth, as you did." His father had nodded to himself. "In the beginning, when magic first comes on, it is very intense. Raw power . . . but balance is what tempers magical ability. It takes a lot of study to have as much power as a newly woken mage. Young mages have little control. But, Call, you must fight it. And you must never use your magic again. If you do, the mages will take you away to their tunnels."

"That's where the school is? The Magisterium is underground?" Call had asked.

"Buried under the earth where no one can find it," his father told him grimly. "There's no light down there. No windows. The place is a maze. You could get lost in the caverns and die and no one would ever know."

Call licked his suddenly dry lips. "But you're a magician, aren't you?"

"I haven't used my magic since your mother died. I'll never use it again."

"And Mom went there? To the tunnels? Really?" Call was eager to hear anything about his mother. He didn't have much. Some yellowed photographs in an old scrapbook, showing a pretty woman with Call's ink-black hair and eyes a color Call couldn't make out. He knew better than to ask his father too many questions about her. He never talked about Call's mom unless he absolutely had to.

"Yes, she did," Call's father told him. "And it's because of magic that she died. When mages go to war, which is often, they don't care about the people who die because of it. Which is the other reason you must not attract their attention."

That night, Call woke up screaming, believing he was trapped underground, earth piling on him as if he were being buried alive. No matter how much he thrashed around, he couldn't breathe. After that, he dreamed that he was running away from a monster made of smoke whose eyes swirled with a thousand different evil colors . . . only he couldn't run fast enough because of his leg. In the dreams, it dragged behind him like a dead thing until he collapsed, with the monster's hot breath on his neck.

Other kids in Call's class were afraid of the dark, the monster under the bed, zombies, or murderers with giant axes. Call was afraid of magicians, and he was even more afraid he was one.

Now he was going to meet them. The same magicians who were the reason his mother was dead and his father hardly ever laughed and didn't have any friends, sitting instead in the work-room he'd made out of the garage and fixing beat-up furniture and cars and jewelry. Call didn't think it took a genius to figure out why his dad was obsessed with putting broken things back together.

They whizzed past a sign welcoming them to Virginia. Everything looked the same. He didn't know what he'd expected, but he'd seldom been out of North Carolina before. Their trips beyond Asheville were infrequent, mostly to go to car-part swap meets and antique fairs, where Call would wander around among mounds of unpolished silverware, collections of baseball cards in plastic sleeves, and weird old taxidermied yak heads, while his dad bargained for something boring.

It occurred to Call that if he didn't mess up this test, he might never go to one of those swap meets again. His stomach lurched and a cold shiver rattled his bones. He forced himself to think about the plan his father had drilled into him: *Make your mind totally blank. Or focus on something that's the opposite of what those monsters want. Or focus your mind on someone else's test instead of your own.*

He let out his breath. His father's nerves were getting to him. It was going to be fine. It was easy to mess up tests.

The car swung off the highway onto a narrow road. The only sign had the symbol of an airplane on it, with the words AIR-FIELD CLOSED FOR RENOVATION beneath it.

"Where are we going?" Call asked. "Are we *flying* some-where?"

"Let's hope not," his dad muttered. The street had turned abruptly from asphalt to dirt. As they bumped over the next few hundred yards, Call grabbed on to the door frame to keep himself from flying up and whacking his head on the roof. Rolls-Royces were not made for dirt roads.

Suddenly, the lane widened and the trees parted. The Rolls was now in a huge cleared space. In the middle was an enormous hangar made out of corrugated steel. Parked around it were about a hundred cars, from beat-up pickup trucks to sedans almost as fancy as the Phantom and a lot newer. Call saw parents and their kids, all about his age, hurrying toward the hangar.

"I think we're late," Call said.

"Good." His father sounded grimly pleased. He pulled the car to a stop and got out, gesturing for Call to follow. Call was glad to see that his father seemed to have forgotten about the crutches. It was a hot day, and the sun beat down on the back of Call's gray T-shirt. He wiped his sweaty palms against his jeans as they walked across the lot and into the big black open space that was the hangar entrance.

Inside, everything was crazy. Kids milled around, their voices carrying in the vast space. Bleachers were set up along one metal wall; even though they could hold many more people than were present, they were dwarfed by the immensity of the room. Bright blue tape marked x's and circles along the concrete floor.

Across the other side, in front of a set of hangar doors that would once have opened to let airplanes taxi out onto runways, were the mages.

CHAPTER TWO

THERE WERE ONLY about a half dozen mages, but they seemed to fill the space with their presence. Call wasn't sure what he'd thought they were going to look like — he knew his father was a mage and he seemed pretty ordinary, if tweedy. He figured most of the other magicians would look much weirder. Maybe pointy hats. Or robes with silver stars on them. He'd hoped that someone would be green-skinned.

To his disappointment, they looked completely normal. There were three women and three men, each wearing loose-fitting, long-sleeved belted black tunics over pants of the same material. There were leather-and-metal cuffs around their wrists, but Call couldn't tell if there was anything special about those or if they were just a fashion statement.

The tallest of the mages, a big, wide-shouldered man with a hawkish nose and shaggy brown hair shot through with threads of silver, stepped forward and addressed the families in the bleachers.

"Welcome, aspirants, and welcome, families of aspirants, to the most significant afternoon of your child's life."

Right, Call thought. *No pressure or anything.*

"Do they all know they're here to try to get into magic school?" he asked quietly.

His father shook his head. "The parents believe whatever they want to believe and hear whatever they want to hear. If they want their child to be a famous athlete, they believe he is getting into an exclusive training program. If they hope she'll be a brain surgeon, this is pre-pre-premed. If they want him to grow up to be wealthy, then they believe this is the sort of prep school where he'll hobnob with the rich and powerful."

The mage went on, explaining how the afternoon was going to go, how long it would take. "Some of you have traveled a great distance to give your child this opportunity, and we want to extend our gratitude —"

Call could hear him, but he heard another voice, too, one that seemed to come from everywhere and nowhere at once.

When Master North finishes speaking, all aspirants should rise and come to the front. The Trial is about to begin.

"Did you hear that?" Call asked his dad, who nodded. Call looked around at the faces all turned to the mages, some apprehensive, some smiling. "What about the kids?"

The mage — Call guessed he must be Master North, according to the disembodied voice — was finishing up his speech. Call knew he should start down the bleachers, since it was going to take him longer than it would take the others. But he wanted to find out the answer.

"Anyone with even a little power can hear Master Phineus — and most of the aspirants will have had some kind of magical occurrence before. Some have already guessed what they are, some already know for sure, and the rest are about to find out."

There was a shuffling as kids got to their feet, making the metal stands shake.

"So that's the first test?" Call asked his father. "Whether we hear Master Phineus?"

His dad barely seemed to register what he was saying. He looked distracted. "I suppose. But the other tests will be much worse. Just remember what I said and it will all be over soon." He caught Call's wrist, startling him — he knew his dad cared about him, but he wasn't touchy-feely most of the time. He gripped Call's hand hard and released it fast. "Now go."

As Call made his way down the bleachers, the other kids were being corralled into groups. One of the female magicians waved Call toward a group at the end. All the other aspirants were whispering to one another, seeming nervous but full of anticipation. Call saw Kylie Myles two groups over. He wondered if he should yell over to her that she wasn't really here for ballet school tryouts, but she was grinning and chatting with some of the other aspirants, so he doubted she would have listened to him anyway.

Ballet school tryouts, he thought grimly. *That's how they get you.*

"I am Master Milagros," the female mage who'd directed Call was now saying as she herded her group expertly out of the big room and down a long, blandly painted hallway. "For this first test, you will all be together. Please follow behind me in an orderly fashion."

Call, almost at the back, hurried a little bit to catch up. He knew that being late was probably an advantage if he wanted them to think that he didn't care about the tests or didn't know what he was doing, but he hated the stares he got when he lagged behind. In fact, he hurried ahead so quickly that he accidentally banged into the shoulder of a pretty girl with large, dark eyes. She shot him an annoyed look from underneath the even darker curtain of her hair.

"Sorry," Call said automatically.

"We're all nervous," the girl said, which was funny, because she didn't look nervous. She looked completely composed. Her eyebrows were perfectly arched. There wasn't a speck of dust on her caramel-colored sweater or her expensive-looking jeans. She wore a delicate filigree hand pendant around her throat that Call recognized from antique store visits as a Hand of Fatima. The gold earrings in her ears looked like they had once belonged to a princess, if not a queen. Call immediately felt self-conscious, as if he were covered in dirt.

"Hey, Tamara!" a tall Asian boy with floppy razor-cut black hair said, and the girl turned away from Call. The boy said something else that Call couldn't hear, sneering as he said it, and Call worried it was about how Call was a cripple who couldn't help lurching into people. Like he was Frankenstein's monster. Resentment bubbled in his brain — especially since Tamara hadn't looked at him like she'd noticed his leg at all. She'd been annoyed with him, like he was a regular kid. He reminded himself that as soon as he failed the exams, he'd never have to see any of these people again.

Also, they were going to die underground.

That thought kept him going down an endless series of halls and into a big white room where rows of desks were laid out in lines. It looked like every other room Call had ever taken a standardized test in. The desks were plain and wooden, attached to rickety chairs. Each desk had a blue book labeled with a kid's name and a pen laid on top. There was a hubbub as everyone went from desk to desk, searching for his or her place card. Call found his in the third row and slid into the seat, behind a kid with pale wavy hair and a soccer team jacket. He looked more like a jock than a candidate for mage school. The boy smiled at Call as though he was genuinely happy to be seated near him.

Call didn't bother smiling back. He opened his blue book, glancing at the pages with questions and empty circles for *A*, *B*, *C*, *D*, or *E*. He had been expecting the tests to be scary, but the only apparent danger was the danger of being bored to death.

"Please keep your books closed until the test has started," Master Milagros said from the front of the room. She was a tall, extremely young-looking Master who reminded Call a little of his homeroom teacher. She had the same sense of awkward nervousness, as if she wasn't used to spending a lot of time around kids. Her hair was black and short, with a streak of pink in it.

Call closed his book and then looked around, realizing he'd been the only person to open it. He decided he wasn't going to tell his father how easy it had been to avoid fitting in.

"First of all, I want to welcome you all to the Iron Trial," Master Milagros went on, clearing her throat. "Now that we're away from your guardians, we can explain in more detail what is going to happen today. Some of you will have received invitations to apply for music school, or a school that concentrates on astronomy or advanced mathematics or horseback riding. But as you may have supposed by now, you are actually here to be evaluated for acceptance into the Magisterium."

She raised her arms, and the walls seemed to fall away. In their place was rough-hewn stone. The kids remained at their desks, but the ground beneath them had changed to mica-flecked rock, which sparkled like strewn glitter. Shimmering stalactites hung from the ceiling like icicles.

The blond boy drew in his breath. All across the room, Call could hear low exclamations of awe.

It was as if they were inside the caves of the Magisterium.

"So cool," said a pretty girl with white beads on the ends of her cornrowed braids.

In that moment, despite everything his father had told Call, he wanted to go to the Magisterium. It no longer seemed dark or scary, but amazing. Like being an explorer or going to another planet. He thought of his father's words:

The magicians will tempt you with pretty illusions and elaborate lies. Don't be drawn in.

Master Milagros went on, her voice gaining in confidence. "Some of you are legacy students, with parents or other family members who have attended the Magisterium. Others have been chosen because we believe you have the potential to become mages. But none of you are assured a place. Only the Masters know what makes a perfect candidate."

Call stuck his hand up and, without waiting to be called on, asked, "What if you don't want to go?"

"Why wouldn't anyone want to go to pony school?" wondered a boy with a mop of brown hair, seated diagonally from Call. He was small and pale, with scrawny long legs and arms sticking out of a blue T-shirt with the faded picture of a horse on it.

Master Milagros looked as if she was so annoyed, she'd forgotten to be nervous. "Drew Wallace," she said. "This is not pony school. You are being tested to see if you possess the qualities that will lead you to be chosen as an apprentice, and to accompany your teacher, called your Master, to the Magisterium. And if you possess sufficient magic, *attendance is not optional.*" She glared at Call. "The Trial is for your own safety. Those of you who are legacies know the dangers untrained mages pose to themselves and others."

A murmur ran around the room. Several of the kids, Call realized, were looking at Tamara. She was sitting very straight in her chair, her eyes fixed ahead of her, her chin jutting out. He knew that look. It was the same look he got when people muttered about his leg or his dead mother, or his weirdo father. It was the look of someone trying to pretend she didn't know she was being talked about.

"So what happens if you don't get into the Magisterium?" asked the girl with the braids.

"Good question, Gwenda Mason," said Master Milagros encouragingly. "To be a successful mage, you must possess three things. One is the intrinsic power of magic. That, you all have, to some degree. The second is the knowledge of how to use it. That, we can give you. The third is control — and that, that must come from inside of you. Now, in your first year, as untaught mages, you are reaching the apex of your power, but you have no learning and no control. If you seem to possess neither an aptitude for learning nor one for control, then you will not find a place at the Magisterium. In that case, we will make sure that you — and your families — are permanently safe from magic or any danger of succumbing to the elements."

Succumbing to the elements? What does that *mean?* Call wondered. It sounded like other people were just as confused: "Does that mean I failed a test?" someone asked. "Wait, what does she mean?" another kid said.

"So this definitely isn't pony school?" Drew asked again, wistfully.

Master Milagros ignored all this. The images of the cavern slowly faded away. They were in the same white room they'd always been in.

"The pens in front of you are special," she said, looking as if she'd remembered to be nervous again. Call wondered how old she was. She seemed young, even younger because of the pink hair, but he guessed you had to be a pretty accomplished magician to be a Master. "If you don't use your pen, we won't be able to read your test. Shake it to activate the ink. And remember to show your work. You may begin."

Call opened the book again. He squinted at the first question:

> **1.** A dragon and a wyvern set out at 2 P.M. from the same cavern, headed in the same direction. The average speed of the dragon is 30 mph slower than twice the speed of the wyvern. In 2 hours, the dragon is 20 miles ahead of the wyvern. Find the flight speed of the dragon, factoring in that the wyvern is bent on revenge.

Revenge? Call goggled at the page, then flipped it. The next one was no better.

> **2.** Lucretia is preparing to plant a crop of deadly nightshade this autumn. She will plant 4 patches of common nightshade with 15 plants in each patch. She estimates that 20 percent of the field will be planted with a test crop of woody nightshade. How many nightshade plants are there in all? How many woody nightshade plants were planted? If Lucretia is an earth mage who has crossed three of the gates, how many people can she poison with the deadly nightshade before she is caught and beheaded?

Call blinked at the test. Did he have to actually put effort into figuring out which answers were wrong, so that he didn't accidentally get them right? Should he just put down the same thing over and over, figuring that had to get a low score? By the law of averages, he'd still get about twenty percent right, and that was higher than he wanted.

As he furiously pondered what to do, he picked up the pen, shook it, and tried to mark the paper.

It didn't work.

He tried again, pressing harder. Still nothing. He looked around and it seemed that most of the other kids were writing fine, although a few were struggling with their pens, too.

It figured that he wasn't going to fail the test like a normal nonmagical person — he wasn't even going to be able to *take* it. But what if the mages made you take the test over again if you left it blank? Wasn't that like refusing to show up in the first place?

Scowling, he tried to remember what Milagros had said about the pen. Something about shaking it to get the ink to work. Maybe he just hadn't shaken it enough.

He tightened his fist around the pen and shook it hard, his annoyance at the test putting extra force into the snap of his wrist. *Come on*, he thought. *Come on, you stupid thing, WORK!*

Blue ink exploded from the tip of the pen. He tried to stop the flow, pressing his finger against where he thought the crack might be . . . but that just made the ink shoot harder. It splattered against the back of the chair in front of him; the blond boy, sensing the inky storm that had just been unleashed, ducked to get out of range of the mess. More ink than seemed possible to come from such a small pen was spurting all over the place, and people were starting to glare at him.

Call dropped the pen, which immediately stopped spraying. But the damage was done. His hands and desk, his test book and hair, were covered in ink. He tried to wipe it off his fingers, only succeeding in leaving blue handprints all over his shirt.

He hoped the ink wasn't poisonous. He was pretty sure he'd swallowed some.

Everyone in the class was staring. Even Master Milagros was watching him in what looked alarmingly like amazement, as though no one had ever managed to destroy a pen so thoroughly. Everyone was silent except the lanky kid who'd been talking to Tamara before. He had leaned over to whisper to her again. Tamara didn't crack a smile, but from the smirk on the boy's face, and the superior glint in her eyes, Call could tell they were sneering at him. He felt the tips of his ears pinking.

"Callum Hunt," said Master Milagros in a shocked voice. "Please — please leave the room and clean yourself up, then wait in the hallway until the group rejoins you."

Call staggered to his feet, barely registering that the blond boy who'd almost been soaked with ink threw him what looked like a sympathetic smile. He could still hear someone giggling as he banged out through the door — and still picture Tamara's scornful look. Who cared what she thought — who cared what *any* of them thought, whether they were trying to be friendly or mean or not? They didn't matter. They weren't part of his life. None of this was.

Just a few more hours. He repeated it to himself over and over as he stood in the bathroom, doing his best to scrub off the ink with powdered soap and rough paper towels. He wondered if the ink was magical. It sure wanted to stick. Some of it had dried in his black hair, and there were still dark blue handprints on his white shirt when he emerged from the bathroom and found the other aspirants waiting for him in the hallway. He heard some of them muttering to one another about "the freak with the ink."

"Nice look with the shirt," the boy with the black hair said. He looked rich to Call, rich like Tamara. He couldn't have said why exactly, but his clothes were the kind of tailored casual-fancy that cost a lot of money. "For your sake, I hope the next test doesn't involve explosions. Or, oh, wait — I hope it *does*."

"Shut up," Call muttered, aware that this was hardly the greatest comeback of all time. He slouched against the wall until Master Milagros, reappearing, called them all to order. Silence fell as she called out names in groups of five, directing each group down a corridor and telling them to wait at the other end. Call had no idea how the airplane hangar managed to house such a network of hallways. He suspected it was one of those things his father would say he was better off not thinking about.

"Callum Hunt!" she called out, and Call shuffled along to join his group, which also contained, to his dismay, the black-haired boy, whose name turned out to be Jasper deWinter, and the blond boy he'd spattered ink on earlier, who was Aaron Stewart. Jasper made a big show of hugging Tamara and wishing her luck before he sauntered over to join his group. Once there, he immediately started talking to Aaron, turning his back on Call as if Call didn't exist.

The other two kids in Call's new group were Kylie Myles and a nervous-looking girl named Celia something, who had a big mass of dirty blond hair and had clipped a blue flower behind her bangs.

"Hey, Kylie," Call said, thinking now was the perfect opportunity to warn her that the picture of the Magisterium that Master Milagros was conjuring for them was merely a flattering illusion. He had it on good authority that the real caves were full of dead ends and eyeless fish.

She looked apologetic. "Would you mind . . . not talking to me?"

"What?" They had started moving off down the hall, and Call limped faster to keep up. "Seriously?"

She shrugged. "You know how it is. I'm trying to make a good impression, and talking to you isn't going to help. Sorry!" She skipped ahead, catching up with Jasper and Aaron. Call stared at the back of her head as if he could drill into it with anger.

"I hope the eyeless fish eat you!" he called after her. She pretended not to hear.

Master Milagros led them around a last corner, into a huge room that was set up like a gymnasium. There was a high ceiling, and from the center of it dangled a big red ball, suspended high over their heads. Next to the ball was a long rope ladder with wooden rungs that reached from the roof to brush the floor.

This was ridiculous. He couldn't climb with his leg the way it was. He was supposed to be *throwing* these tests on purpose, not being so terrible at them that he'd never have been able to get into magic school in the first place.

"I will now leave you to Master Rockmaple," Master Milagros said after the last group of five had arrived, indicating a short magician with a bristling red beard and a ruddy nose. He was carrying a clipboard and had a whistle around his neck, like a gym teacher, although he was wearing the all-black outfit the other magicians were in.

"This test is deceptively simple," said Master Rockmaple, stroking his beard in a way that seemed calculated to look menacing. "Simply climb the rope ladder and get the ball. Who would like to go first?"

Several kids shot up their hands.

Master Rockmaple pointed to Jasper. He bounded up to the rope as though being selected first were some kind of indication of how awesome he was, instead of just a measure of how eagerly he'd waggled his hand. Instead of climbing right on, he circled the apparatus, looking up at the ball thoughtfully, tapping his lower lip.

"Are you quite ready?" Master Rockmaple asked, eyebrows raised just slightly, and a few of the other kids snickered.

Jasper, clearly annoyed at being laughed at when he was taking the whole thing so seriously, launched himself violently at the dangling rope ladder. As soon as he'd climbed from one rung to another, the ladder seemed to lengthen, so that the more he climbed, the more he had to climb. Finally, it got the better of him and he toppled to the ground, surrounded by coils and coils of rope and steps of wood.

Now, that was funny, Callum thought.

"Very good," said Master Rockmaple. "Who would like to go next?"

"Let me try it again," said Jasper, a whine creeping into his voice. "I know how to do it now."

"We have a lot of aspirants waiting for their turn," Master Rockmaple said, looking as if he was enjoying himself.

"But it's *not fair*. Someone will get it right and then everyone will know how to do it. I'm being punished for going first."

"It looked to me like you wanted to go first. But very well, Jasper. If there's time after everyone else is done, and you'd still like to try again, you may."

It just figured that Jasper would get another chance. Call assumed that from the way he was acting, his dad was probably somebody important.

Most of the other kids didn't do any better, some making it halfway up and then sliding back down, one never even hauling himself off the ground. Celia got the farthest before losing her grip and falling onto a practice mat. Her flower hair clip wound up a little mangled. Although she didn't want to show she was upset, Call could tell she was by the way she kept anxiously trying to fix the clip back into place.

Master Rockmaple looked at his list. "Aaron Stewart."

Aaron stood in front of the rope ladder, flexing his fingers like he was about to jog onto a basketball court. He looked sporty and confident, and Call felt that familiar ache of jealousy in his stomach, quickly smothered, that he got whenever he watched kids play basketball or baseball and be totally at home in their skin. Team sports weren't an option for Call; the opportunity for embarrassment was too great, even if he'd been allowed to play. Guys like Aaron never had to worry about things like that.

Aaron jogged toward the rope ladder and flung himself onto it. He climbed fast, his feet pushing as his arms pulled him upward in what looked like a single, fluid motion. He was moving so quickly that he was going faster than the rope was falling. Higher and higher he went. Callum held his breath and realized that all around him, everyone else had grown hushed, too.

Aaron, grinning like a maniac, reached the top. He hit the ball with the side of one hand, knocking it free, before slithering back down the ladder and landing on his feet like a gymnast.

Some of the other kids burst into spontaneous applause. Even Jasper seemed happy for him, going over to clap him grudgingly on the back.

"Very good," Master Rockmaple said, using exactly the same words and tone he'd used with everyone else. Callum thought the grumpy old mage was probably just annoyed that someone had beaten his stupid test.

"Callum Hunt," the mage said next.

Callum stepped forward, wishing that he'd thought to bring a doctor's note. "I can't."

Master Rockmaple looked him over. "Why not?"

Oh, come on. Look at me. Just look at me. Call raised his head and stared defiantly at the mage. "My leg. I'm not supposed to do gym stuff," he said.

The mage shrugged. "So don't."

Call fought down a blaze of anger. He could tell the other kids were looking at him, some with pity and others with annoyance. The worst part was that, normally, he'd have jumped at the chance to do something physical. He was just trying to do what he was supposed to and *fail*. "It's not an *excuse*," he said. "My leg bones were shattered when I was a baby. I've had ten operations, and as a result, I've got sixty iron screws in there holding my leg together. Do you need to see the scars?"

Callum fervently hoped Master Rockmaple would say no. His left leg was a mass of red incision lines and ugly bunched tissue. He never let anyone see it; he'd never worn shorts, ever, since he was old enough to know what strangers' glances at his leg were all about. He didn't know why he'd even explained as much as he had, except that he was so mad he had no idea what he was saying.

Master Rockmaple, who had been holding his whistle in one hand, twirled it thoughtfully. "These tests aren't all obvious," he said. "At least try, Callum. If you fail, we move on to the next one."

Call threw up his hands. "Fine. *Fine.*" He stalked toward the rope ladder and put one hand on it. He deliberately put his left leg on the lowest rung and braced his weight on it, reaching up.

Pain shot up his calf and he dropped back down to the floor, still gripping the ladder. He could hear Jasper laughing behind him. His leg ached and his stomach felt numb. He looked up the ladder again, toward the red rubber ball at the very top, and felt his head start to throb with pain. Years and years of being made to sit on the bleachers, of limping behind everyone when they were running laps, rose up behind his eyes and he glared furiously at the ball that he knew he couldn't reach, thinking, *I hate you, I hate you, I hate —*

There was a sharp boom, and the red ball caught on fire. Someone shrieked — it sounded like Kylie, but Call hoped it was Jasper. Everyone, including Master Rockmaple, was staring as the red ball burned merrily away like it had been full of fireworks. The stench of burning chemical nastiness filled the air, and Call jumped back as a big lump of melting plastic meteored to the floor. He scrambled away as more of the goop began to drip from the burning ball, a little of it splattering the shoulder of his T-shirt.

Ink *and* goop. This was a great fashion day for him.

"Get out," Master Rockmaple said as the kids started to choke and cough on smoke. "Everyone, get out of the room."

"But my turn!" Jasper protested. "How am I going to get my second turn now that the freak has totally destroyed the ball? Master Rockmaple —"

"I SAID GET OUT," the mage roared, and the kids surged from the room, Call bringing up the rear, intensely conscious of the fact that both Jasper *and* Master Rockmaple were glaring at him with what looked a lot like hatred.

Like the smell of burning, the word *freak* carried through the air.

CHAPTER THREE

MASTER ROCKMAPLE marched angrily, leading the whole group down a hallway, away from the testing room. Everyone was moving so fast there was no way for Callum to keep up. His leg hurt more than ever and he smelled like a burning tire factory. He limped along behind them, wondering if anyone had ever messed up this badly in the history of the Magisterium. Maybe they'd let him go home early, for his sake and for the sake of everyone else.

"You okay?" Aaron asked him, dropping back so he could walk alongside Callum. He smiled good-naturedly, like there was nothing strange about talking to Call when the rest of the group was avoiding him like the plague.

"Fine," Call said, gritting his teeth. "Never better."

"I have no idea how you did what you did, but that was *epic*. The look on Master Rockmaple's face was like —" Aaron tried to approximate it, furrowing his eyebrows, widening his eyes, and making his mouth gape.

Call started to laugh but stifled it quickly. He didn't want to like any of the other kids, especially not super-competent Aaron.

They turned the corner. The rest of the class was waiting. Master Rockmaple cleared his throat, apparently about to scold Call, when he seemed to notice Aaron standing beside him. Biting off whatever he had been about to say, the mage opened the door to a new room.

Call scrambled into the room along with the rest of the group. It was a boring industrial space like the one they'd been in for the first test, with rows of desks and a single sheet of paper resting atop each one.

How many written tests are there going to be? Callum wanted to ask, but he didn't think that Master Rockmaple was in the mood to answer him. None of these desks had names, so he sat at one and folded his arms over his chest.

"Master Rockmaple!" called out Kylie, sitting down. "Master Rockmaple, I don't have a pen."

"Nor will you need one," said the mage. "This is a test of your ability to control your magic. You will be using the element of air. Concentrate on the paper in front of you until you are able to lift it off the desk, using only the energy of your thoughts. Lift it straight up, without allowing it to wobble or fall. Once that is accomplished, please rise and join me at the front of the room."

Relief washed through Call. All he had to do was make sure the paper didn't fly up into the air, which seemed simple enough. His whole life, he had managed not to make pieces of paper fly around classrooms.

Aaron was sitting across the aisle from him. He had his hand on his chin, his green eyes narrowed. As Call darted a sideways glance toward him, the paper on Aaron's desk rose into the air, perfectly level. It hovered for a moment before fluttering back to the desk. With a grin, Aaron got up to join Master Rockmaple at the front of the room.

Call heard a chuckle to his left. He glanced over and saw Jasper take out what looked like a regular sewing pin and prick his finger. A drop of blood appeared, and Jasper shoved his finger into his mouth, sucking on it. *What a weirdo*, Call thought. But then Jasper slumped back in his chair, in a casual, I-can-do-magic-with-my-hands-tied kind of way. And it seemed like he could, since the paper on his desk was folding and crumpling — rolling itself into a new shape. With a few more folds and tucks, it became a paper airplane, which zoomed off Jasper's desk and flew across the room, hitting Call directly in the forehead. He swatted it away and it dropped to the ground.

"Jasper, that's enough," Master Rockmaple said, though he didn't sound as annoyed as he could have. "Get up here."

Call returned his attention to his paper as Jasper sauntered up to the front of the room. All around him, kids were staring and whispering at the papers on their desks, *willing* them to move. Call's stomach tightened uneasily. What if a gust of air came along and picked up his paper? What if it just . . . fluttered on its own? Would he get points for that?

Stay put, he thought savagely at the paper on his desk. *Don't you move.* He pictured himself holding it down against the wood, fingers splayed, preventing it from twitching. *Man, this is stupid*, he thought. *What a thing to do with your day.* But he stayed where he was, concentrating. This time, he wasn't alone. Several other kids were unable to move their papers, including Kylie.

"Callum?" said Master Rockmaple, sounding weary.

Call sat back. "I can't do it."

"If he can't, he *really* can't," said Jasper. "Just give the loser a zero and let's go before he creates a blizzard and we all die from paper cuts."

"All right," said the mage. "Everyone, bring me your papers and I'll give you your marks. Come on, let's get this room cleaned up for the next group."

Relieved, Call reached for the paper on his desk — and froze. Desperately, he scrabbled at the edges of it with his fingernails, but somehow, he didn't know how, the paper had sunk into the wood of the desk and he couldn't get a grip on it. "Master Rockmaple — there's something wrong with my paper," he said.

"Everyone under the desks!" said Jasper, but no one was paying attention to him. They were all looking at Call. Master Rockmaple stalked over to him and stared down at the paper. It had well and truly become fused to the desk.

"Who did this?" demanded Master Rockmaple. He sounded flabbergasted. "Is this someone's idea of a prank?"

Everyone in the class was silent.

"Did *you* do this?" Master Rockmaple asked Call.

I was just trying to keep it from moving, Call thought miserably, but he couldn't say that. "I don't know."

"You don't know?"

"I don't know. Maybe the paper is defective."

"It's just paper!" the mage shouted, and then seemed to get control of himself. "All right. Fine. You get a zero. No, wait, you are going to be the first aspirant in Magisterium history to get a negative score on one of the Iron Trial tests. You get a minus ten." He shook his head. "I think we can all be grateful that the final test is one you do alone."

By that point, Callum was most grateful that it would all soon be over.

This time, the aspirants stood in the hallway outside a double door and waited to be called inside. Jasper was speaking to Aaron, looking over at Call like he was the subject they were discussing.

Call sighed. This was the last test. Some of the tension drained out of him at the thought. No matter how well he did, one last test wasn't going to make that much of a difference to his terrible score. In less than an hour, he'd be heading home with his dad.

"Callum Hunt," called a mage who hadn't introduced herself before. She had an elaborate snake-shaped necklace wound around her throat and was reading off a clipboard. "Master Rufus is waiting for you inside."

He pushed off the wall and followed her through the double doors. The room was large and empty and dim, with a wooden floor where a single mage sat next to a large wooden bowl. The bowl was filled with water and there was a flame burning at its center, without wick or candle.

Call stopped and stared, feeling a little prickle against the back of his neck. He'd seen plenty of weird things that day, but this was the first time since the illusion of the cave that he'd really felt the presence of magic.

The mage spoke. "Did you know that to obtain good posture, people used to practice walking around with books balanced on their heads?" His voice was low and rumbling, the sound of a distant fire. Master Rufus was a large, dark-skinned man with a bald head as smooth as a macadamia nut. He stood up in one easy motion, lifting the bowl in his wide, callused fingers.

The flame didn't waver. If anything, it shone a little more brightly.

"Wasn't it girls who did that?" Call asked.

"Did what?" Master Rufus frowned.

"Walked around with books on their heads."

The mage gave him a look that made Callum feel as if he'd said something disappointing. "Take the bowl," he said.

"But the flame will go out," Call protested.

"That is the test," said Rufus. "See if you can keep the flame burning, and for how long." He held out the bowl to Call.

So far, none of the tests had been what Call expected. Still, he'd managed to fail each one — either because he'd tried to or because he just wasn't cut out to be a magician. There was something about Master Rufus that made him want to do better, but that didn't matter. There was no way he was going to the Magisterium.

Call took the bowl.

Almost immediately, the flame inside leaped up, as though Call had turned the knob on a gas lamp too high. He jumped and deliberately tilted the bowl to the side, trying to slosh water over the flame. But instead of going out, it burned through the water. Panicking, Call shook the bowl, sending more small waves over the fire. It began to sputter.

"Callum Hunt." It was Master Rufus looking down at him, his face impassive, his arms crossed over his wide chest. "I'm surprised at you."

Call said nothing. He held the bowl with its sloshing water and sputtering flame.

"I taught both your parents at the Magisterium," Master Rufus said. He looked serious and sad. The flame made dark shadows under his eyes. "They were my apprentices. Top of their class, the best marks in the Trial. Your mother would have been disappointed to have seen her son so obviously trying to fail a test simply because —"

Master Rufus never got to finish the sentence, because at the mention of Call's mother, the wooden bowl cracked — not in half, but into a dozen splintered pieces, each sharp enough to stab into Call's palms. He dropped what he was holding, only to see that each part of the bowl had caught fire and was burning steadily, little pyres scattered at his feet. As he looked at the flames, though, he wasn't afraid. It seemed to him, in that moment, as though the fire were beckoning for him to step inside it, to drown his rage and fear in its light.

The flames leaped up as he looked around the room, shooting along the spilled water like it was gasoline. All Call felt was a terrible sweeping anger that this mage had known his mother, that the man right in front of him might have had something to do with her death.

"Stop it! Stop it right now!" Master Rufus shouted, grabbing both of Call's hands and slamming them together. The slap of them made the fresh cuts hurt.

Abruptly, all the fires went out.

"Let me go!" Call yanked his hands away from Master Rufus and wiped his bloody palms on his pants, adding another layer of stains. "I didn't mean to do that. I don't even know what happened."

"What happened is that you failed another test," said Master Rufus, his anger replaced by what seemed like cold curiosity. He was considering Call the way a scientist considered a bug pinned to a board. "You may go back out and join your father on the bleachers to await your final score."

Thankfully, there was a door on the other side of the room, so Call could slink through that and not have to face any of the other aspirants. He could just picture the expression on Jasper's face if he saw the blood on his clothes.

His hands were trembling.

The bleachers were full of bored-looking parents and a few younger siblings toddling around. The low buzz of conversation echoed in the hangar, and Call realized how strangely quiet the corridors had been — it was a shock to hear the noise of people again. Aspirants were exiting through five different doors in a slow trickle and joining their families. Three whiteboards had been set up at the base of the bleachers, where mages were recording scores as they came in. Call didn't look at them. He headed straight for his dad.

Alastair had a book sitting on his lap, closed, as though he'd meant to read it but had never begun. Call noticed the relief that started on his father's face as he got close, immediately replaced by concern once he got a true look at his son.

Alastair jumped to his feet, the book falling to the ground. "Callum! You're covered in blood and ink and you smell like burned plastic. What happened?"

"I messed up. I — I think I really messed up." Call could hear his voice shaking. He kept seeing the burning remains of the bowl and the look on Master Rufus's face.

His dad put a comforting hand on his shoulder. "Call, it's okay. You were *supposed* to mess up."

"I know, but I thought I'd be —" He jammed his hands in his pockets, remembering all the lectures his father had given him about how he was going to have to try to fail. But he hadn't had to try at all. He'd failed at everything because he didn't know what he was doing, because he was bad at magic. "I thought everything would be different."

His father dropped his voice low. "I know it doesn't feel good to fail at anything, Call, but this is for the best. You did really well."

"If by 'really well' you mean 'sucking,'" Call muttered.

His dad grinned. "I was worried for a minute when you got full points for the first test, but then they took them away. I've never seen anyone *lose* points before."

Call scowled. He knew his father meant this as a compliment, but it didn't feel like one.

"You're in last place. There are kids without any magic who did better than you. I think you deserve an ice-cream sundae — the biggest one we can get — on the way home. Your favorite kind, with butterscotch, peanut butter, *and* Gummi Bears. Okay?"

"Yeah," Call said, sitting down. He was too bummed even for the thought of peanut-butter-and-butterscotch-covered Gummi Bears to cheer him up. "Okay."

His father sat again, too. He was nodding to himself now, looking pleased. He looked even more pleased as more scores came in.

Call let himself look at the whiteboards. Aaron and Tamara were at the very top, their total scores exactly identical. Annoyingly, Jasper was three points beneath them, in second place.

Oh, well, Call thought. What did he expect? Mages were jerks, just like his dad said, and the jerkiest jerks of all got the best scores. It figured.

Although it wasn't *all* jerks on top. Kylie had done badly while Aaron had done well. That was good, Call supposed. It seemed like Aaron had really wanted to do well. Except of course that doing well meant you went to the Magisterium, and Call's father had always said that was something he wouldn't wish on his worst enemy.

Call wasn't sure whether to be happy for Aaron, who had at least been nice to him, or sad for him. All he knew was that he was getting a headache thinking about it.

Master Rufus strode out of one of the doors. He didn't say anything out loud, but the whole crowd fell silent as if he had. Scanning the room, Call could see a few familiar faces — Kylie looking anxious, Aaron biting his lip. Jasper looked pale and strained, while Tamara appeared cool and collected, not worried at all. She sat between an elegant dark-haired couple, whose cream-colored clothes set off their brown skin. Her mother wore an ivory dress and gloves, her father an entirely cream-colored suit.

"Aspirants for this year," said Master Rufus, and everyone leaned forward at once, "thank you for being with us today and for working so hard in the Trial. The thanks of the Magisterium also go out to all of the families who brought children and waited for them to finish."

He put his hands behind his back, his gaze sweeping over the bleachers.

"There are nine mages here, and each of them is authorized to choose up to six applicants. Those applicants will be their apprentices for the five years they will spend at the Magisterium, so this is not a choice that a Master undertakes lightly. You must also understand that there are more children here than will qualify for places at the Magisterium. If you are not selected, it is because you are not suitable for this kind of training — please understand there are many possible reasons you might not be suitable, and further exploration of your powers could be deadly. Before you leave, a mage will explain your obligations of secrecy and give you the means to protect yourself and your family."

Hurry up and get this over with, Call thought, barely paying attention to what Rufus was saying. The other students were shuffling uncomfortably, too. Jasper, seated between his Asian mom and white dad, both sporting fancy haircuts, drummed his fingers against his knees. Call glanced at his father, who was staring at Rufus with an expression Call had never seen on his face before. He looked as if he was thinking about running the mage over with the remodeled Rolls, even if it would break the transmission again.

"Does anyone have questions?" Rufus asked.

The room was silent. His dad spoke to Call in a whisper. "It's okay," he said, though Call hadn't done anything to indicate he thought it *wasn't* okay. His father's grip on Call grew firmer, fingers digging into his shoulder. "You won't get picked."

"Very well!" boomed Rufus. "Let the selection process begin!" He stepped back, until he was standing before the board with the scores on it. "Aspirants, as we say your names, please rise to your feet and join your new Master. As the senior mage present after Master North, who will not be taking any apprentices, I will begin the selection." His gaze swept out over the crowd. "Aaron Stewart."

There was a scatter of applause, though not from Tamara's family. She sat incredibly still and rigid, looking like she'd been embalmed. Her parents appeared furious. Her father leaned forward to say something in her ear, and Call saw her flinch in response. Maybe she was human after all.

Aaron rose to his feet. *Totally unexpected choice*, Call thought sarcastically. Aaron looked like Captain America, with his blond hair, athletic build, and goody-two-shoes demeanor. Call wanted to throw his father's book at Aaron's head, even if he was nice. Captain America was nice, too, but it didn't mean you wanted to have to compete with him.

Then, with a start, Call realized that though other people in the audience were clapping, Aaron had no family sitting on either side of him. No one hugging him or slapping him on the back. He must have come alone. Swallowing, Aaron smiled and then jogged down the stairs between the bleachers to stand next to Master Rufus.

Rufus cleared his throat. "Tamara Rajavi," he said.

Tamara stood, her dark hair flying. Her parents clapped politely, as if they were at an opera. Tamara didn't pause to hug either of them, just walked steadily to stand beside Aaron, who gave her a congratulatory smile.

Call wondered if it annoyed the other mages that Master Rufus got to pick first and went straight for the top of the list. It would have annoyed Call.

Master Rufus's dark eyes raked over the room one more time. Call could feel the hush over everyone as they waited for Rufus to call out the next name. Jasper was already half out of his seat.

"And my last apprentice will be Callum Hunt," Master Rufus said, and the bottom fell out of Call's world.

There were a few surprised gasps from the other aspirants and confused muttering from the audience as each of them scanned the whiteboards for Call's name and found it, absolutely dead last, with a negative score.

Call stared at Master Rufus. Master Rufus stared back, entirely blank. Next to him, Aaron was giving Call an encouraging smile while Tamara looked at him with an expression of total astonishment.

"I said *Callum Hunt*," Master Rufus repeated. "Callum Hunt, please come down here."

Call started to get up, but his father shoved him back down into his seat.

"Absolutely not," Alastair Hunt said, standing. "This has gone far enough, Rufus. You can't have him."

Master Rufus was looking up at them as if there was no one else in the room. "Come now, Alastair, you know the rules as well as anyone. Stop making a fuss over something inevitable. The boy needs to be taught."

Mages were ascending the bleachers on either side of where Call was sitting, his father holding him in place. The mages, in their black clothes, looked as sinister as his father had ever described them. They looked ready for battle. Once they reached Call's row of benches, they stopped, waiting for his father's first move.

Call's dad had given up magic years ago; he had to be completely out of practice. There was no chance the other mages weren't going to mop the floor with him.

"I'll go," he told his father, turning toward him. "Don't worry. I don't know what I'm doing. I'll get kicked out. They won't want me for long and then I'll come home and everything will be the same —"

"You don't understand," Call's father said, hauling him to his feet with a clawlike grip. Everyone in the whole room was staring, and no wonder. His father looked unhinged, his eyes wide and bulging. "Come on. We're going to have to run."

"I *can't*," he reminded his father. But his father was beyond listening.

Call's dad pulled him through the bleachers, hopping from bench to bench. People made way for them, dodging to one side or jumping up. The mages on the stairs rushed toward them. Call staggered along, focusing on keeping his balance as they descended.

As soon as they hit the floor of the hangar, Rufus stepped in front of Call's father.

"Enough," Master Rufus said. "The boy stays here."

Call's dad came to a jerking stop. He put his arms around Call from the back, which was weird — his father practically never hugged him, but this was more of a wrestling grip. Call's leg was aching from their race through the bleachers. He tried to twist around to look at his father, but his dad was staring at Master Rufus. "Haven't you killed enough of my family?" he demanded.

Master Rufus dropped his voice so that the mass of people sitting on the benches couldn't hear them, though Aaron and Tamara obviously could. "You haven't taught him anything," he said. "An untrained mage wandering around is like a fault in the earth waiting to crack open, and if he does crack, he will kill a lot of other people as well as himself. So don't talk to me about death."

"Okay," said Call's father. "I'll teach him myself. I'll take him and I'll teach him. I'll get him ready for the First Gate."

"You've had twelve years to teach him and you haven't used them. I'm sorry, Alastair. This is how it has to be."

"Look at his score — he shouldn't qualify. He doesn't want to qualify! Right, Call? Right?" Call's father shook him as he said it. The boy couldn't get any words out even if he'd wanted to.

"Let him go, Alastair," said Master Rufus, his deep voice full of sadness.

"No," Call's father said. "He's my child. I have rights. I decide his future."

"No," said Master Rufus. "You don't."

Call's father jerked back, but not fast enough. Call felt arms grabbing at him as two mages wrenched him out of his dad's grip. His father was shouting and Call was kicking and pulling, but it didn't make a difference as he was dragged over to where Aaron and Tamara stood. They both looked absolutely horrified. Call flung a sharp elbow out at one of the mages who was holding him. He heard a grunt of pain, and his arm got jerked up behind his back. He winced and wondered what all the parents in the bleachers, here to send their kids to aerodynamics school, were thinking now.

"Call!" His father was being restrained by two other mages. "Call, don't listen to anything they say! They don't know what they're doing! They don't know anything about you!" They were dragging Alastair toward the exit. Call couldn't believe what was happening.

Suddenly, something glinted in the air. He hadn't seen his dad's arm pull free from the mages' grip, but it must have. A dagger now soared toward him. It flew straight and true, farther than a dagger should be able to go. Call couldn't take his eyes off it as it whirled at him, blade first.

He knew he should do something.

He knew he had to get out of the way.

But somehow he couldn't.

His feet felt rooted to the spot.

The blade stopped inches from Call, plucked out of the air by Aaron as easily as if he were plucking an apple off the low-hanging branch of a tree.

Everyone was still for a moment, staring. Call's father had been pulled through the far doors of the hangar by the mages. He was gone.

"Here," said a voice at Call's elbow. It was Aaron, holding out the dagger. It wasn't anything Call had ever seen before. It was a glinting silver color, with whorls and scrolls in the metal. The hilt was shaped like a bird with its wings outspread. The word *Semiramis* was etched along the blade in an ornate script.

"I guess this is yours, right?" Aaron said.

"Thanks," said Call, taking the dagger.

"*That* was your father?" Tamara asked under her breath,

without turning her face toward him. Her voice was full of cool disapproval.

Some of the mages were looking over at Call like they thought he was crazy and they could see how he got to be that way. He felt better with the dagger in his hand, even if the only thing he'd ever used a knife for was spreading peanut butter or cutting up steak. "Yeah," Call told her. "He wants me to be safe."

Master Rufus nodded to Master Milagros and she stepped forward.

"We're very sorry for that disruption. We appreciate that you all remained in your seats and stayed calm," she said. "We hope that the ceremony will proceed without any further delays. I will be selecting my apprentices next."

The crowd quieted again.

"I have chosen five," said Master Milagros. "The first will be Jasper deWinter. Jasper, please come down and stand by me."

Jasper rose and walked to his place beside Master Milagros, with a single hateful look in Call's direction.

CHAPTER FOUR

THE SUN WAS beginning to set by the time all the Masters had picked their apprentices. Lots of kids had gone away crying, including, to Call's satisfaction, Kylie. He would have traded places with her in a second, but since that wasn't allowed, at least he got to really annoy her by being forced to stay. It was the only perk he could think of, and as the time to leave for the Magisterium drew closer, he was clinging to any comfort.

Call's father's warnings about the Magisterium had always been frustratingly vague. As Call stood there, singed and bloody and soaked with blue ink, his leg hurting more and more, he had nothing to do but go back over those warnings in his mind. *The mages don't care about anyone or anything except advancing their studies. They steal children from their families. They are monsters. They experiment on children. They are the reason your mother is dead.*

Aaron tried to make conversation with Call, but Call didn't feel like talking. He played with the hilt of the dagger, which he had stuck through his belt, and tried to look frightening.

Eventually, Aaron gave up and started to chat with Tamara. She knew a lot about the Magisterium from an older sister who, according to Tamara, was the best at absolutely every single thing at the school. Troublingly, Tamara was vowing to be even better. Aaron seemed happy just to be going to magic school.

Call wondered if he should warn them. Then he remembered the horrified tone in Tamara's voice when she'd seen who his father was. *Forget it*, he thought. They could get eaten by wyverns traveling at twenty miles an hour and bent on revenge for all he cared.

Finally, the ceremony was over, and everyone was herded out into the parking lot. Parents tearfully hugged and kissed their kids good-bye, loading them down with suitcases and duffel bags and care packages. Call stood around with his hands in his pockets. Not only was his dad not there to say good-bye to him, but Call didn't have any luggage, either. After a few days with no change of clothes, he was going to smell even worse than he did now.

Two yellow school buses were waiting, and the mages began to divide the students into groups according to their Masters. Each bus carried several groups. Master Rufus's apprentices were put with Master Milagros's, Master Rockmaple's, and Master Lemuel's.

As Call waited, Jasper walked up to him. His bags were as expensive-looking as his clothes, with initials — *JDW* — monogrammed onto the leather. He had a sneer plastered on his face as he looked at Call.

"That spot in Master Rufus's group," Jasper said. "That was *my* spot. And you took it."

Although it should have made him happy to annoy Jasper, Call was tired of people acting like getting picked by Rufus was some great honor. "Look, I didn't do anything to make it happen. I didn't even mean to get picked at all, okay? I don't want to be here."

Jasper was shaking with rage. Up close, Call saw with bemusement that his bag, though fancy, had holes in the leather that had been carefully and repeatedly patched. Jasper's cuffs were an inch or so too short, too, Call realized, as if his clothes were hand-me-downs, or he'd almost grown out of them. Call bet that even his name was a hand-me-down, to match the monogram.

Maybe his family used to have money, but it didn't seem like they had it anymore.

"You're a liar," Jasper said desperately. "You did something. Nobody winds up getting picked by the most prestigious Master at the Magisterium by accident, so you can forget trying to fool me. When we get to school, I'm going to make it my mission to get that spot back. You're going to be *begging* to go home."

"Wait," Call said. "If you beg, they let you go home?"

Jasper stared at Call as if he'd just spouted off a bunch of sentences in Babylonian. "You have no idea how important this is," he said, gripping the handle of his bag so tightly that his knuckles turned white. "No idea. I can't even stand to be on the same bus as you." He spun away from Call, marching toward the other Masters.

Call had always hated the school bus. He never knew who to sit next to, because he'd never had a friend along the route — or any friend, really. Other kids thought he was weird. Even during the Trial, even among people who wanted to be *mages*, he seemed to stand out as strange. On this bus, at least, there was enough space that he got a row of seats to himself. *The fact that I smell like burning tires probably has something to do with that*, he thought. But it was still a relief. All he wanted was to be left alone to think about what had just happened. He wished his dad had gotten him a phone when he'd begged on his last birthday. He just wanted to hear his father's voice. He just wanted his last memory of his dad not to be of him being dragged away screaming. All he wanted to know was what to do next.

As they pulled onto the road, Master Rockmaple stood and began talking about the school, explaining that Iron Year students would be staying through the winter because it wasn't safe for them to go home partially trained. He also told them how they'd work with their Masters all week, have lectures with other Masters on Fridays, and participate in some kind of big test once every month. Call found it hard to concentrate on the details, especially when Master Rockmaple listed the Five Principles of Magic, which all appeared to have something to do with balance. Or nature. Or something. Call tried to pay attention, but the words seemed to wash away before he could commit them to memory.

After an hour and a half of driving, the buses pulled into a rest stop, where Call realized that in addition to not having luggage, he also didn't have any money. He pretended not to be hungry or thirsty while everyone else bought candy bars and chips and soda.

When they reboarded the bus, Call sat behind Aaron.

"Do you know where they're taking us?" Call asked.

"The Magisterium," Aaron said, sounding a little worried about Call's brain. "You know, the *school*? Where we're going to be *apprentices*?"

"But where is it exactly? Where are the tunnels?" Call asked. "And do you think they lock us in our rooms at night? Are there bars on the windows? Oh, wait, nope — because there aren't going to be any windows, right?"

"Uh," Aaron said, holding out his open bag of cheesy-garlic-bread-flavored Lays. "Chip?"

Tamara leaned across the aisle. "Are you actually deranged?" she asked, not really like she was insulting him this time, but more like she honestly wanted to discuss it.

"You do know that when we get there, we're going to die, right?" Call said, loud enough for the whole bus to hear him.

That was met with a resounding silence.

Finally, Celia piped up. "All of us?"

Some of the other kids snickered.

"Well, no, not all of us, *obviously*," said Call. "But some of us. That's still bad!"

Everyone was staring at Call again, except Master Rufus and Master Rockmaple, who were sitting up front and not paying any attention to what the kids were doing in back. Being treated like he was nuts had happened to Call more times that day than it had happened to him in his entire life, and he was getting sick of it. Only Aaron wasn't looking at Call like he was crazy. Instead, he crunched a chip.

"So who told you that?" he asked. "About us dying."

"My father," said Call. "He went to the Magisterium, so he knows what it's like. He says the mages are going to experiment on us."

"Was that the guy who was screaming at you at the Trial? Who threw that knife?" asked Aaron.

"He doesn't usually act like that," Call muttered.

"Well, he obviously went to the Magisterium and *he's* still alive," Tamara pointed out. She'd lowered her voice. "And my sister's there. And some of our parents went."

"Yeah, but my mother is dead," said Call. "And my father hates everything about the school. He won't even talk about it. He says my mom died because of it."

"What happened to her?" Celia asked. She had a package of root beer gummies open on her lap, and Call was tempted to ask her for one because it reminded him of the sundae he was never going to get and also because she sounded kind, like she was asking him because she wanted him not to worry about the mages, rather than because she thought he was a raving weirdo. "I mean, she had you, so she didn't die at the Magisterium, right? She must have graduated first."

Her question threw Call. He'd lumped it all together and hadn't thought about the timeline much. There had been a fight somewhere, part of some magic war. His father had been vague about the details. What he'd focused on was how the mages had let it happen.

When mages go to war, which is often, they don't care about the people who die because of it.

"A war," he said. "There was a war."

"Well, that's not very specific," said Tamara. "But if it was your mother, it had to be the Third Mage War. The Enemy's war."

"All I know is that they died somewhere in South America."

Celia gasped.

"So she died on the mountain," Jasper said.

"The mountain?" asked Drew from the back, sounding nervous. Call remembered him as the one who had been asking about pony school.

"The Cold Massacre," said Gwenda. He remembered the way she'd stood up when she'd been chosen, smiling like it was her birthday, her many braids with their beads swinging around her face. "Don't you know anything? Haven't you heard of the Enemy, Drew?"

Drew's expression froze. "Which enemy?"

Gwenda sighed with annoyance. "The *Enemy of Death*. He's the last of the Makaris and the reason for the Third War."

Drew still looked puzzled. Call wasn't sure he understood what Gwenda had said either. Makaris? Enemy of Death? Tamara looked back and caught sight of their expressions.

"Most mages can access the four elements," she explained. "Remember what Master Rockmaple said about us drawing on air, water, earth, and fire to make magic? And all that stuff about chaos magic?"

Call remembered something from the lecture at the front of the bus, something about chaos and devouring. It had sounded bad then and it wasn't sounding any better now.

"They bring something from nothing and that's why we call them Makaris. Makers. They're powerful. And dangerous. Like the Enemy."

A shiver went down Call's spine. Magic sounded even creepier than his father had said. "Being the Enemy of Death doesn't sound that bad," he said, mostly to be contrary. "It's not like death is so great. I mean, who would want to be the Friend of Death?"

"It's not like that." Tamara folded her hands in her lap, clearly annoyed. "The Enemy was a great mage — maybe even the best — but he went crazy. He wanted to live forever and make the dead walk again. That's why they called him the Enemy of Death, because he tried to conquer death. He started pulling chaos into the world, putting the power of the void into animals . . . and even people. When he put a piece of the void into people, it turned them into mindless monsters."

Outside the bus, the sun was gone, with only a smear of red and gold at the very edge of the horizon to remind them how recently it had become night. As the bus trundled along, farther into the dark, Call could pick out more and more stars in the canopy of the sky out the bus window. He could pick out only vague shapes in the woods they passed — it was just leafy darkness and rock as far as Call could see.

"And that's probably what he's still doing," said Jasper. "Just waiting to break the Treaty."

"He wasn't the only Makari of his generation," said Tamara, as if telling a story she'd learned by rote or reciting a speech she'd heard many times. "There was another one. She was our champion and her name was Verity Torres. She was only a little older than we are now, but she was very brave and led the battles against the Enemy. We were winning." Tamara's eyes shone, talking about Verity. "But then, the Enemy did the most treacherous thing anyone could ever do." Her voice dropped again so that the Masters up in the front of the bus couldn't possibly hear. "Everyone knew a big battle was coming. Our side, the good magicians, had hidden their families and children in a remote cave so they couldn't be used as hostages. The Enemy found out where the cave was and instead of going to the battlefield, he went there to kill them all."

"He expected them to die easily," Celia added, jumping in, her voice soft. She'd obviously heard the story lots of times, too. "It was just kids and old people and a few parents with babies. They tried to hold him off. They killed the Chaos-ridden in the cave, but they weren't strong enough to destroy the Enemy. In the end, everyone died and he slipped away. It was brutal enough that the Assembly offered the Enemy a truce and he accepted."

There was a horrified silence. "None of the good magicians lived?" asked Drew.

"Everybody lives in pony school," Call muttered. He was suddenly glad that he hadn't had enough money to buy any food at the rest stop, because he was pretty sure he would have thrown it up now. He knew his mother had died. He even knew she'd died in a battle. But he'd never heard the details before.

"What?" Tamara turned on him, icy fury on her face. "What did you say?"

"Nothing." Call sat back with his arms crossed. He knew from her expression he'd gone too far.

"You're unbelievable. Your mother died during the Cold Massacre, and you joke around about her sacrifice. You act like it was the mages' fault instead of the Enemy's."

Call looked away, his face hot. He felt ashamed of what he'd said, but he felt angry, too, because he should know about these things, shouldn't he? His father should have told him. But he hadn't.

"If your mother died on the mountain, where were you?" Celia interrupted, clearly trying to make peace. The flower in her hair was still crumpled from her fall at the Trial, and one corner of it was slightly singed.

"In the hospital," Call said. "My leg was messed up when I was born and I was having an operation. I guess she should have just stayed in the hospital waiting room, even if the coffee was bad." It was always like this when he was upset. It was like he couldn't control the words coming out of his mouth.

"You are a disgrace," Tamara spat, no longer the chilly, restrained girl she'd been throughout the Trial. Her eyes danced with anger. "Half the legacy kids at the Magisterium have family who died on the mountain. If you keep talking that way, somebody's going to drown you in an underground pool and no one will be sorry, including me."

"Tamara," Aaron said. "We're all in the same apprentice group. Give him a break. His mother died. He's allowed to feel any way he wants about it."

"My great-aunt died there, too," Celia said. "My parents talk about her all the time, but I never knew her. I'm not mad at you, Call. I just wish it didn't happen to either of us. To any of them."

"Well, I'm mad," said a guy in the back. Call thought his name might be Rafe. He was tall, with a thicket of curly dark hair, and he wore a T-shirt with a grinning skull on it that glowed a faint green in the dim light.

Call felt even worse. He almost said something apologetic to Celia and Rafe, until Tamara turned to Aaron and said fiercely: "But it's like he doesn't care. They were heroes."

"No, they weren't," Call burst out, before Aaron could speak. "They were victims. They got killed because of *magic*, and it can't be fixed. Not even by your Enemy of Death, right?"

There was a shocked silence. Even people who had been involved in other conversations in other parts of the bus turned around and gaped at Call.

His father had blamed the other mages for his mother's death. And he trusted his dad. He did. But with all of their eyes on him, Call wasn't sure what to think.

The silence was broken only by the sound of Master Rockmaple snoring. The bus had turned onto a bumpy dirt path.

Very quietly, Celia said, "I hear there are Chaos-ridden animals near the school. From the Enemy's experiments."

"Like horses?" Drew asked.

"I hope not," Tamara said with a shudder. Drew looked disappointed. "You wouldn't want a Chaos-ridden horse if you had one. Chaos-ridden creatures are the Enemy's servants. They've got a piece of the void in them and it makes them smarter than other animals, but bloodthirsty and insane. Only the Enemy or one of his servants can control them."

"So they'd be like evil-possessed zombie horses?" Drew asked.

"Not exactly. You'd know them by their eyes. Their eyes coruscate — pale, with spiraling colors inside of them — but otherwise they just look regular. That's the scary part," put in Gwenda. "I hope we don't have to go outside much."

"I do," said Tamara. "I hope we learn how to recognize and kill them. I want to do *that*."

"Oh, yeah," Call said under his breath. "*I'm* the crazy one. Nothing to worry about at the ole Magisterium. Evil pony school, here we come."

But Tamara wasn't paying attention to him. She was leaning out from her seat, listening to Celia say, "I hear there's a new type of Chaos-ridden where you can't tell from the eyes. The creature doesn't even know what it is until the Enemy makes it do what he wants. So, like, your cat could be spying on you or —"

The bus stopped with a jerk. For a second, Call thought maybe they'd gone to another gas station, but then Master Rufus rose to his feet. "We've arrived," he said. "Please file off the bus in an orderly fashion." And for a few minutes, everything was really ordinary, as if Call were just on a field trip. Kids grabbed their luggage and bags and jostled toward the front of the bus. Call got off just after Aaron and, since he didn't have to collect any baggage, was the first one to really take a second to look around.

CHAPTER FIVE

CALL WAS STANDING in front of a sheer mountain face. To the left and right was forest, but in front of him was a set of massive double doors. They were a weathered gray color with iron hinges that turned into curved swirls, bending inward on one another. Call imagined that from a distance or without the glow of the bus headlights, they would have been nearly invisible. Carved into the rock over the doors was an unfamiliar symbol:

Beneath it were the words: *Fire wants to burn, water wants to flow, air wants to rise, earth wants to bind, chaos wants to devour.*

Devour. The word sent a shiver through him. *Last chance to run,* he thought. But he wasn't very fast and there was nowhere to run to anyway.

The other kids had gotten their gear and were now standing around like he was. Master Rufus walked to the doors, and all of them grew quiet. Master North stepped forward.

"You are about to enter the halls of the Magisterium," he said. "For some of you, this may be the fulfillment of a dream. For others, we hope it may be the beginning of one. To all of you, I say, the Magisterium exists here for your own safety. You have a great power, and without training, that power is dangerous. Here, we will help you to learn control and teach you about the great history of mages like yourself, dating back through time. Each of you has a unique destiny, one outside the normal path you might have walked, one you will find here. You may have guessed this when you saw the first stirrings of your power. But as you stand at the entrance to the mountain, I imagine at least a few of you are wondering just what you've gotten yourselves into."

Some of the kids laughed self-consciously.

"Long ago, in the very beginning, the first mages wondered much the same thing. Intrigued by the teachings of the alchemists, particularly Paracelsus, they sought to explore elemental magic. They had limited success, until one alchemist realized that his young son was able to easily do the same exercises with which he struggled. The mages discovered that magic could be performed by those with an inborn power and was performed best by the young. After that, the mages found new students to teach and to learn from, seeking all over Europe for children with power. Very few have it, perhaps one in twenty-five thousand, but the mages gathered up those they could and began the first school of magic. Along the way, they heard stories of untrained boys and girls who had set fire to houses and burned in the flames, who had drowned in rainstorms or had been drawn up into tornados or pulled down into sinkholes. With teaching, the mages learned to walk through lava unscathed, to explore the deepest parts of the sea without an oxygen tank, even to fly."

Something inside Call leaped at what Master North was saying. He remembered being very small and asking his father to swing him through the air, but his dad wouldn't and told him to stop pretending. Could he really learn how to fly?

If you could fly, whispered a small, treacherous part of his brain, *it wouldn't matter so much that you can't run.*

"Here, you will encounter elementals, creatures of great beauty and danger that have existed in our world since the dawn of time. You will shape earth, air, water, and fire, bending them to your will. You will study our past as you become our future. You will discover what your ordinary self would never have had the privilege to see. You will learn great things and you will do greater things.

"Welcome to the Magisterium."

There was applause. Call looked around: Everyone's eyes were shining. And as much as he fought against it, he was sure he looked the same.

Master Rufus stepped forward. "Tomorrow, you will see more of the school, but for tonight, follow your Masters and get yourselves settled in your rooms. Please stay close as they lead you through the Magisterium. The tunnel system is complex, and until you know it well, it's easy to become lost."

Lost in the tunnels, Call thought. It was the exact thing he'd been scared of since he'd first heard of this place. He shivered as he remembered his nightmare about being trapped underground. Some of his doubts were creeping back, his father's warnings echoing in his head.

But they're going to teach me how to fly, he thought, as though arguing with someone who wasn't there.

Master Rufus held up one large hand, fingers splayed, and said something under his breath. The metal of his wristband began to glow, as though it had turned white-hot. A moment later, with a loud creaking that sounded almost like a scream, the doors began to open.

Light poured out from between them, and the kids moved forward, gasping and exclaiming. Call overhead a lot of "Cool!" and "Awesome!"

A minute later, he had to grudgingly admit it *was* kind of awesome.

There was a vast entrance hall, bigger than any inside space Call could have ever imagined. It could have held three basketball courts and still have room left over. The floor was the same glittering mica he'd seen in the illusion back at the airplane hangar, but the walls were covered with flowstone, which made it look like thousands of melting candles had slicked the walls in dripped wax. Stalagmites rose up all along the edges of the room, and huge stalactites hung down, nearly touching one another in places. There was a river, a bright glowing blue like luminous sapphire, cutting through the room, flowing in through an archway in one wall and out through another, a carved rock bridge crossing it. Patterns were cut into the sides of the bridge, patterns Call didn't recognize yet, but they reminded him of the markings on the dagger his dad had thrown to him.

Call hung back as all the apprentices from the Trial flooded in around him, forming a knot in the middle of the room. His leg felt stiff from the long bus ride and he knew he would be moving slower than ever. He hoped it wasn't a long walk to where they were supposed to sleep.

The huge doors closed behind them with a crash that made Call jump. He spun around just in time to see a row of sharply pointed stalactites, one after another, drop from the roof and thud into the ground, effectively blocking off the doors.

Drew, behind Call, swallowed audibly. "But — how are we supposed to get back out?"

"We're not," Call said, happy to have an answer for this, at least. "We're not ever supposed to get out."

Drew edged away. Call supposed he couldn't blame him, though he was getting a little tired of being treated like a freakazoid just for pointing out the obvious.

A hand took hold of his sleeve. "Come on." It was Aaron.

Call turned and saw that Master Rufus and Tamara were already starting to move. Tamara had a swagger in her step that hadn't been there before, under the watchful eyes of her parents. Muttering under his breath, Call followed the three of them through one of the archways and into the tunnels of the Magisterium.

Master Rufus held up one hand, and a flame appeared in his palm, flickering like a torch. It reminded Call of the fire resting on the water in the final test. He wondered what he should have done to really fail — to fail in a way that wouldn't have meant his coming here.

They walked one by one through a narrow corridor that smelled faintly of sulfur. It spilled into another room, this one with a series of pools, one of which bubbled away muddily and another full of pale, eyeless fish that dispersed at the sound of the humans' footfalls.

Call wanted to make a joke about how Chaos-ridden eyeless fish might be undetectable if they were servants of the Enemy of Death, because, well, no eyes, but he managed to creep himself out instead, imagining them spying on all the students.

Next they came upon a cavern with five doors set into its far wall. The first was made of iron; the second, copper; the third, bronze; the fourth, silver; and the last of gleaming gold. All of the doors reflected the fire in Master Rufus's hand, making flames dance eerily in the mirror of their polished surfaces.

High above him, Call thought he saw the flash of something shining, something with a tail, something that moved quickly into the shadows and was gone.

Master Rufus didn't lead them into the cavern and through any of the doors but kept them walking until they came to a big, round, high-ceilinged room with five arched passageways leading in as many different directions.

On the ceiling, Call spotted a group of lizards with gems on their backs, some seeming to burn with blue flames.

"Elementals," Tamara gasped.

"This way," Master Rufus said, the first words he'd spoken, his sonorous voice echoing in the empty space. Call wondered where all the other magicians were. Maybe it was later than he thought and they were asleep, but the emptiness of the rooms they'd passed through made it seem that they were all alone here, underground.

Finally, Master Rufus stopped in front of a large square door with a metal panel on the front where a door knocker would usually be. He raised his arm, and his wristband glowed again, this time a quick flash of light. Something clicked inside the door, and it swung open.

"Can we do that?" Aaron asked in an awed voice.

Master Rufus smiled down at him. "Yes, you certainly will be able to get into your own rooms with your wristbands, although you won't be able to go everywhere. Come inside your room and see where you're all going to spend the Iron Year of your apprenticeship."

"Iron Year?" Call echoed, thinking of the doors.

Master Rufus went inside, sweeping his arm around what looked like a combination living room and study area. The cave walls were high and arced upward to a dome. From the center of the dome hung a huge coppery chandelier. It had a dozen curving arms, each carved with designs of flame, each holding a burning torch. On the stone floor were three desks grouped in a loose circle and two deep, plush sofas facing each other in front of a fireplace big enough to roast a cow in. Not just a cow, a *pony*. Call thought of Drew and hid a sideways smile.

"It's amazing," Tamara said, turning around to look at everything. For a moment, she seemed like a regular kid rather than a mage from some ancient mage family.

Veins of bright quartz and mica ran through the stone walls, and as the torchlight hit them, they became a pattern of five symbols like those over the entrance — a triangle, a circle, three wavy lines, an arrow pointing up, and a spiral.

"Fire, earth, water, air, and chaos," said Aaron.

He must have been paying attention on the bus.

"Very good," said Master Rufus.

"Why are they arranged like that?" Call asked, pointing.

"It makes the symbols into a quincunx. And now, these are for you." He lifted three wristbands off a table that seemed carved out of a single piece of rock. They were wide leather bands with a strip of iron riveted into the cuffs and fastened with a buckle of the same metal.

Tamara picked hers up as though it were some kind of holy object. "Wow."

"Are they magic?" asked Call, eyeing his skeptically.

"These wristbands mark your progression through the Magisterium. Providing that you pass your test at the end of the year, you'll earn a different metal. Iron, then copper, bronze, silver, and finally gold. Once you complete your Gold Year, you will be considered no longer an apprentice but a journeyman mage, able to enter the Collegium. In answer to your question, Call, yes, these are magic. They've been made by a metal shaper and act as keys, allowing you access to classrooms in the tunnels. You will get additional metals and stones to attach to your cuff, signifying your achievements, so that by the time you graduate, it will be a reflection of your time here."

Master Rufus went over to a small kitchen area. Above an odd-looking stove with circles of stones where burners usually went, he reached into a cabinet and brought down three empty wooden plates. "We generally find it better to let new apprentices settle in their rooms the first night instead of getting over-whelmed in the Refectory, so you'll eat here this evening."

"Those plates are *empty*," Call pointed out.

Rufus reached into his pocket, bringing out a package of bologna and then a loaf of bread, two things that couldn't possibly have fit in there. "So they are. But not for long." He opened the bologna and made three sandwiches, placing each one on a plate and then carefully cutting them in halves. "Now picture your favorite meal."

Call looked from Master Rufus to Tamara and Aaron. Was this some kind of magic that they were supposed to be doing? Was Master Rufus suggesting that if you pictured something delicious while you ate a bologna sandwich, the bologna would taste better? Could he *read Call's mind*? What if the mages had been monitoring his thoughts the whole time and —

"Call," Master Rufus intoned, making him jump. "Is anything the matter?"

"Can you hear my thoughts?" Call blurted out.

Master Rufus blinked at him once, slowly, like one of the creepy lizards on the Magisterium ceiling. "Tamara. Can I read Call's thoughts?"

"Mages can only read your thoughts if you're projecting them," she said.

Master Rufus nodded. "And by projecting, what do you think she means, Aaron?"

"Thinking really hard?" he answered after a moment.

"Yes," said Master Rufus. "So please think very hard."

Call thought about his favorite foods, going over and over them in his mind. He kept getting distracted by other stuff, though, stuff that would be really funny if he pictured. Like a pie that was baked inside a cake. Or thirty-seven Twinkies stacked in the shape of a pyramid.

Then Master Rufus brought up his hands, and Call forgot to think of anything. The first sandwich began to spread, tendrils of bologna unfurling, coils growing across the plate. Delicious smells rose from it.

Aaron leaned in, clearly hungry despite the chips he'd eaten on the bus. The bologna coalesced into a plate, a bowl, and a carafe — the bowl was full of macaroni and cheese covered in bread crumbs, steaming as though it had just come out of an oven; the plate held a brownie heaped with ice cream; and the carafe was full of an amber liquid that Call guessed was apple juice.

"Wow," Aaron said, astonished. "It's exactly what I pictured. But is it real?"

Master Rufus nodded. "As real as the sandwich. You might recall the Fourth Principle of Magic — *You can change a thing's shape but not its essential nature.* And since I didn't alter the food's nature, it was truly transformed. Now you, Tamara."

Call wondered whether that meant Aaron's mac and cheese would taste like bologna. But at least it appeared Call wasn't the only one who didn't remember the principles of magic.

Tamara stepped forward to take her tray as her food formed. It held a big plate of sushi with a lump of green stuff on one end and a bowl of soy sauce on the other. With it was another plate with three round pink mochi balls. She'd received hot green tea to drink and actually looked happy about it.

Then it was Call's turn. He reached for his tray skeptically, not sure what he would find. But it really did hold his favorite dinner — chicken fingers with ranch dressing for dipping, a side bowl of spaghetti with tomato sauce, and a peanut butter sandwich with cornflakes for dessert. In his mug was hot chocolate with whipped cream and colored marshmallows dotted over the top.

Master Rufus looked pleased. "And now, I leave you to settle in. Someone will be along soon with your things —"

"Can I call my father?" Call asked. "I mean, is there a phone I could use? I don't have one of my own."

There was a silence. Then Master Rufus said, more gently than Call expected, "Cellular phones don't work in the Magisterium, Callum. We're too far below ground for that. Nor do we have landline phones. We use the elements to communicate. I would suggest we give Alastair some time to calm down, and then you and I will contact him together."

Call bit back any protest. It hadn't been a mean no, but it was a definite no. "Now," Master Rufus went on, "I expect the three of you up and dressed at nine tomorrow — and furthermore, I will expect you to be sharp-witted and ready to learn. We have much work to do together, and I would be very sorry if you didn't live up to the promise you showed at the Trial."

Call guessed that he meant Tamara and Aaron, since if he lived up to his promise, it would mean setting the underground river on fire.

After Master Rufus left, they sat down on stalagmite stools at the smooth stone table to eat together.

"What if you get ranch dressing on your spaghetti?" asked Tamara, glancing at Call's plate with her chopsticks poised in the air.

"Then it will be even more delicious," said Call.

"Gross," said Tamara, dabbing her wasabi into her soy sauce, without splashing a drop outside the dish.

"Where do you think they got fresh fish for your sushi, since we're in a cave?" Call asked, popping a chicken finger in his mouth. "Bet they took a net down to one of those underground pools and nabbed whatever came up. Glurp lurp."

"Guys," said Aaron in a long-suffering way. "You're putting me off my macaroni."

"Glurp lurp!" said Call again, closing his eyes and waving his head back and forth like an underground fish. Tamara picked up her food and stalked over to the couches, where she sat down with her back to Call and began eating.

They finished the rest of their food in silence. Despite hardly having eaten all day, Call couldn't finish his dinner. He pictured his father at home, eating at the cluttered kitchen table. He missed all of it, more than he'd ever missed anything.

Call shoved back his tray and stood up. "I'm going to go to bed. Which one is mine?"

Aaron leaned back in his chair and looked over. "Our names are on the doors."

"Oh," Call said, feeling foolish and a bit creeped out. His name was there, picked out in veins of quartz. *Callum Hunt.*

He went inside. It was a luxurious room, much bigger than his room at home. A thick rug covered the stone floor. It was woven with the repeating patterns of the five elements. The furniture seemed to be made of petrified wood. It shone with a sort of soft golden glow. The bed was huge and covered with thick blue blankets and big pillows. There was a wardrobe and a chest of drawers, but since Call had no clothes to put away and no stuff coming, he flopped down on the bed and put the pillow over his face. It only helped a little bit. Out in the common room, he could hear Tamara and Aaron giggling. They hadn't been talking like that before. They must have been waiting for him to leave.

Something was poking into his side. He had forgotten about the dagger his father had given him. Pulling it out of his belt, he looked at it in the torchlight. *Semiramis.* He wondered what the word meant. He wondered if he would spend the next five years alone in this room with his weird knife while people laughed at him. With a sigh, he dropped the knife onto the bedside table, kicked his feet under the blankets, and tried to go to sleep.

But it was hours before he did.

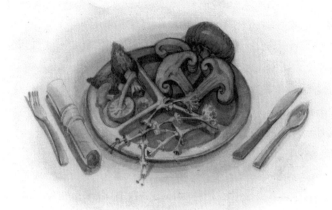

CHAPTER SIX

CALL WOKE UP to a sound like someone screaming in his ear. He threw himself sideways and fell off the bed, landing in a crouch and banging his knee against the cavern floor. The horrible sounds went on and on, echoing through the walls.

The door of his room flew open as the screams began to die away. Aaron appeared, and then Tamara. They were both wearing first-year uniforms: gray cotton tunics over loose-fitting pants made of the same material. Both of them had their iron cuffs clamped around their wrists: Tamara's on her right wrist, Aaron's on his left. Tamara had done her long hair in two dark braids on either side of her head.

"Ow," Call said, sitting back on his heels.

"It was just the bell," Aaron told him. "It means it's time for breakfast."

Call had never been woken up for school by an alarm before. His father had always come in and woken him by shaking his shoulder gently until Call rolled over, sleepy-eyed and grumbling. Call swallowed hard, missing home fiercely.

Tamara pointed behind Call, her perfectly tweezed eyebrows raised. "Did you sleep with your *knife*?"

A glance back at the bed showed that the knife his father had given him had been knocked off his bedside table — probably struck by one of his flailing arms — and onto his pillow. He felt his cheeks get hot.

"Some people have stuffed animals," Aaron said with a shrug. "Other people have knives."

Tamara crossed the room to sit on his bed, picking up the blade as Call pulled himself to his feet. He didn't hang on to the post of the bed to keep his balance, even though he wanted to. With his clothes crumpled from sleeping and his hair sticking up every-where, he was conscious of them watching him and of how slowly he had to move to avoid twisting his already hurting leg.

"What does it say?" Tamara asked, holding the knife up and turning it at an angle. "Down the side. Semi . . . ram . . . mis?"

Upright, Call said, "I bet you're pronouncing it wrong."

"And I bet you don't even know what the name means," Tamara smirked.

It hadn't even occurred to Call that the word on the blade was the knife's *name*. He didn't really think of knives as things that had names. Though he supposed King Arthur had Excalibur and in *The Hobbit*, Bilbo had Sting.

"You should call her Miri for short," Tamara said, handing it back to him. "She's a nice knife. Really well made."

Call searched her expression to see if she was mocking him, but she seemed serious. Apparently, she respected a good weapon. "Miri," he repeated, turning the knife over in his hand so that light sparked off the blade.

"Come on, Tamara," said Aaron, tugging on her sleeve. "Let Call get dressed."

"I don't have a uniform," Call admitted.

"Sure you do. It's right there." Tamara pointed to the foot of the bed as Aaron pulled her out of the room. "We all got them. They must have been brought by air elementals."

Tamara was right. Someone had left a neatly folded uniform, exactly Call's size, on top of his blanket, along with a leather school bag. When had that happened? When he was asleep? Or had he really not noticed it the night before? He put it on warily, shaking it out first in case there were any sharp bits or buttons that might stick him. The material was smooth and soft and completely comfortable. The boots he found resting beside the bed were heavy and held Call's weak ankle in a vise grip, steadying it. The only problem was that there was no pocket to put Miri in. Eventually, he wrapped the knife in his old sock and stuck it in the top of his boot. Then he pulled the strap of the leather bag over his head and went out into the common room, where Tamara and Aaron were sitting while a glowering Master Rufus stood over them with his arms folded.

"The three of you are late," he said. "The morning alarm is a call to breakfast in the Refectory. It's not your personal alarm clock. This had better not happen again or you will miss breakfast entirely."

"But we —" Tamara began, starting to look toward Call.

Master Rufus swung his gaze to her, pinning her in place. "Are you going to tell me that you were ready and someone else made you late, Tamara? Because then I would tell you that it is the responsibility of my apprentices to look after one another, and the failure of one is the failure of all. Now what was it you were about to say?"

Tamara lowered her head, braids swinging. "Nothing, Master Rufus," she said.

He nodded once, opened the door, and swept out into the hall, leaving them to follow him. Call limped toward the door, hoping fervently that this wouldn't be a long walk and hoping even more fervently that he could avoid getting in more trouble before he got something to eat.

Suddenly, Aaron appeared next to him. Call almost yelped in surprise. Aaron had an amazing habit of doing that, he thought, clicking into place beside him like a determined blond magnet. He bumped Call's shoulder and looked meaningfully down at his hand. Call followed his gaze and saw that there was something dangling from Aaron's fingers. It was Call's wristband. "Put it on," Aaron whispered. "Before Rufus sees. You're supposed to wear them all the time."

Call groaned, but he took the band and clicked it on to his wrist, where it glinted, gunmetal gray, like a handcuff.

That makes sense, Call thought. *After all, I'm a prisoner here.*

As Call had hoped, the Refectory wasn't far away. It didn't sound that different from his school cafeteria from a distance: the din of kids talking, the clatter of cutlery.

The Refectory was in another large cavern with more of the giant pillars that looked like melted ice cream turned to stone. Chips of mica sparkled in the rock, and the roof of the cave disappeared into shadow above their heads. It was too early in the morning for Call to be overly awed by the grandeur, though. He really just wanted to go back to sleep and pretend yesterday had never happened and that he was home with his father, waiting for the bus to take him to his regular school, where they let him wear regular clothes and sleep in a regular bed and eat regular food.

It certainly wasn't regular food that waited for him at the front of the Refectory. Steaming stone cauldrons along one side held an assortment of bizarre-looking food: stewed purple tubers, greens so dark they were almost black, fuzzy lichen, and a red speckled mushroom cap as large as a pizza and sliced up like a pie. Brown tea floating with pieces of bark steamed in a nearby bowl. Kids in uniforms of blue, green, white, red, and gray, each color denoting a different Magisterium year, were ladling it into carved wooden cups. Their wristbands flashed in gold and silver and copper and bronze, many with various colored stones attached. Call wasn't sure what the stones signified, but they looked pretty cool.

Tamara was already putting a scoop of the green stuff onto her plate. Aaron, however, was staring at the selection with the same expression of horror that Call felt.

"Please tell me that Master Rufus is going to turn this into something else," Aaron said.

Tamara bit back a laugh and looked almost guilty. Call got the feeling she didn't come from a family where people laughed very much. "You'll see," she said.

"Will we?" Drew squeaked. He seemed a little lost without his pony T-shirt, now dressed plainly in the high-necked gray tunic and pants that was the uniform of the Iron Year students. He reached dubiously for a bowl of lichen, knocked it over, and then edged away, pretending it hadn't been him.

One of the mages behind the tables — Call had seen her, and her elaborate snake necklace, at the Trial — sighed and went to clear it up. Call blinked as her snake necklace seemed to move for a second. Then he decided he was seeing things. He probably was suffering from caffeine withdrawal.

"Where's the coffee?" he asked Aaron.

"You can't drink coffee," Aaron said, squinting as he took a slice of mushroom. "It's bad for you. Stunts your growth."

"But I drank it all the time back home," Call protested. "I always drink coffee. I drink *espresso*."

Aaron shrugged, which seemed to be his default move when presented with some new Callum-related craziness. "There's that weird tea."

"But I love coffee," Call told the green sludge in front of him, plaintively.

"I miss bacon," said Celia, who was behind Call in line. She had a new bright clip in her hair, this one a ladybug. Despite how cheery it looked, she appeared woebegone.

"Caffeine withdrawal makes you crazy," he told her. "I could snap and kill someone."

She giggled like he'd made a really funny joke. Maybe she thought he had. She was pretty, he realized, with her blond hair and the spray of freckles across her slightly sunburned nose. He remembered that, along with Jasper and Gwenda, she was one of Master Milagros's apprentices. A wave of sympathy swept over him that she had to live in the same room as a weenus like Jasper.

"He *could* kill someone," Tamara said casually, looking back over her shoulder. "He has a huge knife in his —"

"Tamara!" Aaron interrupted her.

She gave him an innocent smile before heading back to Master Rufus's table with her plate. For the first time, Call wondered if he had something in common with Tamara after all — an instinct for troublemaking.

The whole room was filled with stone tables at which groups of apprentices sat on stools, some Second and Third Years with their Masters, and some without. The Iron Year students were all clustered with their Masters — Jasper, Celia, Gwenda, and a boy named Nigel with Master Milagros, the pink in her hair very bright today; Drew, Rafe, and a girl named Laurel with grouchy-looking Master Lemuel. Only a very few students in the white and red uniforms of Fourth and Fifth Years were present, and they all sat together in a corner, having what appeared to be a very serious discussion.

"Where are the rest of the older kids?" Call asked.

"On missions," said Celia. "Older apprentices learn in the field, and some grown-up mages come here to use the facilities for research and experiments."

"See," Call said in a hushed tone. *"Experiments!"*

Celia didn't seem particularly worried. She just grinned at Call and moved off toward her Master's table.

Call thumped into a chair between Aaron and Master Rufus, who was already seated before an austere breakfast containing a single clump of lichen. Call's plate was covered in mushrooms and green stuff — he didn't remember doing that. *I must be cracking up*, he thought. Then he took a forkful of mushroom and shoved it into his mouth.

The taste exploded over his tongue. It was actually good. *Really* good. Crispy at the edges and a little bit sweet, like the way maple syrup tastes on sausages when everything runs together.

"Huh," Call said, taking another bite. The greens were creamy and rich, like porridge with brown sugar. Aaron was shoveling spoonfuls of it into his mouth, looking astonished.

He expected to see Tamara snickering at him for being so surprised, but she wasn't even looking. She waved across the room at a tall, slim girl with the same long dark hair and perfect eyebrows as she had. A copper wristband glittered on the girl's wrist as she lifted her hand in a lazy wave. "My sister," Tamara said proudly. "Kimiya."

Call looked over at the girl, sitting at a table with a few other students in green and Master Rockmaple, and then back at Tamara. He wondered what it would be like to be happy here, to be glad you were chosen, instead of its being a terrible accident.

Tamara and her sister seemed so totally confident that this was a good place — that this wasn't the evil lair his father had described.

But why would his dad lie?

Master Rufus was slicing his lichen in a very strange way, segmenting it like individual pieces of bread in a loaf. Then he cut each of those pieces in half, and half again. This freaked Call out so badly that he turned to Aaron and asked, "So do you have any family here?"

"No," Aaron said, glancing away from Call as though he didn't like talking about it. "No family anywhere. I heard about the Magisterium from a girl I used to know. She saw this trick I did sometimes when I was bored — make dust motes dance around and form into shapes. She said she had a brother who went here and even though he wasn't supposed to tell her about it, he had. After he graduated and she left to go live with him, I started practicing for the Trial."

Call squinted at Aaron across his pile of mushrooms. There was something about the too-casual way he told the story that made Call wonder if maybe there was more to it. He didn't want to ask, though. He hated it when people pried into his life. Maybe Aaron did, too.

Aaron and Call lapsed into silence, pushing their food around their plates. Tamara went back to eating. From the other side of the hall, Jasper deWinter was waving his arms, clearly trying to get her attention. Call nudged her with his elbow and she scowled at him.

Rufus took a small, precise bite of lichen. "I see the three of you have grown very close already."

No one said anything. Jasper's gestures at Tamara were growing somewhat wilder. He was clearly urging her to do something, though Call couldn't tell what. Jump in the air? Throw her porridge?

Tamara turned back to Master Rufus, taking a deep breath as though steeling herself to do something she didn't particularly want to do. "Do you think you would ever reconsider about Jasper? I know it was his dream to be picked by you, and there's room for more in our group —" She stopped speaking, probably because Master Rufus was looking at her like a raptor bird about to bite off the head of a mouse.

When he finally spoke, though, his tone was cool, not angry. "The three of you are a team. You're going to work together and fight together and, yes, even eat together, for the next five years. I have chosen you not just as individuals, but as a combination. No one else will be joining you, because that would alter the combination." He stood up, pushing his chair back with a solid thwack. "Now, rise! We go to our first lesson."

Call's education in the use of magic was about to begin.

CHAPTER SEVEN

CALL WAS PREPARED for a long and miserable walk through the caverns, but Master Rufus led them down a straight corridor to an underground river instead.

It looked to Call a little like a subway tunnel in New York; he'd gone to the city with his dad on the hunt for antiques and remembered looking down into the darkness, waiting for the glow of lights that signaled a train. His gaze followed the river the same way, although now he wasn't sure what he was looking for or what it might signal. A sheer rock wall rose behind them, and water flowed swiftly past them into a smaller cave where they could see only shadows. A damp mineral smell was in the air, and along the shore were seven gray boats tied up in a neat row. They were constructed of wooden planks, each overlapping the other along the side and meeting at the front, affixed with copper rivets, all of it making them look like tiny Viking ships. Call looked around for oars or a motor or even a big pole, but he couldn't see any way to propel the boats.

"Go ahead," said Master Rufus. "Get in."

Aaron scrambled into the first of the boats, reaching out his hand to help Call inside. Resentfully, Call took it. Tamara got in behind them, looking a little nervous herself. As soon as she was settled, Master Rufus stepped into the boat.

"This is the most common way we get around the Magisterium, using the underground rivers. Until you can navigate, I will take you through the caves. Eventually, each of you will learn the paths and how to coax the water to take you where you want to go."

Master Rufus leaned over the side of the boat and whispered to the water. There was a soft ripple across the surface, as if the wind had stirred it, even though there was no wind underground.

Aaron leaned forward to ask another question, but all at once, the boat began to move and he fell back into his seat.

Once, when Call had been a lot younger, his father had taken him to a big park with rides that started like this. He'd cried through all of them, totally terrified, despite the cheerful music and the animated dancing puppets. And those had been rides. This was real. Call kept thinking about bats and sharp rocks and how, sometimes, in caves, there were cliffs and holes that dropped down like a million feet below sea level. How were they going to be able to avoid stuff like that? How were they going to know if they were going the right way in the dark?

The boat cut through the water, into darkness. It was the darkest darkness Call had ever experienced. He couldn't even see his hand in front of his face. His stomach lurched.

Tamara made a tiny sound. Call was glad it wasn't just him who was freaked out.

Then, all around them, the cave came to glowing life. They

passed into a room where the walls shimmered with pale, biolu-
minescent green moss. The water itself turned to light where the
prow of the boat touched it; when Aaron dragged his hand
through the river, it lit around his fingers, too. He flicked water
into the air and it transformed into a cascade of sparks. "Cool,"
Aaron breathed.

It *was* kind of cool. Call started to relax as the boat slipped
silently through the glowing water. They passed walls of rock
striped in dozens of colors, and rooms where long pale vines hung
from the ceiling, trailing tendrils in the river. Then they would
slide again into a dark tunnel and emerge into a new stone chamber where quartz stalactites sparkled like knife blades, or where
the stone seemed to grow naturally into the shapes of curved
benches, even tables — they passed two silent Masters in one
chamber, playing checkers with pieces that flew through the air.
"Got you!" said one of them, and the wooden discs started to
rearrange themselves, resetting the board to the beginning.

As though it were being steered by some invisible hand, the
boat docked itself near a small platform with stone steps, rocking
gently in place.

Aaron was out of the boat first, followed by Tamara, and
then Call. Aaron reached out a hand to help him, but Call deliberately ignored it. He used his arms to flip himself over the side
of the boat, landing awkwardly. For a moment, he thought he
was going to fall backward into the river, making a huge biolu-
minescent splash. A large hand clamped down on his shoulder,
steadying him. He looked up in surprise to see Master Rufus
watching him with a strange expression.

"I don't need your help," Call said, startled.

Rufus said nothing. Call couldn't read his expression at all.
He took his hand off Call's shoulder.

"Come," he said, and stalked up a smooth path that cut through the pebbly shore. The apprentices scrambled to follow.

The path led up to a blank granite wall. When Rufus put his hand to the stone, it turned transparent. Call wasn't even surprised. He'd come to expect weirdness. Rufus walked through the wall as if it were made of air. Tamara ducked after him. Call looked at Aaron, who shrugged. Taking a deep breath, Call followed.

He emerged into a chamber whose walls were bare rock. The floor was completely smooth stone. In the center of the room was a pile of sand.

"First, I wish to go over the Five Principles of Magic. You may remember some of these from your first lecture on the bus, but I don't expect any of you — even you, Tamara, no matter how many times your parents have drilled you — to truly comprehend them until you have learned many more things. You may write these down, however, and I do expect you to think on them."

Call scrambled with his pack and tugged out what appeared to be a hand-stitched notebook and one of those annoying pens from the Trial. He shook it lightly, hoping it wasn't going to explode this time.

Master Rufus began to speak and Call scrambled to transcribe fast enough. He wrote:

1. Power comes from imbalance; control comes from balance.

2. All elements act according to their nature: Fire wants to burn, water wants to flow, air wants to rise, earth wants to bind, chaos wants to devour.

3. In all magic, there is an exchange of power.

4. You can change a thing's shape, but not its essential nature.

5. All elements have a counterweight. Fire is the counterweight of water. Air is the counterweight of earth. The counterweight of chaos is the soul.

"During the tests," said Master Rufus, "all of you displayed power. But without focus, power is nothing. Fire can either burn down your house or warm it; the difference is in your ability to control the fire. Without focus, working with the elements is very dangerous. I don't need to tell some of you just how dangerous."

Call looked up, expecting to be the one who Master Rufus was staring at, since Master Rufus seemed to always be looking at Call when he said something ominous. This time, however, he was looking at Tamara. Her cheeks flushed and her chin went up defiantly.

"Four days a week, you three will train with me. On the fifth day, there will be a lecture by one of the other mages, and then, once a month, there will be an exercise in which you will put what you have learned to use. On that day, you may find yourselves either competing against or working with other apprentice groups. Weekends and nights are yours for practice and further study. There is the Library as well as practice rooms, and the Gallery, where you can waste time. Do you have any questions for me before we begin your first lesson?"

No one spoke. Call wanted to say something about how he'd love some directions to that Gallery place, but he held himself back. He remembered telling his father back at the hangar that he was going to get himself thrown out of the Magisterium, but he'd woken up that morning with the sinking feeling that maybe that wasn't such a good idea. Trying to flunk the tests in front of Rufus hadn't worked, after all, so acting out might not either. Master Rufus clearly wasn't going to let him communicate with Alastair until Call settled in as an apprentice. As much as it galled him to do it, he probably had to be on his best behavior until Rufus relaxed and let him contact his father. Then, when he *could* finally talk to Alastair, they'd plan his escape.

He just wished he felt a little more enthusiastic about running away.

"Very well. Can you guess why I've set up the room this way, then?"

"I'm guessing you need help fortifying your sand castle?" muttered Call under his breath. Even his best behavior apparently wasn't all that good. Aaron, standing beside him, stifled a laugh.

Master Rufus raised a single brow but didn't otherwise acknowledge what Call had said. "I want you three to sit in a circle around the sand. You can sit any way that you're the most comfortable. Once you're ready, you must concentrate on moving the sand with your mind. Feel the power in the air around you. Feel the power in the earth. Feel it rise up through the soles of your feet and in the breaths you take. Now *focus* it. Grain by grain, you are going to separate the sand into two piles — one dark and one light. You may begin!"

He said it like they were in a race and he'd given them the green light, but Call, Tamara, and Aaron just stared at him in horror. Tamara was the first to find her voice.

"Separate out the sand?" she said. "But shouldn't we be learning something more useful? Like fighting rogue elementals or piloting the boat or —"

"Two piles," said Rufus. "One light, one dark. Start now."

He turned around and walked away. The wall became transparent again as he approached it, then turned back to stone as he passed through.

"Don't we even get a tool kit?" Tamara called sadly after him.

The three of them were alone in a room with no windows and no doors. Call was glad he didn't have claustrophobia or he'd be chewing off his own arm.

"Well," said Aaron, "I guess we should start."

Even he didn't manage to say it with any enthusiasm.

The floor was cold when Call sat and he wondered how long it would be before the dampness made his leg ache. He tried to ignore this thought as Tamara and Aaron sat down, making a triangle around the sand pile. They all stared at it. Finally, Tamara stuck out her hand, and some sand rose into the air. "Light," she said, sending a grain spinning toward the floor. "Dark." She sent that one on the floor, too, a little distance away. "Light. Dark. Dark. Light."

"I can't believe I was worried magic school was going to be dangerous," Call said, squinting at the sand pile.

"You could die of boredom," said Aaron. Call snickered.

Tamara looked up at them miserably. "The thought of that is the only thing that's going to keep me going."

As difficult as Call had imagined it to be to move tiny grains of sand with his mind, it was even harder than that. He remembered the times he'd moved things before, how he'd accidentally broken the bowl during his exam with Master Rufus and how it had felt like a buzzing in his mind. He concentrated on that buzzing while he stared at the sand, and it started to move. It felt a little like he was operating a device with a remote control — it wasn't his fingers picking up the sand, but he was still making it happen. His hands felt clammy and his neck strained — making a single grain hover in the air for long enough to see whether it was light or dark was tricky. Even worse was setting it down without messing up the pile already there. More than once, his concentration slipped and he dropped a grain into the wrong pile. Then he had to find it and pull it back out, which took time and even *more* concentration.

There were no clocks in the sand room, and neither Call nor Aaron nor Tamara were wearing watches, so Call had no idea how much time was passing. Finally, another student showed up — he was tall and lanky, dressed in blue, with a bronze wristband that indicated he'd been at the Magisterium three years. Call thought he might have been sitting with Tamara's sister and Master Rockmaple in the Refectory that morning.

Call squinted at him to see if he looked particularly sinister, but he just grinned from under a tangle of messy brown hair and dropped a burlap bag of lichen and cheese sandwiches, along with an earthenware pitcher of water, at their feet. "Eat up, kids," he said, and headed out the way he'd come.

Call realized he was starving. He'd been concentrating for hours and his brain felt fuzzy. He was exhausted, much too tired to make conversation as he ate. Worse, as he studied the remaining sand, they'd made it only a small part of the way through the pile. The heap that remained seemed enormous.

This was not flying. This wasn't what he'd pictured when he'd imagined doing magic. This stank.

"Come on," Aaron said. "Or we're going to have to eat dinner down here."

Call tried to concentrate, focusing his attention on a single grain, but then his mind slipped sideways into anger. The sand exploded, all the piles flying sideways, grains splashing the walls and settling into a giant, unsorted mess. All of their hard work was undone.

Tamara sucked in her breath in horror. "What — what did you *do*?"

Even Aaron looked at Call like he was going to strangle him. It was the first time Call had ever seen Aaron look angry.

"I — I —" Call wanted to say he was sorry, but he bit down on the words. He knew they wouldn't matter. "It just happened."

"I'm going to kill you," Tamara said very calmly. "I am going to sort your guts into piles."

"Uh," said Call. He kind of believed her.

"Okay," Aaron said, taking big calming breaths, hands in his hair, like he was trying to press all that rage back into his skull. "Okay, we're just going to have to do it all over again."

Tamara kicked the sand, then crouched down and began the tedious work of moving single grains with her mind. She didn't even look in Call's direction.

Call tried to concentrate again, eyes burning. By the time Master Rufus came and told them they were free to go to dinner and then back to their rooms, Call's head was pounding and he'd decided he never wanted to go to the beach ever again. Aaron and Tamara wouldn't look at him as they made their way through the corridors.

The Refectory was full of kids chatting away amicably, a lot of them giggling and laughing. Call, Tamara, and Aaron stood in the doorway behind Master Rufus and stared blearily ahead of them. All of them had sand in their hair and dirt streaks on their faces. "I will be eating with the other Masters," Master Rufus said. "Do as you like with the rest of your evening."

Moving like robots, Call and the others gathered up food — mushroom soup, more piles of different-colored lichen, and an odd opalescent pudding for dessert — and went over to sit at a table with another clump of Iron Year students. Call recognized a few of them, like Drew, Jasper, and Celia. He sat down across from Celia, and she didn't immediately dump her soup on his head — a thing that had actually happened at his last school — so that seemed like a good sign.

The Masters sat together at a round table across the room, probably brainstorming new tortures for the students. Call was sure he could see several of them smiling in a sinister way. While he was watching, three people in olive green uniforms — two women and a man — came through the doorway. They bowed shallowly to the table of Masters.

"They're Assembly members," Celia informed Call. "It's our governing body, set up after the Second Mage War. They're hoping one of the older kids turns out to be a chaos mage."

"Like that Enemy of Death guy?" Call asked. "What happens if they find chaos mages? Do they kill them, or what?"

Celia lowered her voice. "No, of course not! They *want* to find a chaos mage. They say it takes a Makar to stop a Makar. As long as the Enemy is the only one of the Makaris alive, he has the advantage over us."

"If they even *think* someone here has that power, they'll check it out," said Jasper, moving down so he was closer to the discussion. "They're desperate."

"No one believes that the Treaty will last," said Gwenda. "And if the war starts up again . . ."

"Well, what makes them think anyone here could be what they're looking for?" Call asked.

"Like I said," Jasper told him, "they're desperate. But don't worry — your scores are way too lousy. Chaos mages have to actually be *good* at magic."

For a minute, Jasper had acted like a normal human being, but apparently that minute was over. Celia glared at him.

Everyone launched into a discussion of their first lessons. Drew told them that Master Lemuel had been really tough during their lessons, and he wanted to know if everyone else's Masters were like that. Everyone started talking at once, with a bunch of others describing lessons that sounded a lot less frustrating and more fun than Call's had been.

"Master Milagros let us pilot the boats," Jasper gloated. "There were little waterfalls. It was like white-water rafting. Awesome."

"Great," Tamara said, without enthusiasm.

"Jasper got us all lost," Celia said, serenely munching a piece of lichen, and Jasper's eyes flashed with annoyance.

"Only for a minute," Jasper said. "It was fine."

"Master Tanaka showed us how to make fireballs," said a boy named Peter, and Call remembered that Tanaka was the name of the Master who had chosen after Milagros. "We held the fire and we didn't even get burned." His eyes sparkled.

"Master Lemuel threw rocks at us," said Drew.

Everyone stared at him.

"What?" said Aaron.

"Drew," hissed Laurel, another of Master Lemuel's apprentices. "He did not. He was showing us how you can move rocks with your mind. Drew got in the way of a rock."

That explains the big bruise on Drew's collarbone, Call thought, feeling a little sick. He remembered his father's warnings about how the Masters didn't care about hurting students.

"Tomorrow it's going to be metal," said Drew. "I bet he throws knives at us."

"I'd rather have knives thrown at me than spend all day in a pile of sand," said Tamara, unsympathetic. "At least you can dodge knives."

"Looks like Drew can't," said Jasper with a smirk. For once, he was picking on someone who wasn't Call, but Call didn't get any pleasure from it.

"It can't be all lessons around here," said Aaron, an edge to his usually peaceful voice. "Right? There's got to be something fun. What was that place Master Rufus told us about?"

"We could go to the Gallery after dinner?" Celia said, speaking directly to Call. "There's games."

Jasper looked annoyed. Call knew he should go with Celia to the Gallery, whatever that was. Anything that made Jasper mad was worth doing, and besides, he needed to learn to navigate the Magisterium, make a map like you did in video games.

He needed an escape route.

Call shook his head and forked up a mouthful of lichen. It tasted like steak. He glanced down the table at Aaron, who looked weary, too. Call's body felt leaden. He just wanted to go to sleep. He'd start looking for a way out of the Magisterium tomorrow.

"I don't think I'm up for games," he told Celia. "Another time."

↑ ≈ △○◉

"Maybe today was a test," Tamara said as they headed back to their rooms after dinner. "Like, of our patience or our ability to take orders. Maybe tomorrow we'll get to do real training."

Aaron, trailing one of his hands along the wall as he walked, took a moment to respond. "Yeah. Maybe."

Call didn't say anything. He was too tired.

Magic, he was finding, was hard work.

The next day, Tamara's hopes were dashed when they returned to the place that Call had dubbed the Room of Sand and Boredom to finish sorting. They still had plenty of sand to go. Call felt guilty all over again.

"But when we're done," Aaron said to Master Rufus, "we can do other stuff, right?"

"Concentrate on the task at hand," the mage replied enigmatically, walking out through the wall.

Heaving sighs, they sat down to work. Sand sorting went on for the rest of the week, with Tamara spending all her time after classes with her sister or Jasper or other expensive-looking legacy students, and Aaron spending his time with *everyone*, while Call sulked in their room. Then sand sorting went on for another week after that — the pile of sand to sort seemed to be getting bigger and bigger, as if someone didn't want this test ever to end. Call had heard there was some kind of torture where a single drop of water hit a guy's forehead over and over again until he went insane. He had never understood how that worked before, but he understood it now.

There's got to be an easier way, he thought, but the scheming part of his mind must have been the same part used for magic, because he couldn't think of anything.

"Look," Call said finally, "you guys are good at this, right? The best mages in the tests. Top-ranked."

The other two gazed at him, glassy-eyed. Aaron looked like maybe he'd been hit on the head by a falling boulder when no one was looking.

"I guess," Tamara said. She didn't sound too excited about it. "The best in our year, anyway."

"Okay, well, I'm terrible. The worst. I was in last place and I've already messed things up for us, so obviously I don't know anything. But there must be a faster way. Something we're supposed to be doing. Some lesson we're supposed to be learning. Is there anything you can think of? *Anything?*" A note of pleading had entered his voice.

Tamara hesitated. Aaron shook his head.

Call saw her expression. "What? *Is* there something?"

"Well, there are some magical principles, some . . . special ways of tapping into the elements," she said, her black braids swinging as she moved into a different sitting position. "Stuff that Master Rufus probably doesn't want us to know about."

Aaron nodded eagerly, the hope of making it out of this room lighting his face.

"You know how Rufus was talking about feeling the power in the earth and all that?" Tamara wasn't looking at them. She was staring at the piles of sand like she was focused on something far away. "Well, there's a way to get more power, fast. But you have to open yourself up to the element . . . and, well, eat a grain of sand."

"Eat the sand?" Call said. "You have to be kidding."

"It's kind of dangerous, because of that whole First Principle of Magic thing. But it works for the same reason. You're closer to the element — like if you're doing earth magic, you eat rocks or sand, fire mages can eat matches, air mages might consume blood for its oxygen. It's not a good idea, but . . ."

Call thought of Jasper grinning around his bloody finger at the Trial. His heart started to pound. "How do you know this?"

Tamara looked at the wall. She took a deep breath. "My dad. He taught me how. For emergencies, he said, but he considers doing well on a test an emergency. I've never done it, though, because it scares me — if you get too much power and can't control it, you could get drawn into an element. It burns away your soul and replaces it with fire, air, water, earth, or chaos. You become a creature of that element. Like an elemental."

"One of those lizard things?" Aaron asked.

Call was relieved he hadn't had to be the one to ask that exact same question.

Tamara shook her head. "Elementals come in all sizes. Small like those lizards, or big and bloated on magic, like wyverns and dragons and sea serpents. Or even human size. So we'd have to be careful."

"I can be careful," Call said. "How about you, Aaron?"

Aaron ran grainy hands through his blond hair and shrugged. "Anything is better than this. And if we finish faster than Master Rufus expects, he'll have to give us something else to do."

"Okay. Here goes nothing." Tamara licked the tip of her finger and touched it to the pile of sand. A few grains stuck. Then she put her finger in her mouth.

Call and Aaron copied her. As Call jammed his wet finger into his mouth, he couldn't help wondering what he would have thought if a week ago someone had told him he'd be sitting in an underground cavern eating sand. The sand didn't taste bad — it didn't taste like anything, really. He swallowed the rough grains down and waited.

"Now what?" he asked after a few seconds. He was starting to get a little nervous. Nothing had happened to Jasper at the Trial, he told himself. Nothing would happen to them.

"Now we concentrate," Tamara said.

Call looked at the pile of sand. This time when he slid his thoughts toward it, he could sense each of the tiny grains. Minuscule pieces of shell sparkled in his mind, beside crystal pieces, and yellowish stones honeycombed with crags. He tried to imagine picking up the whole pile of sand in his hands. It would be heavy, and the sand would spill between his fingers and pool on the floor. He tried to blank out everything around him — Tamara and Aaron, the cold stone under him, the faint rush of wind in the room — and narrow his concentration down to the only two things that mattered: himself and the pile of sand. The sand felt completely solid and light, like Styrofoam. It would be easy to lift. He could lift it with one hand. With one finger. With one . . . thought. He imagined it rising and separating. . . .

The sand pile lurched, spilling a few grains from the top, and then drifted upward. It hung over the three of them like a small storm cloud.

Tamara and Aaron both stared. Call fell back on his hands. His legs were prickling with pins and needles. He must have sat on them wrong. He'd been concentrating too hard to notice. "Your turn," he said, and it seemed to him that the walls were closer, that he could feel the pulse of the earth underneath him. He wondered what it would be like to sink into the ground.

"Absolutely," said Aaron. The cloud of sand broke apart into two halves, one composed of lighter sand, the other darker. Tamara raised her hand and drew a lazy spiral on the air. Call and Aaron watched in wonder as the sand swirled into different patterns above them.

The wall opened. Master Rufus stood on the threshold, his face a mask. Tamara made a little squeaking sound, and the hovering pile of sand crashed down, sending up puffs of dust that made Call choke.

"What have you done?" Master Rufus demanded.

Aaron looked pale. "I — we didn't mean —"

Master Rufus gestured sharply toward them. "Aaron, be quiet. Callum, come with me."

"What?" Call began. "But I — that's not fair!"

"Come. With. Me," Rufus repeated. "*Now.*"

Call rose gingerly to his feet, his weak leg stinging. He glanced at Aaron and Tamara, but they were looking down at their hands, not at him. *So much for loyalty*, he thought as he followed Master Rufus out of the room.

↑≈△○@

Rufus led him on a short walk through some twisting corridors to his office. It wasn't what Call expected. The furnishings were modern. Steel bookcases filled one wall, and a sleek leather couch, big enough to nap on, stretched along the other. Tacked to one side of the room were pages and pages of what looked like scrawled equations, but with odd markings instead of numbers. They hung above a rough wooden workstation whose surface was blotched with stains and covered with knives, beakers, and the taxidermied bodies of weird-looking animals. Beside delicate, geared models that looked like mousetraps crossed with clocks, there was a live animal in a small barred cage — one of those lizards with blue flames running along its back. Rufus's desk was tucked into a corner, an old rolltop that was at odds with the rest of the room. On top of it was a glass jar holding a tiny tornado spinning in place.

Call couldn't take his eyes off it, expecting it to burst out of the jar at any moment.

"Callum, sit down," said Master Rufus, indicating the couch. "I want to explain why I brought you to the Magisterium."

CHAPTER EIGHT

CALL STARED. After two weeks of sand sorting, he'd
given up on the idea that Rufus was ever going to be forward
or direct with him. In fact, he realized, he'd given up on the idea
that he'd ever really find out why he was at the Magisterium at all.

"Sit," Rufus said again, and this time Call sat, wincing as his
leg twinged. The couch was comfortable after hours of sitting on
a cold stone floor, and he let himself sink into it. "What do you
think of our school so far?"

Before Call could answer, there was the sound of rushing
wind. He blinked, and realized it was coming from the jar on
Master Rufus's desk. The small tornado inside it was darkening
and condensing into a shape. A moment later, it had taken the
form of a miniature olive-green-uniformed Assembly member. It
was a man with very dark hair. He blinked around.

"Rufus?" he said. "Rufus, are you there?"

Rufus made an impatient noise and flipped the jar over. "Not
now," he said to it, and the image inside became a tornado again.

"Is that like a telephone?" Call asked, awed.

"Something like a telephone," said Rufus. "As I said before, the concentration of elemental magic in the Magisterium interferes with most technology. Besides, we prefer to do things our own way."

"My dad is probaby really worried, not having heard from me in so —" Call started.

Master Rufus leaned against his desk, crossing his arms over his broad chest. "First," he said, "I want to know what you think of the Magisterium and your training."

"It's easy," Call said. "Boring and pointless, but easy."

Rufus gave a thin smile. "What you did in there was very clever," he said. "You want to make me angry because you think that if you do, I'll send you home. And you believe you want to be sent home."

Call had actually given up on that plan. Saying obnoxious things just came naturally to him. He shrugged.

"You must wonder why I chose you," Rufus said. "You, the last of all those ranked. The least competent of all the potential mages. I suppose you imagine that it is because I saw something in you. Some potential the other Masters had missed. Some untapped well of skill. Maybe even something that reminded me of myself."

His tone was lightly mocking. Call was silent.

"I took you on," Rufus continued, "because you do have skill and power, but you also have a great deal of anger. And you have almost no control at all. I did not want you to be a burden on one of the other mages. Nor did I want one of them to choose you for the wrong reasons." His eyes flicked toward the tornado, spinning in its upside-down jar. "Many years ago, I made a mistake with a student. A mistake that had grave consequences. Taking you on is my penance."

Call's stomach felt as if it wanted to curl up inside him like a kicked puppy. It hurt, being told that he was so unpleasant he was someone's punishment.

"So send me home," he burst out. "If you just took me because you don't feel like one of the other mages should have to teach me, send me home."

Rufus shook his head. "You still don't understand," he said. "Uncontrolled magic like yours is a danger. Sending you home to your small town would be the equivalent of dropping a bomb on them. But make no mistake, Callum. If you persist in disobedience, if you refuse to learn to control your magic, then I will send you home. But I will bind your magic first."

"Bind my magic?"

"Yes. Until a mage passes through the First Gate at the end of his Iron Year, his or her magic can be bound by one of the Masters. You would be unable to access the elements, unable to use your power. And we would take your memories of magic, too, so that all you would know was that you were missing something, some essential part of yourself, but you would no longer know what it was. You would spend your life tormented by the loss of something you didn't remember losing. Is that what you want?"

"No," Call whispered.

"If I believe that you're holding back the others or that you're untrainable, you're done here. But if you make it through this whole year and pass through the First Gate, then no one can ever take your magic away. Make it through this year and you can drop out of the Magisterium if you want. You'll have learned enough to no longer be a danger to the world. Think on that, Callum Hunt, as you sort your sand the way I instructed you to. Grain by grain." Master Rufus paused, and then made a dismissive gesture, indicating that Call could go. "Think on that and make your choice."

↑ ≈ △ ○ @

Concentrating on moving the sand was as grueling as ever, more so because of how pleased Call had been with their cleverness in coming up with a better solution. For once, he'd felt that maybe they could really be a team, maybe even friends.

Now Aaron and Tamara concentrated quietly, and when he looked over at them, they wouldn't meet his gaze. They were probably mad at him, Call thought. He'd been the one who'd insisted that someone come up with a better way of doing the exercise. And even though he was the one who'd been dragged into Rufus's office, they were all going to be in trouble. Maybe Tamara even thought he'd finked on her. Plus, it was his magic that had scattered their piles that first day. He was a burden on the group, and they all knew it.

Fine, Call thought. *All Master Rufus said I had to do was get through this year, so I'm going to do it. And I'm going to be the best mage here, just because no one thinks I can be. I never really tried before, but I'm going to try now. I'm going to be better than you both and then, when I've impressed you and you really want me to be your friend, I'm going to turn around and tell you how much I don't need you or the Magisterium. As soon as I pass through the First Gate and they can't bind my magic anymore, I'm going home and no one can stop me.*

That's what I'm going to tell Dad, too, as soon as I get to that tornado phone.

He spent the rest of the day moving sand with his mind, but instead of doing it the way he had the first day, straining to capture each grain, pushing it with all the desperate effort of his brain, today he let himself experiment. He tried a lighter and lighter touch, tried rolling the sand instead of lifting it into the air. Then he tried to move more than one bit of sand at once. He'd done it before, after all. The trick was that he'd thought of it as one thing — a sand cloud — instead of as three hundred individual grains.

Maybe he could do the same thing now, thinking of all the dark grains as one thing.

He tried, *pulling* with his mind, but there were too many and he lost focus. He gave up on that idea and concentrated on five grains of dark sand. These he was able to move, rolling them together toward the pile.

He slumped back, amazed, feeling he'd done something incredible. He wanted to say something to Aaron, but instead, he kept his mouth shut and practiced his new technique, getting better and better at it, until he was moving twenty grains at a time. He couldn't do better than that, though, no matter how hard he struggled. Aaron and Tamara saw what he was doing, but neither one of them said anything, nor did they try to imitate him.

That night, Call dreamed of sand. He was sitting on a beach, trying to build a castle for a naked mole rat caught in a storm, but the wind kept blowing the sand away as the water grew closer and closer. Finally, frustrated, he stood up and kicked at the castle until it came apart and became a huge monster with enormous sand arms and legs. It chased him down the beach, always about to grab him but never quite close enough, as it shouted at him in Master Rufus's voice, *Remember what your father said about magic, boy. It'll cost you everything.*

↑ ≈ △ ○ @

The next day, Master Rufus didn't drop them off and leave as usual. Instead, he sat down in a far corner of the Room of Sand and Boredom, took out a book and a waxed paper packet, and started to read. After about two hours, he unwrapped the packet. It was a ham-and-cheese sandwich on rye bread.

He appeared to be indifferent to Callum's method of moving more than one grain at a time, so Aaron and Tamara started doing it, too. Things moved faster then.

That day, they actually managed to sort all the sand before dinnertime. Master Rufus looked over what they'd done, nodded in satisfaction, and kicked it all back into one big pile again. "Tomorrow, you're going to sort by five gradations of color," he said.

The three of them groaned in unison.

↑ ≈ △○@

Things went on like that for another week and a half. Outside of class, Tamara and Aaron ignored Call, and Call ignored them right back. But they got better at moving sand — better, more precise, and more able to concentrate on multiple grains at once.

Meanwhile, at meals, they heard about the lessons the other apprentices were receiving, which all sounded more interesting than sand — especially when those lessons backfired. Like when Drew set himself on fire and managed to burn up one of the boats and singe Rafe's hair before he was able to put himself out. Or when Milagros's and Tanaka's students were practicing together and Kai Hale dropped a lizard elemental down the back of Jasper's shirt. (Call thought Kai might deserve a medal.) Or when Gwenda decided she liked one of the mushroom cap pizza things so much that she wanted more of it and inflated the mushroom so large that it pushed everyone — even the Masters — out of the Refectory for several days until its growth could be tamed and they could hack their way back in.

Dinner the night they were able to use the Refectory again was lichen and more pudding — no mushrooms at all, anywhere. The interesting thing about the lichen was that it never tasted the same — sometimes it tasted like steak and sometimes like fish tacos or vegetables with spicy hot sauce, even if it was the same color. The gray pudding that night tasted like butterscotch. When Celia caught Call going back for fourths, she tapped his wrist playfully with her spoon.

"Come on, you should come to the Gallery," she said. "There's great snacks there."

Call glanced up the table at Aaron and Tamara, who shrugged agreement. The three of them were still being stiff and silent with one another, only talking when they had to. Call wondered if they planned to forgive him ever, or if this was it, and it was going to be awkward for the rest of the time he was here.

Call dropped his bowl back on the table, and a few minutes later found himself part of a laughing group of Iron Year students making their way toward the Gallery. Call noticed that as they went, the glittering crystals on the walls made it seem like the corridor was covered in a fine layer of snow.

He wondered if any of these corridors led in the direction of Master Rufus's office. Not a day went by that he didn't think about sneaking in there and using the tornado phone. But until Master Rufus taught them how to control the boats, Call needed another route.

They walked through an unfamiliar part of the tunnels, one that seemed to slope gently upward, with a shortcut over an underground lake. For once, Call didn't mind the extra distance, because this part of the caves had a bunch of cool things to look at — a flowstone formation of white calcite that looked like a frozen waterfall, concretions in the shape of fried eggs, and stalagmites that had turned blue and green from the copper in the rock.

Call, moving slower than the others, was in the back, and Celia dropped back to chat with him. She pointed out things he hadn't seen before, like the holes high up in the rocks where bats and salamanders lived. They passed through a big circular room with two passages leading from it. One had the word *Gallery* picked out above it in sparkling rock crystal. The other read *The Mission Gate*.

"What's that?" Call asked.

"It's another way out of the caves," Drew, overhearing, told him. Then he looked weirdly guilty, as if he wasn't supposed to tell.

Maybe Call wasn't the only one who didn't understand the rules of magic school. When he looked closer, he saw Drew looked about as exhausted as Call felt.

"But you can't just leave," Celia added, giving Call a wry look, as if she thought that every time he heard about a new exit, he was going to consider whether or not he could escape that way. "It's only for apprentices on missions."

"Missions?" Call asked, as they followed the others toward the Gallery. He remembered her saying something about them before, when she'd explained why all the apprentices weren't at the Magisterium.

"Errands for Masters. Fighting elementals. Fighting the Chaos-ridden," Celia said. "You know, mage stuff."

Right, Call thought. *Pick up some deadly nightshade and kill a wyvern on your way back. No problem.* But he didn't want to make

Celia mad, since she was pretty much the only person still talking to him, so he kept those thoughts to himself.

The Gallery was huge, with a ceiling at least a hundred feet above them and a lake at one end, stretching off into the distance, with several small islands dotting the surface. A few kids were splashing in the water, which steamed gently. A movie was playing on one crystal wall — Call had seen the movie before, but he was sure what was happening on the screen hadn't actually happened in the version he'd seen.

"I love this part," Tamara said, rushing over to where kids had arranged themselves on rows of oversize, velvety-looking toadstools. Jasper appeared and plunked himself down directly next to her. Aaron looked slightly puzzled but followed anyway.

"You have to try the fizzy drinks," Celia said, pulling Call over to a rocky ledge where an enormous glass beverage dispenser, full of what looked like water, rested beside three stalactites. She picked up a glass, filled it from the twist spout, and stuck it beneath one of the stalactites. A spurt of blue liquid splashed down into the water, and a mini whirlpool appeared inside the glass, spinning the blue liquid and the clear liquid together. Bubbles rose to the top.

"Go on, try it," Celia urged.

Call gave the drink a suspicious look, then took the glass from her and swigged down the liquid.

It felt like crystals of sweet blueberry and caramel and strawberry were bursting inside his mouth.

"This is *fantastic*," he said when he was done swallowing.

"The green is my favorite," Celia said, grinning around a glass she'd poured for herself. "It tastes like a melted lollipop."

There were piles of other interesting-looking snacks on the ledge — bowls of shiny rocks that were clearly spun out of sugar,

pretzels wound into the shapes of alchemical symbols and sparkling with salt, and a bowl of what looked like crispy potato chips
at first glance but were darker gold when you looked at them
closely. Call tried one. It tasted almost exactly like buttered
popcorn.

"Come on," Celia said, grabbing his wrist. "We're missing
the movie." She drew him toward the velvety toadstools. Call
went a little reluctantly. Things were still fraught with Tamara
and Aaron. He thought it might be better to avoid them and
explore the Gallery on his own. But no one was paying attention
to him anyway; they were all watching the movie being projected
on the far wall. Jasper kept leaning over to say things in Tamara's
ear that made her giggle, and Aaron was chatting with Kai on his
other side. Fortunately, there were enough older kids around to
make it easy for Call not to sit too close to the other apprentices
in his group without it seeming intentional.

As Call relaxed into his seat, he realized that the movie
wasn't being *projected* exactly. A solid block of colored air hovered
against the rock wall, colors swirling in and out of it impossibly
fast, creating the illusion of a screen. "Air magic," he said, half to
himself.

"Alex Strike does the movies." Celia was hugging her knees,
intent on the screen. "You probably know him."

"Why would I know him?"

"He's a Bronze Year. One of the best students. He assists
Master Rufus sometimes." There was admiration in her voice.

Call glanced back over his shoulders. In the shadows behind
the rows of toadstool cushions was a taller chair. The lanky
brown-haired boy who'd brought them sandwiches for the
past few days was sitting in it, his eyes intent on the screen in
front of him. His fingers were moving back and forth, a little like

a puppeteer's. As he moved them, the shapes on the screen shifted.

That's really cool, the little, treacherous voice inside Call said. *I want to do that.* He pushed the voice down. He was leaving as soon as he passed through the First Gate of Magic. He was never going to be a Copper Year or Bronze Year or any other year than this one.

When the movie ended — Call was pretty sure he didn't remember a scene in *Star Wars* where Darth Vader made a conga line with Ewoks, but he'd only seen it once — everyone jumped up and clapped. Alex Strike shook his hair back and grinned. When he saw Call looking at him, he nodded.

Everyone soon spread out through the room to play with other fun stuff. It was like an arcade, Call thought, but with no supervision. There was a hot pool of water that bubbled with many colors. Some of the older students, including Tamara's sister and Alex, were swimming in it, amusing themselves by making little whirlpools dance along the surface of the water. Call stuck his legs in it for a while — it felt good after all the walking he'd been doing — and then joined Drew and Rafe in feeding the tame bats, which would sit on their shoulders while they fed them pieces of fruit. Drew kept giggling as the bats' soft wings tickled his cheek. Later, Call joined up with Kai and Gwenda to play a weird game involving batting around a ball of blue fire that turned out to be cold when it struck him in the chest. Ice crystals clung to his gray uniform, but he didn't mind. The Gallery was so much fun that he forgot to worry about Master Rufus, about his father, about bound magic, or even about Aaron and Tamara hating him.

Will it be hard to give this up? he wondered. He imagined being a mage and playing in bubbling springs and conjuring movies out of thin air. He imagined being good at this stuff, one of the Masters, even. But then he thought of his dad sitting at the kitchen table all by himself, worrying over Call, and felt awful.

When Drew, Celia, and Aaron started back toward the rooms, he decided to go with them. If he stayed up any later, he'd be cranky in the morning and, besides, he wasn't sure he knew the way without them. They retraced their steps through the caves. It was the first time in days Call felt relaxed.

"Where's Tamara?" Celia asked as they walked.

Call had seen her standing with her sister when they left and was about to answer when Aaron spoke. "Arguing with her sister."

Call was surprised. "What about?"

Aaron shrugged. "Kimiya was saying that Tamara shouldn't be wasting her time in the Gallery in her Iron Year, playing games. Said she ought to be studying."

Call frowned. He'd always kind of wanted a sibling, but he was suddenly reconsidering.

Beside him, Aaron stiffened. "What's that noise?"

"It's coming from the Mission Gate," Celia replied, looking worried. A moment later, Call heard it, too: the tread of booted feet on stone, the echo of voices bouncing off rock walls. Someone calling for help.

Aaron took off, running up the passage toward the Mission Gate. The rest of them hesitated before following him, Drew hanging back so much that he kept pace with Call's hurrying. The passage started to fill up with people pushing past them, almost knocking Call over. Something clamped on to his arm and he found himself pulled back against a wall.

Aaron. Aaron had flattened himself against the stone and was watching, his mouth a thin line, as a group of older kids —

some of them wearing silver wrist cuffs, some gold — came limping through the passage. Some were being carried on make-shift stretchers strapped together from branches. One boy was being supported by two other apprentices — the whole front of his uniform looked like it had been burned away, the skin underneath red and bubbly. All of them had scorch marks on their uniforms and black soot streaking their faces. Most were bleeding.

Drew looked like he was going to cry.

Call heard Celia, who had pressed herself to the wall next to Aaron, whisper something about fire elementals. Call stared as a boy went by on a stretcher, writhing in agony. His uniform sleeve was burned away and his arm seemed to be glowing from the inside, like a piece of kindling in a fire.

Fire wants to burn, Call thought.

"You! You, Iron Years! You shouldn't be here!" It was Master North, scowling as he detached himself from the group of the wounded. Call wasn't sure how he'd spotted them or why he was there.

They didn't wait to be told twice. They scattered.

CHAPTER NINE

THE NEXT DAY was more sand and more tiredness. That night in the Refectory, Call slumped down at the table with his plate of lichen and a pile of cookies that appeared to sparkle with crystalline chunks. Celia bit into one and it made a sound like cracking glass.

"These are safe to eat, right?" Call asked Tamara, who was spooning up some kind of purple pudding that stained her lips and tongue a deep indigo.

She rolled her eyes. There were dark smudges under them, but she was, as always, otherwise composed. Resentment twinged in Call's chest. Tamara was a robot, he decided. A robot with no human feelings. He hoped she shorted out.

Celia, seeing the ferocious way he was looking at Tamara, tried to say something, but her mouth was full of cookie. A few seats down, Aaron was saying. "All we do is divide sand into piles. For hours and hours. I mean, I'm sure it's for a reason, but —"

"Well, I feel sorry for you," Jasper interrupted. "Master Lemuel's apprentices have been fighting elementals and we've been doing awesome things with Master Milagros. We made fireballs, and she showed us how to use the metal in the earth to levitate ourselves. I got almost an inch off the ground."

"Wow," said Call, his voice dripping contempt. "A whole inch."

Jasper whipped around on Call, eyes bright with anger. "It's because of you that Aaron and Tamara have to suffer. Because you did so badly in the tests. That's why your whole group is stuck in the sandbox while the rest of us get to hit the playing field."

Call felt the blood rush up into his face. It wasn't true. It couldn't be true. He saw Aaron, down the table, shake his head and start to speak. But Jasper wasn't stopping. With a sneer, he added, "And I wouldn't be so snotty about levitating if I was you, Hunt. If you could ever learn to levitate yourself, maybe you wouldn't slow down Tamara and Aaron so much, limping along after them."

The moment after the words left his mouth, Jasper looked shocked, like even he hadn't expected to go so far.

It wasn't the first time anyone had ever said something like that to Call, but it was always like a bucket of cold water being thrown in his face.

Aaron sat up straight, eyes wide. Tamara slammed her hand down on the table. "Shut up, Jasper! We're not sorting sand because of Call. We're sorting sand because of me. It's my fault, okay?"

"What? No!" Jasper seemed totally confused. Clearly, he hadn't meant to upset Tamara. Maybe he'd even hoped to impress her. "You did really well at the Trial. We all did, except him. He took my spot. Your Master felt sorry for him and wanted —"

Aaron stood up, gripping his fork in his hand. He looked furious.

"It wasn't *your* spot," he spat out at Jasper. "It's more than just points. It's about who the Master wants to teach — and I can see exactly why Master Rufus didn't want *you*."

He'd said it loudly enough that people at nearby tables were staring. With a last disgusted look at Jasper, Aaron threw the fork he was holding onto the table and stalked off, his shoulders stiff.

Jasper turned back to Tamara. "I guess you have two crazy people in your group, not just one."

Tamara gave Jasper a long, considering look. Then she picked up her bowl of pudding and turned it upside down on top of his head. Purple goop ran down his face. He yelped in surprise.

For a moment, Call was too shocked to react. Then he burst out laughing. So did Celia. Laughter broke out up and down the table as Jasper wrestled the bowl off his head. Call laughed even harder.

Tamara wasn't laughing, though. She looked like she couldn't believe she'd lost her composure so thoroughly. She stood frozen for a long moment, then stumbled to her feet and ran for the door in the direction Aaron had gone. Across the room, her sister, Kimiya, disapprovingly watched her go, arms crossed over her chest.

Jasper threw his bowl onto the table and shot Call a look of pure, anguished hatred. His hair was coated with pudding.

"Could have been worse," Call said. "Could have been that green stuff."

Master Milagros appeared at Jasper's side. She shoved some napkins at him and demanded to know what had happened. Master Lemuel, who had been sitting at the closest table, rose and came over to lecture everyone, joined halfway through by Master Rufus, whose face was as impassive as ever. The babble of adult voices went on, but Call wasn't paying attention.

In his whole twelve years, Call couldn't remember anyone but his dad ever defending him. Not when people kicked his weak leg out from under him during soccer, or laughed at him for being benched during gym class or picked last for every team. He thought of Tamara dumping the pudding on Jasper's head and then of Aaron saying *It's more than just points. It's about who the Master wants to teach,* and he felt a little warm glow inside.

Then he thought about the real reason Master Rufus wanted to teach him, and the glow went out.

Call walked back to their rooms alone, through echoing rock passageways. When he got there, Tamara was sitting on the couch, her hands curved around a steaming stone cup. Aaron was talking to her in a low voice.

"Hey," Call said, standing awkwardly in the doorway, not sure if he should leave or not. "Thanks for — well, just thanks."

Tamara looked up at him with a sniff. "Are you coming in or not?"

Since it would be even more awkward to linger around in the hallway, Call let the door swing shut behind him and started toward his room.

"Call, stay," Tamara said.

He turned to look at her and Aaron, who was sitting on the arm of the sofa, dividing anxious glances between Call and Tamara. Tamara's dark hair was still perfect and her back straight, but her face was blotchy, like she'd been crying. Aaron's eyes were troubled.

"What happened with the sand was my fault," Tamara said. "I'm sorry. I'm sorry I got you in trouble. I'm sorry I suggested something so dangerous in the first place. And I'm sorry I didn't say something sooner."

Call shrugged. "I asked you to come up with an idea — any idea. It wasn't your fault."

She gave him a strange look. "But I thought you were mad?"

Aaron nodded in agreement. "Yeah, we thought you were angry with us. You didn't say practically anything for *three whole weeks*."

"No," Call said. "You didn't say anything to *me* for three whole weeks. You guys were the ones who were mad."

Aaron's green eyes went wide. "Why would we be mad at you? You got in trouble with Rufus; we didn't. You didn't blame it on us, even though you could have."

"I'm the one who should have known better," said Tamara, gripping her cup so hard her knuckles turned white. "You two hardly know anything about magic, about the Magisterium, about elements. But I do. My . . . older sister . . ."

"Kimiya?" asked Call, puzzled. His leg was aching. He perched himself on the coffee table, rubbing his knee through his cotton uniform.

"I had another sister," Tamara said in a whisper.

"What happened to her?" Aaron asked, his voice hushing to match hers.

"Worse," said Tamara. "She became one of those things I was telling you about — a human elemental. There are these great mages who can swim through the earth like they're fish or make stone daggers shoot out from walls or bring down lightning strikes or make giant whirlpools. She wanted to be one of the great ones, so she pushed her magic until she got taken over by it."

Tamara shook her head, and Call wondered what she was seeing as she told them about this. "The worst part is how proud my dad was of her at first, when she was succeeding. He would tell Kimiya and me how we should be more like her. Now he and my mother won't talk about her at all. They won't even say her name."

"What is her name?" Call asked.

Tamara looked surprised. "Ravan."

Aaron's hand hovered in the air for a second, like he wanted to pat Tamara on the shoulder but wasn't sure if he should. "You're not going to wind up like her," he said. "You don't have to worry."

She shook her head again. "I told myself that I wouldn't be like my father or my sister. I told myself I would never take any chances. I wanted to prove I could do everything the right way and not cut a single corner — and I would *still* be the best. But then I did cut corners — and I taught you how to cut them, too. I didn't prove anything."

"Don't say that," said Aaron. "You proved something tonight."

Tamara sniffed. "What?"

"That Jasper looks better with pudding in his hair," Call suggested.

Aaron rolled his eyes. "That's not what I was going to say . . . although I sure wish I'd seen it."

"It was pretty great," Call said, grinning.

"Tamara, you proved that you care about your friends. And we care about you. And we'll make sure you don't cut any more corners." He looked over at Call. "Won't we?"

"Yeah," said Call, studying the toe of his boot, not sure he was the best person for this assignment. "And, Tamara . . . ?"

She scrubbed the corner of her eye with her sleeve. "What?"

He didn't look up and he could feel the heat of embarrassment creep up his neck and make his ears pink. "No one's ever stuck up for me like you guys did tonight."

"Did you actually say something nice to us?" Tamara asked him. "Are you feeling okay?"

"I don't know," Call said. "I might need to lie down."

But Call didn't lie down. He stayed up talking with his friends for a good part of the night.

CHAPTER TEN

B Y T H E E N D of the first month, Call didn't care if he was about to get creamed by the other apprentices in whatever trial they were going to do, so long as it meant no more Room of Sand and Boredom. He sat listlessly in a triangle with Aaron and Tamara, sorting the light and dark and lightish and darkish piles as if they'd been doing it for a million years. Aaron tried to start a conversation, but Tamara and Call were too bored to talk in more than grunts. But sometimes now, they all looked at one another and smiled the secret smiles of actual friendship. Exhausted friendship, but real friendship nonetheless.

At lunchtime, the wall opened, but for a change, it wasn't Alex Strike. It was Master Rufus, and he was carrying in one hand what looked like a massive wooden box with a trumpet sticking out of it, and in the other, a bag of something colorful.

"Continue as you were, children," he said, setting the box down on a nearby rock.

Aaron boggled. "What is that?" he whispered to Call.

"A gramophone," said Tamara, who was still sorting sand, even as she stared at Rufus. "It plays music, but it works with magic, not electricity."

At that moment, music blasted from the trumpet of the gramophone. It was very loud, and not anything Call recognized immediately. It had a thumping, repetitive sound that was incredibly annoying.

"Isn't that the *Lone Ranger* theme song?" Aaron asked.

"It's the *William Tell* Overture," Master Rufus shouted over the music, capering around the room. "Listen to those horns! Gets your blood pumping! Ready for doing magic!"

What it did was make it really, really, *really* hard to think. Call found himself straining to concentrate, which made it a challenge to get a single grain up into the air. Just when he thought he had the sand under control, the music would soar and his focus would scatter.

He made a noise of frustration and opened his eyes to see Master Rufus opening the bag and pulling out a beet-red worm. Call seriously hoped it was a gummi worm, since Master Rufus started chewing one end of it.

Call wondered what would happen if instead of trying to move the sand, he concentrated on smashing the gramophone against the cave wall. He looked up and saw Tamara glaring at him.

"Don't even *think* about it," she said, as though reading his mind. She looked flushed, her dark hair sticking to her forehead as she struggled to concentrate on the sand despite the music.

A bright blue worm hit Call in the side of the head, causing him to spill his airborne sand all over his lap. The worm bounced to the ground and lay there. *Okay, it's definitely a candy worm,* Call thought, since it didn't have any eyes and looked gelatinous.

On the other hand, that described a lot of things in the Magisterium.

"I can't do this," Aaron panted. He had his hands raised, sand spinning; his face was red with concentration. An orange worm bounced off his shoulder. Rufus had the bag open and was throwing handfuls of worms. "Gah!" Aaron said — the worms didn't hurt, but they really were startling. There was a green one stuck in Tamara's hair. She looked near tears.

The wall opened again. This time it *was* Alex Strike. He had a bag with him, and an odd, almost malicious grin split his face as he looked from Rufus, still hurling worms, to the apprentices, struggling as hard as they could to concentrate.

"Come in, Alex!" said Rufus cheerfully. "Leave the sandwiches just over there! Enjoy the music!"

Call wondered if Alex was remembering his own Iron Year. He hoped Alex wasn't visiting any of the other apprentice groups, ones that were learning cool things with fire or levitation. If Jasper found out any details of what Call had to do today, he would never stop mocking him.

It doesn't matter, Call told himself sternly. *Concentrate on the sand.*

Tamara and Aaron were moving grains, rolling them and pulling them through the air. Slower than before, but they were in the zone, working even when they were smacked in the back of the head with a gummi worm. Tamara now had a blue one tangled up in a braid and didn't even seem to notice.

Call closed his eyes and focused his mind.

He felt the damp cold smack of a worm on his cheek, but this time, he didn't let the sand fall. The music pounded in his ears, but he let all of that slide away. One grain after another at first, and then, as his confidence grew, more and more sand.

That'll show Master Rufus, he thought.

Another hour went by before they took a break to eat their lunch. When they started up again, the mage bombarded them with waltzes. As his apprentices sorted sand, Rufus sat on a boulder and did a crossword. He didn't seem bothered when they went hours over their time and missed dinner in the Refectory.

They tramped back to their rooms, tired and dirty, to discover food laid out for them on the table in the common room. Call found that he was in a surprisingly good mood, considering, and Aaron made him and Tamara crack up over dinner with his impression of Master Rufus waltzing with a worm.

The next morning, Master Rufus showed up at their door just after the alarm, carrying armbands that would distinguish their team during the first test. They all yelled in excitement. Tamara yelled because she was happy, Aaron yelled because he liked it when other people were happy, and Call yelled because he was sure they were going to die.

"Do you know what kind of test it's going to be?" Tamara asked, eagerly winding the armband around her wrist. "Air, fire, earth, or water? Can you give us a hint? Like just a tiny little itty-bitty —"

Master Rufus looked sternly at her until she stopped talking. "No apprentices are given advance knowledge of how they are to be tested," he said. "That would confer an unfair advantage. You must win on your own merits."

"Win?" Call said, startled. It hadn't occurred to him that Master Rufus was expecting them to win the test. Not after a whole month of sand. "We're not going to *win*." He was mostly concerned with whether they would *survive*.

"That's the spirit." Aaron hid a grin. He was already wearing his armband, just above his elbow. Somehow he managed to make it look cool. Call had tied his around his forearm and was fairly sure it looked like a bandage.

Master Rufus rolled his eyes. It worried Call that the corners of his mouth twitched up in an involuntary smile, as though he was actually starting to understand Master Rufus's expressions and responding to them.

Maybe by the time they were in their Silver Year, Master Rufus would communicate complicated theories of magic by the lifting of a single bushy eyebrow.

"Come along," the mage said. With a dramatic swoosh, he spun around and led them out the door and through what Call was starting to think of as the main corridor. Phosphorescent moss flashed and sparkled as they went, down a spiral stair that Call had never seen before, into a cavern.

At his other school, he'd always wanted to be allowed to play sports. At least here, they were giving him a chance. Now it was his job to keep up.

The cavern was the size of a stadium, with massive stalactites and stalagmites jutting up and down like teeth. Most of the other Iron Year apprentices were there with their Masters. Jasper was talking to Celia, gesturing wildly at the stalagmites in one corner, which had grown together in a complicated loop shape. Master Milagros hovered slightly above the ground, encouraging one of the kids to hover with her. Everyone was moving with restless energy. Drew looked especially on edge, whispering with Alex. Whatever Alex was saying, Drew didn't look happy about it.

Walking farther into the room, Call glanced around, trying to anticipate what might happen. Along one wall was a large cave that appeared to have bars in front of it, like a cage made of calcite. Looking at it, Call worried that the test was going to be even scarier than he'd imagined. He rubbed his leg absently and wondered what his father would say.

This is the part where you die, probably.

Or maybe it was an opportunity to show Tamara and Aaron that he was worth sticking up for.

"Iron Year apprentices!" Master North said as a few more students trickled in after Master Rufus. "I give you your first exercise. You are going to fight elementals."

Hushed gasps of dread and excitement spread around the room. Call's spirits plunged. Were they kidding? None of the apprentices were prepared for that, he was willing to bet. He looked to Aaron and Tamara to see if they disagreed. They had both gone pale. Tamara was gripping her armband.

Call frantically tried to remember the lecture Master Rockmaple had given them two Fridays back, the one on elementals. *Dispersing rogue elementals before they can cause harm is one of the important tasks mages are responsible for*, he'd said. *If they feel threatened, they can disperse back into their element. It takes them a lot of energy to coalesce again.*

So all they had to do was scare the elementals. Great.

Master North furrowed his brow, as though he'd just noticed that the students looked concerned. "You'll do fine," he assured them.

This struck Call as unearned optimism. He imagined them all lying dead on the floor while wyverns bent on revenge swooped overhead, with Master Rufus shaking his head and saying, *Maybe the apprentices will be better next year.*

"Master Rufus," Call hissed, trying to keep his voice down. "We can't do this. We didn't practice —"

"You know what you need to know," said Rufus, cryptically. He turned to Tamara. "What do the elements want?"

Tamara swallowed. *"Fire wants to burn,"* she said. *"Water wants to flow, air wants to rise, earth wants to bind, chaos wants to devour."*

Rufus clapped a hand down on her shoulder. "You three think about the Five Principles of Magic and about what I taught you, and you'll do fine." With that, he strode away to join the other mages on the far side of the room. They'd shaped the rocks into seats and were lounging there in apparent comfort. Some other mages were coming in behind them. There were a few other older students, too, along with Alex, the cave light glinting off their bracelets. That left the Iron Year apprentices in the middle of the room as the lights dimmed, until they were surrounded by darkness and silence. Slowly, the apprentice groups started to shuffle together into a single large mass, facing the portcullis as it opened up into the unknown.

For a long moment, Call stared into the dark beyond, until he started to wonder if anything was there. Maybe the test was to see if the apprentices actually believed the mages would do something as ridiculous as letting twelve-year-olds fight wyverns in gladiatorial combat.

Then he saw shining eyes in the gloom. Great clawed feet crunched through the dirt as three creatures emerged from the cave. They were as tall as two men and stood on their back legs, bodies hunched over, dragging spiked tails behind them. Vast wings beat the air where arms might have been. Wide, toothy mouths snapped at the ceiling.

All Call's father's warnings beat inside his head, making him feel like he couldn't breathe. He was more scared than he could remember being before. All the monsters of his imagination, every beast that hid in closets or under beds was dwarfed by the nightmares that clawed hungrily toward him.

Fire wants to burn, Call thought to himself. *Water wants to flow. Air wants to rise. Earth wants to bind. Chaos wants to devour. Call wants to live.*

Jasper, apparently possessed of an entirely different feeling about his own survival, broke away from the huddle of the apprentices and, with a great howl, ran directly toward the wyverns. He lifted his hand and thrust it, palm out, toward the monsters.

A very small ball of fire shot from his fingers, flying past one of the wyvern's heads.

The creature roared in fury, and Jasper balked. He thrust out his palm again, but now only smoke rose from it. No fire at all.

A wyvern stepped toward Jasper, opening its mouth, thick blue fog pouring from its jaws. The fog curled through the air slowly, but not so slowly that Jasper was able to evade it. He rolled to one side, but the fog blew over him, surrounding him. A moment later, he was rising through it, floating up like a soap bubble.

The other two wyverns sprang into the air.

"Oh, crap," said Call. "How are we supposed to fight that?"

Rage flashed across Aaron's face. "It's not fair."

Jasper was yelling now, bobbing back and forth on the plumes of wyvern breath. Lazily, the first wyvern batted at him with its tail. Call couldn't suppress a spark of pity. The other apprentices stood frozen, staring upward.

Aaron took a deep breath and said, "Here goes nothing." As Call and the others watched, he dashed forward, throwing himself at the closest wyvern's tail. He managed to catch it on the down stroke, and the wyvern let out a cry of surprise that sounded like a thunderclap. Aaron clung on grimly as the tail swung around, tossing him up and down as if he were riding a bucking bronco. Jasper, in his bubble, rose up and bobbled around at the ceiling among the stalactites, yelling and kicking out with his legs.

The wyvern cracked its tail like a whip, and Aaron went flying. Tamara gasped. Rufus flung out a hand, and flecks of ice crystals shot from it, coming together in midair, forming a handlike shape that caught Aaron inches from the floor and then froze that way.

Call felt a burst of relief in his chest. He hadn't realized until that moment how much he'd been worried that the Masters wouldn't lift a hand to help them — that they'd just let them die.

Aaron struggled against the fingers, trying to get free. A few of the other Iron Year apprentices moved together in a pack, advancing toward the second wyvern. Gwenda made fire spark between her hands, blue as the flame on the lizards' backs. The wyvern yawned at them lazily, sending out slow tendrils of breath. One by one, they began to rise through the air, shouting. Celia shot out a blast of ice as she rose. It missed, striking just to the left of the second wyvern's head, making it roar.

"Call!" He whirled around at Tamara's urgent whisper, just in time to see her dive behind a thicket of stalagmites. Call started to move after her, only to stop at the sight of Drew standing frozen, off to the side of the group.

Call wasn't the only one who noticed. The third wyvern, eyes narrowed in a predatory yellow glare, curled around to face the frightened apprentice.

Drew flung both his arms down, palms facing the ground, as he muttered frantically. Then he rose slowly off the ground, lifting himself to the wyvern's eye level.

He's mimicking being hit by the smoke, Call realized. *Smart.*

Drew called up a ball of wind into his hand and aimed. The wyvern snorted in surprise, breaking Drew's concentration and pinwheeling him in the air. Not wasting any time, the wyvern darted its head forward and snapped its beak, catching the very edge of Drew's trouser leg. The cloth ripped as Drew kicked the air frantically.

Call rushed forward to help — just as the second wyvern swooped down from the cavern ceiling, straight toward him.

"Call, run!" Drew yelled. "Go!"

It was a good suggestion, Call thought, if only he *could* run. His weak leg twisted as he tried to dart away over the uneven ground, and he stumbled, righting himself quickly, but not quickly enough. The cold black eyes of the wyvern were focused on him, its talons extended as it grew closer and closer. Call broke into a shambling run, his leg aching as he thumped his foot down against the rock. He wasn't fast enough. Looking over his shoulder, he tripped and went flying, slamming against gravel and sharp stone.

He rolled over onto his back. The wyvern reared up over him. Some part of Call was telling him that the Masters would step in before anything too serious happened, but a much bigger part of him was howling with fear. The wyvern seemed to take up his whole field of vision, its jaws opening, revealing a scaly maw and sharp teeth. . . .

Call flung out his arm. He felt a burst of dull heat explode around him. A wave of sand and rock cascaded up from the ground, hammering against the wyvern's chest.

The beast flew back and was knocked hard against the cave wall, before slumping to the ground. Call blinked, pushing himself slowly to his feet. When he was up, he looked around with new eyes.

Oh, he thought, seeing the mayhem unfolding all over the room, the fire streaking past and kids spinning in circles as they lost their concentration and their magic tossed them from side to side. He understood, all at once, why they'd been practicing in the sand room for so long. Against all odds, magic had become automatic to him. He knew the concentration it needed.

His wyvern was struggling to its feet, but now Call was ready. He focused, throwing his hand out, and three stalactites cracked free, slamming down and pinning the wyvern to the ground by its wings.

"Ha!" said Call.

The beast opened its beak, and Call moved to retreat, knowing he wouldn't be fast enough to avoid the monster's breath —

"Give me Miri," Tamara yelled, coming from the shadows. "Quick!"

Reaching for his belt, Call pulled out the knife and tossed it to her. The wyvern's mouth was open, smoke just beginning to curl out. With two quick strides, Tamara walked through the smoke to the wyvern and moved to stab the blade through the wyvern's eye. Just as it was about to hit, the monster disappeared in a great gust of blue smoke, returning to its element with a howl of rage. Tamara began to float upward.

Call grabbed her leg. It was a little bit like holding the string of a balloon, since she continued to bob in the air.

She grinned down at him. She was smudged all over with dirt and sand, her hair loose and tumbling around her face. "Look," she said, gesturing with Miri, and Call turned in time to see Aaron, free of the ice, sending a flood of small rocks toward a wyvern. Celia, from her perch, rained down more stones. In the air, they became a massive boulder that dispersed the creature with a single strike before it crashed into rubble against the far wall.

"Only one more," Call said, panting.

"No more," Tamara told him gleefully. "I got two. Although, I mean, you did help a little with the second."

"I could just let you go right now." Call tugged on her leg threateningly.

"Okay, okay, you helped a lot!" Tamara laughed, just as the room broke into applause. The Masters were clapping — looking, Call realized, at him and Tamara and Aaron and Celia. Aaron was breathing hard, glancing from his hands to the place where the wyvern had disappeared, as if he couldn't believe he'd thrown a boulder. Call knew how he felt.

"Whee!" said Tamara, waving her arms up and down as she bobbed. A moment later, the apprentices who had floated up to the ceiling were slowly floating down, Call letting go of Tamara's ankle so she could land on the floor feetfirst. She handed Miri back to him as the other apprentices landed, some laughing, some — like Jasper — silent and grim-faced.

Tamara and Call made their way toward Aaron among the hubbub of voices. People were cheering and clapping them on the backs; it was a little like what Call had always imagined winning a basketball game would be like, though he'd never won one. He'd never even played for a team.

"Call," said a voice behind him. He turned to see Alex, a big grin on his face. "I was rooting for you guys," he said.

Call blinked. "Why?" It wasn't as if they'd talked much, or at all.

"Because you're like me. I can tell."

"Yeah, right," Call said. That was ridiculous. Alex was the kind of guy who, back home, would have been pushing Call into a mud puddle. The Magisterium was different, but it couldn't be *that* different.

"I didn't really do much, anyway," Call went on. "I just stood there until I remembered to run — except then, I remembered that I *can't* run." He saw Master Rufus circling through the crowd to approach his apprentices. He wore a small smile, which for Master Rufus was like leaping and cartwheeling down the hallways.

Alex grinned. "You don't need to run," he said. "Here, they'll teach you how to fight. And trust me, you're going to be good at it."

↑ ≋ △ ○ @

Call, Tamara, and Aaron went back to their rooms feeling that, for the first time since they'd gotten to the Magisterium, everything was falling into place. They'd done better than all the other apprentice groups, and everyone knew it. Best of all, Master Rufus had gotten them pizza. *Real* pizza from a *cardboard box* with melty cheese and lots of toppings that weren't lichen or bright purple mushrooms or anything else weird that grew underground. They ate it in the common room, friendly-fighting over who got the most pieces. Tamara won by eating the fastest.

Call's fingers were still a little greasy as he pushed open the door to his bedroom. Full from pizza and soda and laughing, he felt the best he had in a long time.

But the minute he saw what was waiting on his bed, that all changed.

It was a box — a cardboard box taped up heavily, with his name scrawled in Call's father's spidery, unmistakable handwriting:

CALLUM HUNT
THE MAGISTERIUM
LURAY, VA

For a moment, Call stood and stared. He moved slowly over to the box and touched it, running his fingers along the duct-taped seams. His father always used the same heavy tape to pack up boxes, like when he had to ship something that had been ordered from out of town. They were practically impossible to open.

Call took Miri out of his belt. The knife's sharp blade tore through the cardboard as if it were a sheet of paper. Clothes spilled out onto the bed — Call's jeans, jackets, and T-shirts, packets of his favorite sour gummi candy, a windup alarm clock, and a copy of *The Three Musketeers*, which Call and his dad had been reading together.

When Call picked up the book, a folded-up note fell from between the pages. Call lifted it and read:

Callum,

I know this isn't your fault. I love you and I am sorry for everything that happened. Keep your chin up at school.

Affectionately,
Alastair Hunt

He had signed it with his full name, as though Call were someone he hardly even knew. Holding the letter in his hand, Call sank down onto the bed.

CHAPTER ELEVEN

CALL COULDN'T SLEEP that night. He was keyed up from the fight, and his mind kept going over the words of his dad's note, trying to puzzle out what they meant. It didn't help that Call had immediately eaten all but one package of the gummi candy he'd received, making him about ready to bounce off the cave roof without the need for wyvern breath to propel him. If his father had sent Call's skateboard (and it was annoying that he hadn't), he would've been careening into walls with it.

His dad had written that he wasn't angry, and the words he picked didn't sound angry either, but he sounded something else. Sad. Cold, maybe. Distant.

Maybe he was worried about the magicians stealing Call's mail and reading it. Maybe he was afraid of writing anything private. It was an understatement to say that his dad could be a little paranoid sometimes, especially about mages.

If only Call could talk to him, just for a second. He wanted to reassure his father that he was doing fine and that no one had opened the package but him. As far as he could tell, the Magisterium wasn't so bad. It was even kind of fun.

If only the Magisterium had telephones.

Call's mind went immediately to the tiny tornado on Master Rufus's desk. If Call waited to be taught how to pilot the boats to sneak back there, he might be waiting *forever* to talk with his father. He'd proved at the test that he could adapt his magic to many situations he hadn't been specifically trained for. Maybe he could adapt to this one, too.

After so long with only the two uniforms, it was awesome to have a bunch of clothes to choose from. Part of him wanted to put them all on at once and waddle through the Magisterium like a penguin.

In the end, he settled for black jeans and a black T-shirt with a faded Led Zeppelin logo on it, the outfit he deemed most suitable for sneaking around. As an afterthought, he buckled Miri's sheath through a loop of his belt, and ducked out through the darkened common room.

Looking around, he was suddenly aware of how much his and Tamara's stuff was spread all over the place. He'd left his notebook on the counter, his bag tossed haphazardly on the couch, one of his socks on the floor beside a plate of crystalline cookies with a bite missing. Tamara had scattered even more — books from home, hair ties, dangly earrings, pens with feathered ends, and bangle bracelets. But of Aaron, there was nothing. What little stuff he had was in his room, which he kept super clean, the bed made as tightly as if this were a military school.

He could hear Tamara and Aaron's steady breathing coming from their rooms. For a moment, he wondered if he should just go back to bed. He still didn't know the tunnels very well and remembered all the warnings about getting lost. They weren't supposed to be out of their rooms this late without permission from their Master, either, so he was risking getting in trouble.

Taking a quick breath, he pushed all doubts out of his mind. He knew the way to Master Rufus's office during the day. He just had to figure out the boats.

The hall outside the common room was lit by the dim glow of rocks and had fallen utterly, eerily silent. The quiet was punctuated only by distant drips of sediment falling from stalactite to stalagmite.

"Okay," Call muttered. "Here goes nothing."

He started down the path he knew led toward the river. His footsteps beat a pattern, step-shuffle, in the quiet.

The room the river ran through was even more dimly lit than the hall. The water was a dark, heaving rush of shadow. Carefully, Call picked his way along the rocky path to where one of the boats was tied up at the river's edge. He tried to brace himself, but his bad leg wobbled; he had to get down on his knees to crawl into the boat.

Part of Master Rockmaple's lecture on elementals had covered those that could be found in the water. According to him, they were often easily persuaded by a small amount of power to do a mage's bidding. The only problem was that Master Rockmaple had talked theory but hadn't explained any *technique*. Call had no idea how to do this.

The boat rocked under his knees. Mimicking Master Rufus, he leaned over the edge and whispered, "Okay, I feel really stupid doing this. But, uh, maybe you could help me out. I'm trying to get downstream and I don't know how to — look, could you try to keep the boat from knocking into walls and spinning around? Please?"

The elementals, wherever they were and whatever they were doing, didn't offer any response.

Luckily, the current already ran in the direction he was going. Leaning out, he pushed off the riverbank with the heel of his hand, sending the boat wobbling toward the center of the river. He felt a moment of heady success, before realizing he had no way to *stop* the boat.

Recognizing there wasn't much he could do, he slumped against the seat at the stern and resigned himself to worrying about that on the other end. Water lapped against the side of the boat, and every so often, a fish would rise, pale and glowing, to dart across the surface before disappearing into the depths again.

Unfortunately, it didn't seem that he'd done the right thing when whispering to the elementals. The boat turned through the water, making Call dizzy. At one point, he had to shove off a stalagmite to keep the boat from running aground.

Finally, he came to a riverbank he recognized, the one near Rufus's office. He looked around for some way to steer toward the shore. The idea of sticking his hand into the cold, black water didn't appeal to him much, but he did it anyway, paddling frantically.

The prow bumped against the shore, and Call realized he was going to have to jump out into the shallow water, since he couldn't get the boat to press itself against a ledge like Master Rufus did. Bracing himself, he stepped over the side and sank immediately in the silt. He lost his balance, falling and banging his bad leg against the side of the boat. For a long moment, the pain took his breath away.

When he recovered, he realized his situation was even worse. The boat had drifted into the middle of the water, out of his reach.

"Come back," he yelled to the boat. Then, realizing his mistake, he concentrated on the water itself. Even as he strained, all he was able to do was make the water swirl a little. He'd spent a month working with sand and no time at all working with the other elements.

He was soaked and soon his boat would be gone, disappearing into a tunnel and flowing deeper into the caves. Groaning, he splashed his way onto shore. His jeans were heavy and sodden, clinging to his legs. They were also cold. He was going to have to walk all the way back like that . . . if he could find the way back.

Pushing concerns about later out of his mind, Call headed to the heavy wood door of Master Rufus's office. Holding his breath, he tried the knob. It swung open without even a squeak.

The small tornado was still spinning on Master Rufus's rolltop desk. Call took a step toward it. The small lizard in the cage was on the workstation as before, flames flickering along its back. It watched Call with luminous eyes.

"Let me out," the lizard said. It had a whispery croaking voice, but the words had been clear. Call stared at it in confusion. The wyverns hadn't spoken during the exercise; no one had said a single thing about elementals *talking*. Maybe fire elementals were different.

"Let me out," it said again. "The key! I will tell you where he keeps the key and you will let me out."

"I'm not going to do that," Call told the lizard, frowning. He still couldn't quite get over the fact that it talked. Backing away from it, he moved closer to the tornado on the desktop.

"Alastair Hunt," he whispered to the spinning sand.

Nothing happened. Maybe it wasn't going to be as easy as he'd hoped.

Call put his hand to the side of the glass. As hard as he could, he pictured his father. He pictured his father's beaky profile, and the familiar sound of him repairing things in the garage. He pictured his dad's gray eyes, and the way his voice rose when he was cheering on a sports team or lowered if he was talking about dangerous things, like magicians. He pictured the way his father had always read him to sleep with a book, and how his woolly jackets smelled like pipe smoke and wood cleaner.

"Alastair Hunt," he said again, and this time the spinning sand contracted and solidified. In seconds, he was looking at the figure of his father, his glasses pushed up on his head. He was wearing a sweatshirt and jeans and had a book open on his lap. It was as if Call had just walked in on him reading.

Abruptly, his father stood up, looking in his direction. The book slid away, vanishing from view.

"Call?" his father asked, disbelief tingeing his voice.

"Yes!" Call said excitedly. "It's me. I got the clothes and your letter and I wanted to find some way to contact you."

"Ah," said his father, squinting as though he was trying to see Call better. "Well, that's good, that's really good. I'm glad your things made it."

Call nodded. Something about his father's cautious tone took the edge off the pleasure he felt at seeing him.

Call's father pushed his glasses higher on his nose. "You look well."

Call looked down at his clothes. "Yeah. I'm okay. It's really not so bad here. I mean, it can be boring sometimes — and scary other times. But I'm learning stuff. I'm not such a bad mage. I mean, so far."

"I never thought that you would be unskilled, Call." His

father stood up and seemed to move toward where Call was standing. His expression was strange, as though he was steeling himself to some difficult task. "Where are you? Does anyone know you're speaking with me?"

Call shook his head. "I'm in Master Rufus's office. I'm, uh, borrowing his miniature tornado."

"His what?" Call's father's brows knitted in confusion, then he sighed. "Never mind — I'm glad to have a chance to remind you of what's important. The mages aren't what they seem. The magic they're teaching you is dangerous. The more you learn about the magical world, the more you will be drawn into it — drawn into its old conflicts and dangerous temptations. Whatever *fun* you're having —" Call's father said the word *fun* like it was poisonous. "Whatever friends you're making, don't forget that this life isn't the life for you. You must get away as soon as you can."

"Are you telling me to run?"

"It would be the best thing for everyone," Alastair said with perfect sincerity.

"But what if I decide I want to stay here?" Call asked. "What if I decide I'm happy at the Magisterium? Will you still let me come home sometimes?"

There was a silence. The question hung in the air between them. Even if he was a magician, he still wanted to be Alastair's son, too.

"I don't — I —" His father took a deep breath.

"I know you hate the Magisterium because Mom died in the Cold Massacre." Call spoke rapidly, trying to get the words out before his courage failed.

"*What?*" Alastair's eyes went wide. He looked furious — and afraid.

"And I get why you never told me about it. I'm not mad. But that was war. They have a truce now. Nothing's going to happen to me here in the —"

"Call!" Alastair barked. His face was pale. "You absolutely cannot stay at the school. You don't understand — it's too dangerous. Call, you must listen to me. You don't know what you are."

"I —" Call was cut off by a crashing noise behind him. He spun around to see that the lizard had somehow managed to knock its cage off the edge of the workstation. It was lying on its side on the floor, covered by a flurry of papers and the remains of one of Rufus's models. From inside, the elemental was muttering weird words like *Splerg!* and *Gelferfren!*

Call spun back to the tornado, but it was too late. His concentration had been broken. His father had vanished, his last words hanging in the air.

You don't know what you are.

"You stupid lizard," Call yelled, kicking one leg of the workstation. More papers slipped onto the floor.

The elemental went quiet. Call fell back into Rufus's chair, putting his head in his hands. What had his father been saying? What could he have meant?

Call, you must listen to me. You don't know what you are.

A shiver went down Call's spine.

"Let me out," repeated the lizard.

"No!" Call yelled, glad to have a target for his rage. "No, I'm not going to let you out, so just stop asking!"

The lizard watched beadily from its cage as Call knelt down and began to pick up papers and gears from the model. Reaching for an envelope, Call's fingers closed on a small package that must have also been knocked off the table. He pulled it toward him, when he noticed his father's unmistakable spidery hand-writing yet again. It was addressed to William Rufus.

Oh, Call thought. *A letter from Dad. That can't be good.*

Should he open it? The last thing he needed was his father saying crazy things to Master Rufus and begging for Call to be sent home. Besides, Call was already going to be in trouble for sneaking around, so maybe he couldn't get in much *more* trouble for opening mail.

He cut the tape free with the jagged edge of a gear and unfolded a note very like the one he had received. It read:

Rufus,

If ever you trusted me, if ever you felt any loyalty to me for my time as your student and for the tragedy we shared, you must bind Callum's magic before the end of the year.

Alastair

CHAPTER TWELVE

FOR A LONG moment, Call was so angry that he wanted to smash something, and at the same time, his eyes burned like he was about to cry.

Trying to hold back his temper, Call pulled out the object that had been tucked into the package beneath his father's letter. It was the wristband of an older Silver Year student, studded with five stones — one red, one green, one blue, one white, and one as black as the pools of dark water that ran through the caves. He stared at it. Was it his father's bracelet, from the time he'd been in the Magisterium? Why would Alastair send that to Rufus?

One thing is for sure, Call thought. *Master Rufus is never going to get this message.* He jammed the letter and envelope into his pocket and clapped the wristband around his wrist. It was too big on him, so he pushed it high up his arm, above his own cuff, and tugged his sleeve down over it.

"You're stealing," said the lizard. The flames still burned

along its back, blue with flashes of green and yellow. They made shadows dance along the walls.

Call stopped cold. "So what?"

"Let me out," the lizard said. "Let me out or I'll tell that you stole Master Rufus's things."

Call groaned. He hadn't been thinking straight. Not only did the elemental know he'd opened the package, but it also knew what he'd said to his dad. It had heard his father's cryptic warning. Call couldn't let it repeat those things to Master Rufus.

He knelt down and lifted the cage by the iron handle on its top, setting it back on Rufus's work table. He looked at the lizard more closely.

Its body was longer than one of his father's boots. It looked a little like a miniature version of a Komodo dragon — it even had a beard of scales, and eyebrows — yeah, it definitely had eyebrows. Its eyes were big and red, glowing steadily like embers in a fire. The whole cage smelled vaguely of sulfur.

"Sneaking," said the lizard. "You're sneaking, stealing, and your father wants you to run away."

Call didn't know what to do. If he let the elemental out of its cage, it could still tell Master Rufus what it had seen. He couldn't risk being discovered. He didn't want to get his magic bound. He didn't want to let down Aaron and Tamara, not when they'd just started to be friends.

"Yup," Call said. "And guess what else I'm stealing. *You*."

With a last look around the office, Call left, carrying the lizard's cage with him. The elemental ran back and forth inside, causing the cage to rattle. Call didn't care.

He walked down to the water, hoping a new boat might have drifted by. There was nothing but the underground river lapping at a stony beach. Call wondered if he could swim back, but the water was icy cold, the current was running in the wrong direction, and he'd never been the strongest swimmer. Plus, he had the lizard to think about and he doubted its cage would float.

"The currents of the Magisterium are dark and strange," said the elemental, its red eyes glowing bright in the gloom.

Call tilted his head, studying the creature. "Do you have a name?"

"Only the name you give me," said the lizard.

"Stonehead?" Call suggested, looking at the crystal rocks on the lizard's head.

A puff of smoke came from the lizard's ears. It looked annoyed.

"You said I should name you," Call reminded it, squatting down on the bank with a sigh.

The lizard's head squeezed between the bars. Its tongue shot out to curl around a tiny fish and pull it back between its jaws. It crunched away with disturbing satisfaction.

This had happened so fast that Call jumped, nearly dropping the cage. That tongue was scary.

"Fireback?" he suggested, standing, pretending he wasn't freaked out. "Fishface?"

The lizard ignored him.

"Warren?" Call suggested. It was the name of one of the guys who sometimes came by to play poker with Call's father on Sunday nights.

The lizard nodded in satisfaction. "Warren," it said. "Warrens are there, under the earth, where creatures dwell. Warrens to sneak and spy and hole up tight!"

"Uh, great," Call said, thoroughly unnerved.

"There are other ways than the river. You don't know the way back to your nest, but I do."

Call regarded the elemental, who looked up at him through the stone bars of its cage in return. "A shortcut back to my room?"

"Anywhere. Everywhere! No one knows the Magisterium better than Warren. But then you will let me out of the cage. You'll agree to get me out of the cage."

How much did Call trust a weird lizard that wasn't really a lizard?

Maybe if he *drank* some of the water — which was gross, full of eyeless fish and weird sulfur and minerals — maybe he could do better magic. Like the way he had with the sand. Like he wasn't supposed to. Maybe he could draw the current backward and bring the boat to him.

Yeah, right. He had no idea how to do that.

Call, you must listen to me. You don't know what you are.

Apparently, he didn't know lots of things.

"Fine," said Call. "If you get me back to my room, I'll let you out of the cage."

"Let me out now," wheedled the elemental. "We could go faster."

"Nice try." Call snorted. "Which way?"

The little lizard directed him, and he began to walk, his clothes still wet and cold against his skin.

They passed sheets of rock that seemed to melt into one another, columns of limestone and curtains of it, falling like draperies. They passed a bubbling stream of mud snaking back and forth between Call's feet. Warren urged him ahead, the blue flame on his back turning the cage into a lantern.

At one point, the corridor narrowed so much that Call had to turn sideways and squeeze himself between the sheets of stone. He finally popped out the other side like a cork out of a bottle, a long tear in his shirt where it had caught on an edge of rock.

"Shhh," whispered Warren, crouching ahead of him. "Quiet, little mage."

Call was standing in the dark corner of a huge cavern full of echoing voices. The cavern was almost circular, the stone ceiling overhead sweeping up into a massive dome. The walls were decorated with jewel formations that illustrated various weird, possibly alchemical symbols. In the center of the room was a rectangular stone table with a candelabra rising out of it, each of a dozen tapers dripping thick streams of wax. The big, high-backed chairs around the table were filled by Masters who looked like rock formations themselves.

Call flattened himself into the shadows so he wouldn't be spotted, pressing the cage behind him to hide the light.

"Young Jasper showed bravery in throwing himself in front of the wyverns," said Master Lemuel, with a glance at Master Milagros, amusement showing on his face. "Even if he was unsuccessful."

Anger raced through Call's veins. He and Tamara and Aaron had worked hard to do well on that test and they were talking about *Jasper*?

"Bravery will only get you so far," said Master Tanaka, the tall, thin Master who taught Peter and Kai. "The students who returned from our most recent mission had plenty of bravery, and yet those were some of the worst injuries I've seen since the war. They barely made it back alive. Even the fifth years weren't prepared for elementals working together like that —"

"The Enemy is behind this," Master Rockmaple interrupted, running a hand through his ruddy beard. The image of the injured students, bloody and burned, coming through the gate had stuck with Call, and he was glad to know that wasn't how students returned from a typical mission. "The Enemy is breaking the truce in ways he thinks we won't be able to trace back to him. He is getting ready to return to war. I'll wager that, while we've deluded ourselves into thinking he's staying in his remote sanctuary, working on his horrible experiments, he's actually been making greater and more devastating weapons, not to mention alliances."

Master Lemuel snorted. "We have no proof. This could simply be a change among the elementals."

Master Rockmaple whirled on him. "How can you trust the Enemy? Anyone who wouldn't balk at putting a piece of the void inside animals and even children, who slaughtered the most vulnerable among us, is capable of anything."

"I'm not saying I trust him! I just don't want to prematurely panic that the truce has been broken. World forefend that *we* break it because of our fears and, by doing so, incite a new war, one worse than the last."

"Everything would be different if we had a Makar on our side." Master Milagros tucked her pink lock of hair behind her ear nervously. "This year's entering students had exceptional Trial scores. Is it possible that our Makar could be among them? Rufus, you've had experience with this before."

"It's too soon to tell anything," said Rufus. "Constantine himself didn't start showing signs of an affinity with chaos magic until he was fourteen."

"Maybe you just refused to look for them then as you refuse to look for them now," said Master Lemuel disagreeably.

Rufus shook his head. His face was rough-edged in the flickering light. "It doesn't matter," he said. "We need a different plan. The Assembly needs a different plan. It is too great a burden to set upon the shoulders of any child. We should all remember the tragedy of Verity Torres."

"I agree, a plan is needed," Master Rockmaple said. "Whatever the Enemy's scheme, we can't just bury our heads in the sand and act like it will go away. Nor can we simply wait forever for something that might never happen."

"Enough of this bickering," said Master North. "Master Milagros was saying earlier that she's discovered a possible error in the third algorithm of folding air into metal. I thought perhaps we could discuss the anomaly."

Anomaly? Figuring that there was no point risking discovery to listen to something he wouldn't understand anyway, Call slid back into the gap between the rocks. He wriggled through, emerging on the other side with his mind full of his father's words. What was it he had said? *The more you learn about the magical world, the more you will be drawn into it — drawn into its old conflicts and dangerous temptations.*

The war with the Enemy had to be the conflict Call's father had been talking about.

Warren stuck his scaly nose through the bars, his tongue flicking in the air. "We go a new way. Better way. Fewer Masters. Safer."

Call grunted, and followed Warren's directions. He was beginning to wonder if Warren actually knew where they were going, or if he was just leading Call deeper into the caves. Maybe he and Warren would spend the rest of their lives wandering the twisty caverns. They would become a legend to new apprentices who would speak about the lost student and his caged cave lizard in hushed tones of dread.

Warren pointed and Call scrambled up the side of a pile of rocks, sending shards flying.

The corridors were bigger now, zigzagged with sparkling patterns that teased Call's mind, as if they could be read if he only knew how. They passed through a cave full of odd underground plants: big red-tipped ferns that stood in still pools of glittering water, long fronds of lichen drifting from the ceiling and brushing against Call's shoulders. He looked up and thought he saw a pair of glittering eyes disappearing into the shadows. He stopped.

"Warren —"

"Here, here," the lizard urged, flicking his tongue toward an arched doorway at the other end of the room. Someone had carved words into the highest part of the arch:

Thoughts are free and subject to no rule.

Beyond the archway flickered an odd light. Call moved toward it, curiosity getting the better of him. It gave off a golden glow, like that of a fire, though it was no warmer when he stepped through the door than it had been on the other side. He was in another large space, a cavern that seemed to spiral down along a steep and winding path. All along the walls of the room were shelves holding thousands upon thousands of books, most with yellowed pages and ancient bindings. Call stepped to the center of the room, where the sloping path began, and looked over the edge. There were levels and levels, all illuminated with the same golden light and ringed with more bookshelves.

Call had found the Library.

And other people were there, too. He could hear the echoes of their hushed conversation. More Masters? No. Glancing around, he saw Jasper three tiers down, in his gray uniform. Celia was standing across from him. It had to be really, really late, and Call had no idea why they were out of their rooms.

Jasper had a book open on a stone table, his hand extended in front of him. Again and again he thrust out his fingers, gritting his teeth and scrunching up his eyes, until Call started to worry he was going to make his head explode, trying to force the magic to come. Again and again, there was a spark or a puff of smoke between his fingers, but nothing else. Jasper looked ready to scream with disappointment and frustration.

Celia paced back and forth on the other side of the table. "You promised that if I helped you, you'd help me, but it's almost two in the morning and you haven't helped me with *anything*."

"We're still on *me*!" Jasper yelled.

"Fine," Celia said long-sufferingly, sitting down on a stone stool. "Try again."

"I've got to get this right," Jasper said softly. "I've got to. I am the best. I am the *best* Iron Year mage at the Magisterium. Better than Tamara. Better than Aaron. Better than Callum. Better than everyone."

Call wasn't sure if he belonged on that list of people Jasper clearly worried he wasn't better than, but he was flattered. He was also a little disappointed that Celia was hanging out with Jasper.

Warren scrabbled in his cage. Call turned to see what the fussing was about.

The lizard was staring at a framed illustration of a man with huge, red-orange spiraling eyes magnified and diagrammed to one side of the body. *Chaos-ridden,* Call thought. A shudder ran through him at the sight — along with something else, some feeling he couldn't quite put his finger on, as if the inside of his head was itchy or he was hungry or thirsty.

"Who's there?" Jasper said, looking up. He raised his hand defensively, half shielding his face.

Feeling stupid, Call waved. "It's just me. I got a little — lost — and I saw light coming from in here, so I —"

"Call?" Jasper stepped away from the book, his hands flailing. "You were spying on me!" he shouted. "Did you follow me here?"

"No, I —"

"Are you going to tell on us? Is that the idea? You going to get me in trouble so I don't do better than you at the next test?" Jasper sneered, though he was clearly shaken.

"If we want to do better than you on the next test, all we have to do is wait until the next test," said Call, unable to resist.

Jasper looked like he was going to burst. "I'm going to tell everyone you were sneaking around at night!"

"Fine," said Call. "I'll tell everyone the same thing about you."

"You wouldn't dare," Jasper said, grabbing the edge of the table.

"You wouldn't, would you, Call?" Celia asked.

All of a sudden, Call didn't want to be there anymore. He didn't want to be fighting with Jasper, or threatening Celia, wandering around in the dark, or hiding in a corner while the Masters talked about things that made the hair rise up on his neck. He wanted to be in bed, thinking over his conversation with his dad, trying to figure out what Alastair had meant and if there was any way that it wasn't as bad as it had seemed. Plus, he wanted to hunt around the bottom of his box for any last gummi candies.

"Look, Jasper," he said. "I didn't take your spot on purpose. You should at least be able to tell by now that I actually, really, didn't want it."

Jasper dropped his hand. His expensive haircut was growing out, his black hair falling over his eyes. "Don't you get it? That makes it worse."

Call blinked at him. "What?"

"You don't know," Jasper said, his hands curling into fists. "You just don't know what it's like. My family lost everything in the Second War. Money, reputation, everything."

"Jasper, stop." Celia reached for him, clearly trying to snap him out of his rant. It didn't work.

"And if I make something of myself," Jasper said, "if I'm the *best* — it could change all of that. But for you, being here means *nothing*." He slammed his hand down on the table. To Call's surprise, sparks flew up from around Jasper's fingers. Jasper jerked his hand back, staring at it.

"I guess you made it work," Call said. His voice sounded strange in the room, soft after all Jasper's yelling. For a second, the two boys looked at each other. Then Jasper turned away and Call, feeling awkward, started to back toward the door of the Library.

"I'm sorry, Call!" Celia called after him. "He'll be less crazy in the morning."

Call didn't reply. It wasn't fair, he thought — Aaron having no family and Tamara having her scary family and now Jasper. Soon, there would be no one left for him to hate without feeling bad about it.

He grabbed the cage and headed for the nearest passageway. "No more detours," he told the lizard.

"Warren knows the best way. Sometimes the best way isn't the fastest."

"Warren shouldn't talk about himself in the third person," Call said, but he let the elemental lead him the rest of way back to his room. As Call raised his cuff to open the door, the lizard spoke.

"Let me out," he said.

Call paused.

"You promised. Let me out." The lizard looked up at him imploringly with his burning eyes.

Call set the cage down on the stone floor outside of his door and knelt down next to it. As he reached for the latch, he realized that he had failed to ask the one question he should have asked from the start. "Uh, Warren, *why* did Master Rufus have you in a cage in his office?"

The eyebrows on the elemental went up. "Sneaky," he said.

Call shook his head, not sure which one of them Warren was talking about. "What does that mean?"

"Let me out," said the lizard, his raspy voice sounding more like a hiss. "You promised."

With a sigh, Call opened the cage. The lizard raced up the wall toward a spiderwebby alcove in the ceiling. Call could barely see the fire along his back. Call took the cage and stowed it behind a cluster of stalagmites, hoping he could get rid of it in a more permanent fashion the next morning.

"Okay, well, good night," said Call before he went inside. As the door opened, the elemental raced in ahead of him.

Call tried to shoo him back out, but Warren followed him into his bedroom and curled up against one of the glowing rocks on the wall, becoming nearly invisible.

"Staying over?" Call asked.

The lizard remained as still as stone, his red eyes at half-mast, his tongue poking slightly out of the side of his mouth.

Call was too exhausted to worry about whether having an elemental, even a sleeping elemental, hanging around was safe. Pushing the box and all the stuff his father sent onto the floor, he curled up on his bed, one hand clasped on his dad's wristband, fingers tracing the smooth stones as he slipped into slumber. His last thought before he dropped off was of the spiraling bright eyes of the Chaos-ridden.

CHAPTER THIRTEEN

CALL WOKE THE next day scared that Master Rufus would say something about the scattered papers, wrecked model, and missing envelope in his office . . . and even more scared that he would say something about the missing elemental. He dragged his heels all the way to the Refectory, but when he got there, he overheard a heated argument between Master Rufus and Master Milagros.

"For the last time, Rufus," she was saying in the tone of someone much aggrieved, "*I don't have your lizard!*"

Call didn't know whether to feel bad or laugh.

After breakfast, Rufus led them down to the river, where he instructed them to practice picking up water, tossing it into the air, and catching it without getting wet. Pretty soon Call, Tamara, and Aaron were breathless, laughing, and soaked. By the time the day was over, Call was exhausted, so exhausted that what had happened the day before seemed distant and unreal. He headed back to his room to puzzle over his father's letter and the wristband but was sidetracked by the fact that Warren had eaten one of his shoelaces, slurping it up like a noodle.

"Dumb lizard," he muttered, hiding the armband he'd worn in the wyvern exercise, and the crumpled letter from his father, in the bottom drawer of his desk and shoving it closed so the elemental wouldn't eat them, too.

Warren said nothing. His eyes had gone a grayish color; Call suspected the shoelace was disagreeing with him.

The biggest distraction from trying to puzzle out what his dad had meant turned out, to Call's surprise, to be his classes. There was no more Room of Sand and Boredom; instead, there was a roster of new exercises that made the next few weeks go by quickly. The training was still hard and frustrating, but as Master Rufus revealed more of the magical world, Call found himself growing increasingly fascinated.

Master Rufus taught them to feel their affinity with the elements and to better understand the meaning behind what he called the Cinquain, which, along with the rest of the Five Principles of Magic, Call could now recite in his sleep.

Fire wants to burn.

Water wants to flow.

Air wants to rise.

Earth wants to bind.

Chaos wants to devour.

They learned how to kindle small fires and to make flames dance on their palms. They learned to make waves in the cave pools and call over the pale fish (although not to operate the boats, which continued to annoy Call to no end). They even began to learn Call's favorite thing — levitating.

"Focus and practice," Master Rufus said, leading them to a room covered with bouncy mats stuffed with moss and pine needles from the trees outside the Magisterium. "There are no shortcuts, mages. There's only focus and practice. So get to it!"

They took turns trying to draw energy from the air around them and use it to push themselves upward from the soles of their feet. It was much harder to balance than Call would have thought. Over and over, they fell giggling onto the mats, on top of one another. Aaron wound up with one of Tamara's pigtails in his mouth, and Call with Tamara's foot on his neck.

Finally, almost at the end of the lesson, something clicked for Call, and he was able to hover in the air, a foot above the ground, without wobbling at all. There was no gravity pushing down on his leg, nothing that might keep him from soaring sideways through the air except his own lack of practice. Dreams of the day that he could fly through the halls of the Magisterium far faster than he could ever have run exploded through his head. It would be like skateboarding, only better, faster, higher, and with even crazier stunts.

Then Tamara crossed her eyes at him and he lost his concentration and thumped back to the mat. He lay there for a second, just breathing.

For those moments that he'd hung in the air, his leg hadn't hurt, not even a little.

Neither Tamara nor Aaron had managed to get really airborne before the end of the lesson, but Master Rufus seemed delighted with their lack of progress. Several times, he declared it to be the funniest thing he'd seen in a long while.

Master Rufus promised them that by the end of the year, they'd be able to call up a blast of each element, walk through fire, and breathe underwater. In their Silver Year, they would be able to call on the less evident powers of the elements — to shape air into illusions, fire into prophecies, earth into bindings, and water into healing. The thought of being able to do those things thrilled Call, but whenever he thought of the end of the year, he recalled the words of his father's note to Rufus.

You must bind Callum's magic before the end of the year.

Earth magic. If he made it to his Silver Year, maybe he'd learn what binding things entailed.

In one of the Friday lectures, Master Lemuel taught them more about counterweights, warning them that if they overextended themselves and felt themselves being drawn into an element, they should reach for its opposite, just as they had reached for earth when battling an air elemental.

Call asked how you were supposed to reach for *soul*, since that was the counterweight of chaos. Master Lemuel snapped that if Call were battling a chaos mage, it wouldn't matter what he reached for, because he'd be about to die. Drew gave him a sympathetic look. "It's okay," he said, under his breath.

"Stop that, Andrew," said Master Lemuel in a frozen voice. "You know, there was a time when apprentices who failed to show respect to their Masters were whipped with saplings."

"Lemuel," said Master Milagros anxiously, noting the horrified looks on the faces of her own students, "I don't think —"

"Unfortunately, that was centuries ago," said Master Lemuel. "But I can assure you, Andrew, that if you keep whispering behind my back, you'll be sorry you ever came to the Magisterium." His thin lips curled into a smile. "Now come up here and demonstrate how you reach for water when you're using fire. Gwenda, if you would come up to assist him with the counterweight?"

Gwenda walked to the front; after hesitating, Drew shuffled up beside her, his shoulders hunched. He endured twenty minutes of merciless teasing from Lemuel when he couldn't extinguish the flame in his hand, even though Gwenda was holding out a bowl of water to him with so much hopeful enthusiasm that some of it slopped onto his sneakers. "Come on, Drew!" she kept whispering until, eventually, Master Lemuel told her to be quiet.

It made Call appreciate Master Rufus more, even when he gave them a lecture about the duties of mages, most of which seemed really obvious, like keeping magic a secret, not using magic for personal gain or evil ends, and sharing all knowledge gleaned from magical study with the rest of the mage community. Apparently, mages who'd achieved mastery in their study of the elements were required to take apprentices as part of that "sharing all knowledge" thing — meaning there were different Masters at the Magisterium at different times, though those who'd found their vocation as teachers were there permanently.

Being forced to take apprentices explained a lot about Master Lemuel.

Call was more interested in Master Rockmaple's second lecture about elementals. Mostly, it turned out, they weren't sentient creatures. Some kept the same shapes they'd held for centuries, while others fed on magic to become large and dangerous. A few had even been known to absorb wizards. It made Call shudder to think of Warren after hearing that. What had he let loose in the Magisterium? What exactly was sleeping above his bed and eating his shoelaces?

Call learned more about the Third Mage War, too, but none of it gave him any more idea why his father wanted Call's magic bound.

Tamara laughed more as time went on, often with a guilty look, while, oddly, Aaron became more serious as the three of them settled more and more into the Magisterium. Call felt he'd learned his way around and was no longer afraid of getting lost on his way to the Library, the classrooms, or even the Gallery.

Nor did he think it was weird anymore to eat mushrooms and piles of lichen that tasted like delicious roasted chicken or spaghetti or lo mein.

He and Jasper still kept their distance, but Celia stayed his friend, acting like nothing weird had happened that night.

Call began to dread the end of the year, when his father would want him to come home for good. He had real friends for the first time in his life, friends who didn't think he was too weird or messed up because of his leg. And he had magic. He didn't want to give any of it up, even though he'd vowed he would.

It was hard to keep track of seasons passing underground. Sometimes, Master Rufus and the other Masters would take them outside for various earth exercises. It was always kind of cool to see what the other students were good at — when Rufus showed them how to blend elemental magic to make plants grow, Kai Hale made a single seedling sprout and grow so huge that the next day, Master Rockmaple had to come out with an axe and chop it down. Celia was able to summon animals from underground (though not, to Call's disappointment, any naked mole rats). And Tamara was amazing at using the magnetism of the earth to find paths when everyone got lost.

As the outside world started to catch fire in fall colors, the caves grew colder. Big metal bowls full of hot stones lined the corridors, heating the air, and a blazing fire was always in the Gallery now when they went there to watch movies.

The cold didn't bother Call. He felt as if he was getting tougher somehow. He was fairly sure he had grown at least an inch. And he could walk farther, despite his leg, probably because Master Rufus was fond of taking them on hikes through the caverns, or bouldering among the big rocks aboveground.

At night sometimes, Call would take out the wristband from the bedside table and read over both letters from his dad. He wished he could tell his father about the things he was doing, but he never did.

They were well into winter when Master Rufus announced that it was time they started exploring the caves on their own, without his assistance. He'd already shown them how to find their way among the deeper caverns by using earth magic to light up individual rocks and create a path back.

"You want us to get lost on purpose?" Call asked.

"Something like that," said Rufus. "Ideally, you will follow my instruction, find the room you are meant to find, and return without getting lost at all. But that part is up to you."

Tamara clapped her hands together and smiled a slightly devilish smile. "Sounds like fun."

"*Together*," Master Rufus told her. "No running off and leaving those two stumbling around in the dark."

Her smile dimmed a little. "Oh, okay."

"We could make a bet," Call said, thinking of Warren. If he could use some of the shortcuts the lizard had shown him, he might out-navigate her. "See who finishes first."

"Did either of you hear me?" Master Rufus asked. "I said —"

"Together," said Aaron. "I'll make sure we stick by each other."

"See that you do," said Master Rufus. "Now, here is your assignment. At the depths of the second level of the caves is a place called the Butterfly Pool. It's fed from a spring above-ground. The water there is heavy with minerals that make it excellent for smithing weapons, like that knife on your belt." He gestured to Miri, making Call touch the hilt self-consciously. "That blade was made here, in the Magisterium, with water from the Butterfly Pool. I want the three of you to find the room, gather some of the water, and return to me here."

"Do we get a bucket?" Call asked.

"I think you know the answer to that, Callum." Rufus drew a rolled-up parchment from his uniform and handed it to Aaron. "Here is your map. Follow it closely to reach the Butterfly Pool, but remember to light stones to mark your way. You can't always rely on a map to bring you back."

Master Rufus settled down on a large boulder, which gently shaped and reformed itself underneath him until it resembled an armchair. "You will take turns carrying the water. If you drop it, then you'll just have to return for more."

The three apprentices exchanged glances. "When do we start?" asked Aaron.

Master Rufus drew a heavy bound book from his pocket and began to read. "Immediately."

Aaron spread the paper out on a rock in front of him, scowling, then looked over at Master Rufus. "Okay," he said quickly. "We head down and east."

Call crowded close, looking at the map over Aaron's shoulder. "Past the Library looks like the quickest way."

Tamara turned the map with a smirk. "Now north is actually pointing north. That should help."

"Library's still the right way," Call said. "So it didn't help that much."

Aaron rolled his eyes and stood, folding the map. "Let's go, before you two get out compasses and start measuring distances with string."

They headed out, at first going through the familiar parts of the cave. They passed into the Library, following its spirals down, like navigating the inside of a nautilus shell. The very bottom led out into the lower levels of the caves.

The air grew heavier and colder and the smell of minerals hung thick in the air. Call felt the change immediately. The passageway they were in was cramped and narrow, the roof low overhead. Aaron, the tallest of the three, almost had to bend down to walk along it.

Finally, the passageway opened out into a larger cavern. Tamara touched one of the walls, lighting up a crystal and illuminating the roots. They hung down in creepy, spidery vines to almost touch the tops of a vivid orange stream that smoked sulfurously, filling the room with a burnt odor. Massive mushrooms grew along the sides of the stream, striped in unnaturally bright greens and turquoises and purples.

"I wonder what would happen if we ate them?" Call mused as they picked their way among the plants.

"I wouldn't try it to find out," said Aaron, raising his hand. He had taught himself to make a ball of glowing blue fire the week before and was very excited about it. He was constantly making balls of glowing fire, even when they didn't need light or anything. He held the fire up in one hand, and the map in the other. "That way," he said, gesturing to a passage off to the left. "Through the Root Room."

"The rooms have names?" Tamara said, stepping gingerly around the mushrooms.

"No, I'm just calling it that. I mean, we won't forget it if it has a name, right?"

Tamara furrowed her brow, considering. "I guess."

"Better than Butterfly Pool," Call said. "I mean, what kind of name is that for a lake that helps make weapons? It should be called Killer Lake. Or the Pond of Stabbings. Or Murder Puddle."

"Yeah," Tamara said drily. "And we can start calling you Master Obvious."

The next chamber had thick stalactites, white as giant shark's teeth, clumped together as though they might really be attached to the jaw of some long-buried monster. Passing beneath this scarily sharp overhang, Call, Aaron, and Tamara next walked through a narrow, circular opening. Here, the rock was pocked with cave formations that looked eaten away, as though they were in some kind of oversize termite nest. Call concentrated and a crystal in the far corner began to glow, so they wouldn't forget they'd been this way.

"Is this place on the map?" he asked.

Aaron squinted. "Yeah. In fact, we're almost there. Just one room to the south . . ." He disappeared through a dark archway, then reappeared a moment later, flushed with victory. "Found it!"

Tamara and Call crowded in after him. For a moment, they were silent. Even after seeing all sorts of spectacular underground rooms, including the Library and the Gallery, Call knew he was seeing something special. From a gap high in one wall, a torrent of water poured out, splashing down into a huge pool that glowed blue, as if lit from the inside. The walls were feathery with bright green lichen, and the contrast of the green and the blue made Call feel as if he were standing inside a huge marble. The air was redolent with the odor of some unfamiliar and tantalizing spice.

"Huh," Aaron said after a few minutes. "It *is* kind of weird that it's called the Butterfly Pool."

Tamara walked up to the edge. "I think that's because the water is the color of those blue butterflies — what are they called?"

"Blue monarchs," Call said. His father had always been a fan of butterflies. He had a whole collection of them, pinned under glass over his desk.

Tamara put her hand out. The pool shuddered, and a sphere of water rose up from it. Even as it shifted and rippled across the surface, it kept its shape.

"There," Tamara said, a little breathlessly.

"Great," said Aaron. "How long do you think you can hold it?"

"I don't know." She tossed back a thick dark braid, trying not to let any strain show on her face. "I'll tell you when my concentration starts to give."

Aaron nodded, smoothing the map out against one of the damp walls. "Now we just need to find our way —"

At that moment, the map in his hands burst into flames.

Aaron yelled and pulled his fingers away from the blackening pages sparking through the air. The pages fell in a shower of embers and hit the floor. Tamara yelped, losing her focus. The water she'd been suspending splashed down over her uniform and turned into a puddle at their feet.

The three of them looked at one another, wide-eyed. Call straightened his shoulders. "I guess that's what Master Rufus meant," he said. "We're supposed to follow our lighted stones or marks or whatever in order to get back. That map was only good for the way here."

"Should be easy," Tamara said. "I mean, I only lit one of them, but you guys lit more, right?"

"I lit one, too," said Call, looking hopefully in Aaron's direction. Aaron didn't look back.

Tamara frowned. "Ugh, fine. We'll figure out the way back. You carry the water."

With a shrug, Call went over to the lake and concentrated on shaping a ball. Call drew on the air around him to move the water and felt the push-pull of the elements inside him. He wasn't as good at it as Tamara, but he did okay. His ball dripped only a little as it hovered.

Aaron frowned and pointed. "We came in there. This way. I think . . ."

Tamara followed Aaron, and Call went after her, the ball of water spinning over his head as if he had his own personal storm cloud. The next room was familiar: the underground stream, the colorful mushrooms. Call navigated among them carefully, afraid that at any moment his water ball would fall directly on his head.

"Look," Tamara was saying. "There's lit-up stones over here. . . ."

"I think those are just bioluminescence," Aaron said in a worried voice. He tapped at them and then turned back to her with a shrug. "I don't know."

"Well, I do. We go this way." She set off with a determined stride. Call followed, left-right-left, through a cavern full of huge stalactites growing in the shapes of leaves, *don't drop the water*, around a corner, through a gap between boulders, *keep it together, Call*. There were sharp rocks all around and Call nearly walked right into a wall because Tamara and Aaron had stopped dead. They were arguing.

"I told you it was just glowing lichen," Aaron said, clearly frustrated. They were in a large room with a stone cistern in the center, bubbling gently. "Now we're lost."

"Well, if you'd remembered to light up stones as we went —"

"*I* was reading the map," Aaron said, exasperated. In a way, Call thought, it was kind of nice to know that Aaron could get irritated and unreasonable. Then Aaron and Tamara turned to glare at Call, and Call nearly dropped the spinning globe he'd been balancing. Aaron had to throw out a hand to stabilize the water. It hovered in the air between them, shedding droplets.

"What?" Call said.

"Well, do *you* have any idea where we are?" said Tamara.

"No," Call admitted, glancing around at the smooth walls. "But there must be some way to find our way back. Master Rufus wouldn't just send us down here to get lost and die."

"That's pretty optimistic, coming from you," said Tamara.

"Funny." Call made a face to show her exactly how funny it wasn't.

"Stop it, both of you," Aaron said. "Arguing isn't going to get us anywhere."

"Well, following you is going to get us *somewhere*," Call said. "And that *somewhere* is about as far away as you can get from where we need to be."

Aaron shook his head, disappointed. "Why do you have to be such a jerk?" he asked Call.

"Because you never are," Call told him staunchly. "I have to be a jerk for both of us."

Tamara sighed and then, after a moment, laughed. "Can we admit that we're all at fault? We *all* messed up."

Aaron looked like he didn't want to admit it, but finally he nodded. "Yeah, I forgot that we weren't allowed to use the map on the way back."

"Yeah," said Call. "Me, too. Sorry. Aren't you good at finding paths, Tamara? What about all that tapping into the metal of the earth stuff?"

"I can try," Tamara said, her voice a little hollow. "But that just lets me know which way north is, not how these passageways intersect. But we've got to come across something familiar eventually, right?"

It was scary to think about wandering through the tunnels, to think about the pits of darkness they could fall into, the sucking mud pools and the weird choking steam rising from them. But Call didn't have a better plan. "Okay," he said.

They began to walk.

This was pretty much exactly what his father had warned him about.

"You know what I miss from home?" Aaron asked as they went, picking their way past concretions that looked like tattered tapestries. "It's going to sound super lame, but I miss fast food. Like the greasiest possible burger and a mound of fries. Even the smell of them."

"I miss lying out in the backyard in the grass," Call said. "And video games. I definitely miss video games."

"I miss wasting time online," Tamara said, surprising Call. "Don't give me that face — I lived in a town just like the kind you guys grew up in."

Aaron snorted. "Not like where I grew up."

"I mean," she said, taking over the maintenance of the spinning blue globe of water, "I grew up in a town full of people who weren't mages. There was a bookshop where the few mages met up or left messages for one another, but other than that, it was normal."

"I'm just surprised your parents let you go online," Call said. It was such a regular, non-fancy way to waste time. When he imagined her outside the Magisterium, having fun, he imagined her riding a polo pony, although he wasn't exactly sure what that was or how it was different from a regular pony.

Tamara smiled at him. "Well, they didn't exactly *let* me. . . ."

Call wanted to know more about that, but as he opened his mouth to ask, his breath caught at the sight of the remarkable room that had just appeared in front of him.

CHAPTER FOURTEEN

T HE CAVERN WAS quite large, the ceiling carved to be vaulted like the ceiling of a cathedral. There were five tall archways, each flanked by marble pillars, each inlaid with a different metal: iron, copper, bronze, silver, or gold. The walls were marble, indented with thousands of human handprints, a name carved over each one.

A bronze statue of a young girl with long, wind-whipped hair was in the center of the room. Her face was upturned. The plaque beneath her read: *Verity Torres.*

"What is this place?" Aaron asked.

"It's the Hall of Graduates," said Tamara, whirling around, her expression awed. "When apprentices become journeymen and journeywomen mages, they come here and press their handprints into the stone. Everyone who's ever graduated from the Magisterium is here."

"My mom and dad," Call said, walking through the room, looking for their names. There was his father's — *Alastair Hunt* — high up the wall, too high for Call to reach. His father must have levitated to get his hand there. A smile pulled at the corner of Call's mouth, as he imagined his father, this very young version of his father, flying just to show he could.

He was surprised that his mother's handprint wasn't next to his father's, since he assumed they'd been in love even as students — but maybe the handprints didn't work that way. It took a few minutes more, but finally he found it, over on a far wall — *Sarah Novak*, pressed into the base of a stalagmite, the name scrawled in a fine point, like it had been done with a weapon. Call crouched down and rested his hand inside the place his mother's had been. Her hands were shaped like his; his fingers fit neatly inside the phantom ones of a girl long dead. At twelve, his hands were as big as hers had been at seventeen.

He wanted to feel something, with his hand pressed inside his mother's, but he wasn't sure he felt anything at all.

"Call," Tamara said. She touched him gently on the shoulder. Call glanced back at his two friends. Both of them had the same concerned looks on their faces. He knew what they were thinking, knew they were feeling sorry for him. He shot to his feet, shaking off Tamara's hand.

"I'm fine," he said, clearing his throat.

"Look at this." Aaron was standing in the middle of the room, in front of a large archway made of a shimmering white stone. Carved across the front were the words *Prima Materia*. Aaron ducked under it, popping out the other side with a curious look. "It's an archway to nowhere."

"*Prima materia,*" Tamara murmured, and her eyes widened. "It's the First Gate! At the end of every year at the Magisterium, you go through a gate. It's for when you've learned to control your magic, to use your counterweights properly. After, you get your Copper Year armband."

Aaron went pale. "You mean I just went through the gate early? Am I going to be in trouble?"

Tamara shrugged at him. "I don't think so. It doesn't seem like it's activated." They all squinted at it. It stood there, being a stone archway in a dark room. Call had to agree that it didn't seem exactly operational.

"Did you see anything like that on the map?" Call asked.

Aaron shook his head. "I don't remember."

"So even though we found a landmark, we're just as lost as before?" Tamara kicked the wall.

Something dropped down. A large, lizardy thing with shining eyes and flames all down its back and . . . eyebrows.

"Oh, my God," said Tamara, her eyes rounding into saucers. The ball of water took a dangerous dip toward the floor as Aaron stared, and this time Call had to stabilize it.

"Call! Always lost, Call. You should stay in your room. It's warm there," Warren said.

Tamara and Aaron turned to Call, shooting him both exclamation points and question marks with their eyes.

"This is Warren," Call said. "He's, uh, this lizard I know."

"That's a fire elemental!" Tamara said. "What are you doing, knowing an elemental?" She stared at Call.

Call opened his mouth to disavow friendship with Warren — it wasn't like they were *close*! But that didn't seem the best way to persuade Warren to help them — and Call knew that, at this point, they really needed Warren's help.

"Didn't Master Rufus say some of them were into, you know . . . absorbing?" Aaron's gaze followed the lizard.

"Well, he hasn't absorbed me yet," Call said. "And he slept in my room. Warren, can you help us? We're lost. Really lost. We just need you to lead us back."

"Shortcuts, slippery paths, Warren knows all the hidden places. What will you trade for the way back?" The lizard scrambled closer to them, spraying gravel from between its toes.

"What do you want?" Tamara asked, rooting around in her pockets. "I have some gum and a hair tie, but that's about it."

"I have some food," Aaron offered. "Candy, mostly. From the Gallery."

"I'm holding the water," Call said. "I can't go through my pockets. But, uh, you can have my shoelaces."

"All of it!" said the lizard, head bobbing up and down with excitement. "I will have all of it when we get there and then my Master will be pleased."

"What?" Call frowned, not sure he'd heard the elemental quite right.

"Your Master will be pleased when you are back," the lizard said. "Master Rufus. Your Master." Then he ran along the cave wall, fast enough that Call had to breathe hard to keep up and keep the ball of water moving at the same time. A few drops got lost in the rush.

"Come on," he said to Tamara and Aaron, his leg aching from the effort.

With a shrug, Aaron followed.

"Well, I did promise him my gum," Tamara said, jogging after them.

They followed Warren though a sulfur-streaked hall, orange and yellow and weirdly smooth on all sides — Call felt as though they were walking through the throat of some enormous giant. The floor was unpleasantly moist with reddish lichen, thick and spongy. Aaron nearly tripped, and Call's feet sank into it, sending the ball of water wobbling as he steadied himself. Tamara stabilized it with a flick of her fingers as they passed into a cavern whose walls were covered with crystalline formations that looked like icicles. A huge mass of crystals hung from the center of the ceiling like a chandelier, glowing faintly.

"This isn't the way we came," Aaron complained, but Warren didn't pause, except to take a bite out of one of the dangling crystals as he went by it. He bypassed all the obvious exits and headed straight for a small dark hole, which turned out to be an almost lightless tunnel. They had to get on their knees and crawl, the globe of water wobbling precariously between them. Sweat was running down Call's back from the cramped position, his leg was killing him, and he'd begun to worry that Warren was leading them in the totally wrong direction.

"Warren —" he started.

He broke off as the passageway suddenly widened out into a vast chamber. He staggered slowly to his feet, his bad leg punishing him for pushing it so hard. Tamara and Aaron followed, looking pale with the effort of both crawling and holding the water steady at the same time.

Warren scuttled toward an archway leading out. Call followed as fast as his leg would allow.

He was so distracted by the effort that he didn't notice when the air became warmer, filling with the smell of something burning. It wasn't until Aaron exclaimed, "We're been here before — I recognize the water," that he looked up and saw that they were back in the room with the smoking orange stream and the huge vines that hung down like tendrils.

Tamara exhaled with clear relief. "This is great. Now we just —"

She broke off with a cry as a creature rose out of the smoking stream, making her stumble back and Aaron yell out loud. The ball of water that had hung between them crashed to the floor. The water sizzled as if it had been dumped onto a hot skillet.

"Yes," said Warren. "Just like I was bid. He told me to bring you back, and now you are here."

"He told you," Tamara echoed.

Call stared openmouthed at the huge being rising out of the stream, which had started to boil, huge red and orange bubbles appearing on the surface with the ferocity of lava. The creature was clumped and dark and stony, as if it were made out of shards of jagged rock, but it had a human face, a man's face, the planes seemingly cut from granite. Its eyes were just holes into darkness.

"Greetings, Iron Mages," it said, voice echoing as though the thing spoke from some great distance. "You are far from your Master."

The apprentices were speechless. Call could hear Tamara's breath rasping in the quiet.

"Have you nothing to say to me?" The creature's granite mouth moved: It was like watching stone fissure and split apart. "I was once like you, children."

Tamara made a horrible sound, half sob and half gasp. "No," she said. "You can't be one of us — you can't still speak. You . . ."

"What is it?" Call hissed. "What is it, Tamara?"

"You're one of the Devoured," Tamara said, her voice breaking. "Consumed by an element. Not human anymore. . . ."

"Fire," the thing breathed. "I became fire long ago. I gave myself to it, and it to me. It burned away what was human and weak."

"You're immortal," Aaron said, his eyes looking very big and green in his pale, grimy face.

"I am so much more than that. I am eternal." The Devoured leaned close to Aaron, close enough that Aaron's skin began to flush, the way skin pinkens when someone stands close to a fire.

"Aaron, don't!" Tamara said, taking a step forward. "It's trying to burn you, absorb you. Get away from it!"

Her face shone in the flickering light, and Call realized there were tears on her cheeks. He thought suddenly of her sister, consumed by elements, doomed.

"Absorb *you*?" The Devoured laughed. "Look at you, little flickering sparks, barely grown. Not much life to be squeezed out of you."

"You must want something from us," Call said, hoping the Devoured would swing its attention away from Aaron. "Or you wouldn't have bothered to show yourself."

The thing turned to him. "Master Rufus's surprise apprentice. Even the rocks have whispered of you. The greatest of the Masters has chosen strangely this year."

Call couldn't believe it. Even the Devoured knew about his crappy entrance scores.

"I see through the masks of skin you wear," the Devoured continued. "I see your future. One of you will fail. One of you will die. And one of you is already dead."

"What?" Aaron's voice rose. "What does that mean, 'already dead'?"

"Don't listen to it!" Tamara cried. "It's a thing, not human —"

"Who would desire to be human? Human hearts break. Human bones shatter. Human skin can tear." The Devoured, already close to Aaron, reached to touch his face. Call leaped forward as fast as his leg would let him, knocking into Aaron, sending them both tumbling against one of the walls. Tamara whirled to face the Devoured, her hand raised. A swirling mass of air bloomed in her palm.

"Enough!" roared a voice from the archway.

Master Rufus stood there, forbidding and terrible, power seeming to pour off of him.

The thing took a step back, flinching. "I mean no harm."

"Begone," said Master Rufus. "Leave my apprentices be or I will dispel you as I would any elemental, no matter who you once were, Marcus."

"Don't call me by a name that is no longer mine," the Devoured said. Its gaze fell on Call, Aaron, and Tamara as it subsided back to the sulfurous pool. "You three I will see again." It disappeared in a ripple, but Call knew it still remained beneath the surface somewhere.

Master Rufus looked momentarily shaken. "Come along," he said, ushering his apprentices through a low archway. Call looked back for Warren, but the elemental was gone. Call was briefly disappointed. He wanted to scream at Warren for betraying them — and also to disinvite him from his bedroom *forever*. But if Master Rufus saw Warren, it would be obvious that Call was the one who'd stolen him from Rufus's office, so maybe it was good he was gone.

They walked for a while in silence.

"How did you know to come find us?" Tamara asked finally. "That something bad was happening?"

"You don't think I'd let you wander the depths of the Magisterium unwatched, do you?" said Rufus. "I sent an air elemental to follow you. It reported back to me once you had been drawn into the cavern of the Devoured."

"Marcus — the Devoured — told us some . . . he told us our futures," Aaron said. "What did that mean? Was that — was the Devoured really once an apprentice like us?"

Rufus looked uncomfortable for the first time Call could remember. It was amazing. He had finally acquired an expression.

"Whatever he said means nothing. He's gone completely mad. And yes, I suppose he was an apprentice like you once, but he became one of the Devoured long, long after that. He was a Master by then. My Master, in fact."

They were silent all the way back to the Refectory.

↑ ≈ △○◎

At dinner that night, Call, Aaron, and Tamara tried to act like their day had been normal. They sat at the long table with the other apprentices but didn't say much. Rufus was off with Master Milagros and Master Rockmaple, sharing a lichen pizza and looking somber.

"Looks like your orienteering lesson didn't go so well," smirked Jasper, his dark eyes flicking from Tamara to Aaron to Call. Admittedly, they all looked exhausted and dirty, their faces smudged. Tamara had hollows under her eyes, as if she'd had a nightmare. "Get lost in the tunnels?"

"We ran into one of the Devoured," Aaron said. "Down in the deep caves."

The table burst into chatter. "One of the *Devoured*?" Kai demanded. "Are they like people say? Hideous monsters?"

"Did it try to absorb you?" Celia's eyes were round. "How did you get away?"

Call saw that Tamara's hands were shaking as she held her cutlery. He said abruptly, "Actually, it told us our futures."

"What do you mean?" asked Rafe.

"It said that one of us would fail, one of us would die, and one of us was already dead," said Call.

"Think we know who's going to fail," Jasper said, eyeing Call. Call suddenly remembered he hadn't told anyone about

Jasper being in the Library, and began to reconsider that decision.

"Thanks, Jasper," said Aaron. "Always contributing."

"You shouldn't let it bother you," Drew said earnestly. "That's just babble. It doesn't mean anything. None of you are going to die and you're obviously not dead. For Pete's sake."

Call saluted Drew with his fork. "Thanks."

Tamara put her cutlery down. "Excuse me," she said, and slipped out of the room.

Aaron and Call immediately stood up to follow her. They were halfway down the corridor outside the Refectory when Call heard someone call his name — Drew, hurrying along after them. "Call," he said. "Can I talk to you for a second?"

Call exchanged a look with Aaron. "You go ahead," Aaron said. "I'll go check on Tamara. Meet you back at the room."

Call turned back to Drew, pushing his tangled and cave-dusty hair out of his eyes. "Is everything okay?"

"Are you sure that was a good idea?" Drew's blue eyes were wide.

"What?" Call was totally confused.

"Telling everyone about that. About the Devoured! About the prophecy!"

"You said it was just babble," Call protested. "You said it didn't mean anything."

"I just said that because —" Drew searched Call's face, his own expression turning from confusion, to concern, to dawning horror. "You don't know," he said finally. "How can you not know?"

"Not know what?" Call demanded. "You're freaking me out, Drew."

"Who *are* you?" Drew said, half in a whisper, and then

175

backed up a step. "I was wrong about everything," he said. "I have to go."

He turned around and ran. Call watched him go, totally bewildered. He resolved to ask Tamara and Aaron about it, but by the time he got back to the room, exhaustion had clearly overtaken them. Tamara's door was shut and Aaron was asleep on one of the couches.

CHAPTER FIFTEEN

C ALL WOKE UP to the sound of someone moving outside his door. His first thought was that it was Tamara or
Aaron working late in the common room. But the footsteps were
too heavy to belong to either of his friends, and the raised voices
that followed were definitely adult.

He couldn't help hearing Alastair's voice in his head. *They
don't have any mercy, not even for children.*

Call lay sleeplessly staring upward until one of the crystals
set in the walls sputtered into brightness. He took Miri out of
her drawer and slid from the bed, wincing as his shoeless feet hit
the cold stone floor. Without the heavy blankets, he could feel the
chill air through his thin pajamas.

He hoisted Miri just as the door opened. Three Masters
stood in the doorway, looking in at him. They were dressed in
their black uniforms, and their faces were grave and serious.

Master Lemuel's gaze flicked from Call's face to the blade.
"Rufus, your apprentice is well trained."

Call didn't know what to say to that.

"You won't need any weapons tonight, though," said Master Rufus. "Leave Semiramis on your bed and come with us."

Looking down at his LEGO pajamas, Call scowled. "I'm not dressed."

"Well trained in preparedness," said Master North. "Less well trained in obedience." He snapped his fingers. "Put the knife down."

"North," said Master Rufus. "Leave the discipline of my apprentices to me." He moved closer to Call, who didn't quite know what to do. Between Drew's bizarre behavior, his father's warnings, and the Devoured's creepy prophecy, he was feeling deeply unsettled. He didn't want to give up his knife.

Rufus's hand closed around Call's wrist, and Call let Miri go. He didn't know what else he could do. Call knew Master Rufus. He'd eaten meals with him for months and been taught lessons by him. Rufus was a person. Rufus had saved him from the Devoured. *He wouldn't hurt me*, Call told himself. *He wouldn't. No matter what my father said.*

An odd expression flickered across Rufus's face and was gone immediately. "Come along," he said.

Call followed the Masters into the common room, where Tamara and Aaron were already waiting. Both of them were in their pajamas — Aaron was wearing a T-shirt that was practically transparent with washing and sweatpants with a hole in the knee. His blond hair stuck up like duck fluff and he looked barely awake. Tamara looked tense. Her hair was carefully braided and she wore pink pajamas that said I FIGHT LIKE A GIRL across the front. Under the words was a screen print of cartoon girls executing deadly ninja moves.

What's going on? Call mouthed to them silently.

Aaron shrugged and Tamara shook her head. Clearly, they didn't know any more than he did. Although Tamara seemed to know enough to look like she was going to jump out of her skin.

"Seat yourselves," said Master Lemuel. "Please don't dawdle."

"You can clearly see that none of them were trying to . . ." said Master Rufus in a low voice that faded out at the end as though he didn't want to speak the rest out loud.

"This is very important," Master North said as Call, Aaron, and Tamara sat down together on one couch. Tamara yawned hugely and forgot to cover her mouth, which meant she was really tired. "Have you seen Drew Wallace? Several people told us that he followed you out of the Refectory and he seemed upset. Did he say anything to you? Discuss his plans?"

Call frowned. The last time he saw Drew was way too weird to talk about. "What plans?"

"We talked about our lessons," Aaron volunteered. "Drew followed us into the hall — he wanted to talk to Call."

"About the Devoured. I think he was really scared." Call didn't know what else to say. He had no other explanation for Drew's behavior.

"Thank you," said Master North. "Now we need you to go back to your rooms and put on your uniforms. We're going to need your help. Drew left the Magisterium sometime after ten tonight, and it was only due to another apprentice getting up for a midnight glass of water and finding his note that we discovered he was gone at all."

"What did the note say?" Tamara asked. Master Lemuel glowered at her, and Master North looked surprised to be interrupted. Clearly, neither of them knew Tamara very well.

"That he was running away from the Magisterium," Master Lemuel said quietly. "You know how dangerous it is for half-trained mages to be loose in the world? And that's to say nothing of the Chaos-ridden animals that make their homes in the neighboring woods."

"We have to find him," Master Rufus said, nodding slowly. "The whole school will help search. We can cover more ground that way. I hope that explanation is sufficient, Tamara. Because time really is of the essence."

Flushing, Tamara rose and headed toward her room, and Aaron and Call went to theirs. Call slowly drew on his winter clothes: his gray uniform, a thick sweater, a zip-up hoodie. The adrenaline of being woken by the mages was burning off and he was starting to realize how little sleep he'd had, but the idea of Drew stumbling through the dark made him blink himself awake. What had made Drew run?

Reaching for his wristband, Call's fingers trailed over Alastair's cuff and the mysterious note to Master Rufus. He remembered his father's words: *Call, you must listen to me. You don't know what you are. You must get away as soon as you can.*

He was supposed to be the one running, not Drew.

After a knock, the door to his room opened and Tamara came in. She wore her uniform, and her hair was pulled into two braids pinned tightly around her head. She looked a lot more awake than he felt.

"Call," she said. "Come on, we've got to — what's that?"

"What's what?" He glanced down and realized he still had the drawer pulled open, Alastair's wristband and letter on full display. He fished the wristband out and leaned back, pushing the drawer closed with his weight. "I — this is my father's wristband. From when he was at the Magisterium."

"Can I see?" Tamara didn't wait for an answer, just reached out and plucked it from his hand. Her dark eyes widened as she looked at it. "He must have been a really good student."

"What makes you say that?"

"Those stones. And this —" She broke off, blinking. "This can't be your father's wristband."

"Well, I guess it could be my mother's. . . ."

"No," Tamara said. "We saw their handprints in the Hall of Graduates. They both graduated, Call. Whoever's wristband this is, it ends at Silver Year. There's no gold." She handed it back to him. "This bracelet belonged to someone who never graduated from the Magisterium."

"But —" Call broke off as Aaron came in, his wavy hair pasted down to his forehead. He looked like he'd splashed water on his face to wake up.

"Come on, guys," he said. "Master Lemuel and Master North went on ahead, but Rufus seems about to break the door down."

Call shoved the wristband into his pocket, remaining conscious of Tamara's curious gaze on him as they followed Master Rufus through the tunnels. Call's leg was stiff, the way it was most mornings, so it was slow going for him. Aaron and Tamara were careful to match their speed to his, though. For once, he wasn't mad about it.

On the way out, they ran into the rest of the apprentices being led by their Masters, including Lemuel and North. The kids looked as confused and worried as Master Rufus's apprentices did.

A few more turns and they came to a door. Master Lemuel opened it and they stepped into another cave, this one with an opening at the end that wind blew through. They were going outside — and not the way they'd come in that first day. This cave was open at the far end. In the stone was set a pair of giant metal gates.

They had clearly been forged by a Master of metal. They were wrought iron, tapering to sharp points at the top that almost brushed the cave ceiling. Across the the gates, the metal bent into words: *Knowledge and action are one and the same.*

It was the Mission Gate. Call remembered the boy strapped to the stretcher of branches, his skin half burned off, and realized that in the confusion, he'd never noticed much about the gate itself.

"Call, Tamara, Aaron," Master Rufus said. Beside him was tall, curly-haired Alex, looking uncharacteristically somber. He wore his uniform and a thick cloaklike coat over it. There were gloves on his hands. "Alexander will be leading you. Do *not* leave his side. The rest of us will be within shouting distance. We want you to cover an area near one of the Magisterium's less-used exits. Look for any trace of Drew, and if you see him, call out for him. We think it more likely that he will trust one of his own Iron Years than a Master or even an older student like Alex."

Call wondered why the Masters thought Drew would be more likely to trust another student over them. He wondered if they knew more about why Drew had run away than they were letting on.

"Then what do we do?" Aaron asked.

"Once you've spotted him, Alex will signal the Masters. Just keep him talking until we arrive. You and Master Milagros's apprentices will go east." He waved across the crowded grounds, and Master Milagros started toward him, trailed by Celia, Jasper, and Gwenda. "The Bronze Years will head west, the Copper Years will go north, and the Silver and Gold Years who are not assisting Masters will go south and north."

"What about the Chaos-ridden animals in the woods?" Gwenda asked. "Aren't they dangerous to us, too?"

Master Milagros looked toward Alex and another older student. "You won't be alone out there. Stick together and signal us immediately if there's a problem. We will keep close by."

Already, some of the apprentice groups were moving out into the night — summoning glowing orbs that flew through the air like disembodied lanterns. A low hum of whispers and mutterings accompanied them as they made their way into the dark woods.

Call and the others followed Alex. When the last apprentice passed through the gate, it shut with a disturbingly final clang behind them.

"That's the sound it always makes," Alex said, looking at Call's expression. "Come on — we're going this way."

He headed toward the woods, along a dark path. Call stumbled over a root. Aaron, always looking for an excuse, summoned his sparking blue ball of energy, looking pleased that it would be useful. He grinned as it spun above his fingers, lighting the air around them.

"Drew!" Gwenda called. Echoes of other Iron Year students could be heard in the distance. "Drew!"

Jasper rubbed his eyes. He was wearing what appeared to be a fur-lined coat and a hat with earflaps that was slightly too big for his head. "Why do we have to be put in danger just because some dweeb decided he couldn't handle it anymore?" he demanded.

"I don't understand why he'd leave in the middle of the night," Celia said, her arms around herself, shivering even in her long bright blue parka. "None of this makes any sense."

"We don't know any more than you do," said Tamara. "But if Drew ran away, he must have had a reason."

"He's a coward," said Jasper. "That's the only possible reason for leaving."

The forest floor was covered in a thin dusting of snow, and the trees hung low all around them, Aaron's blue light illuminating just enough to emphasize the eeriness of the sharp branches.

"What do you think he has to be afraid of?" Call asked.

Jasper didn't answer.

"We've got to stay together," Alex told them, conjuring three golden balls of flame that whirled around them, charting the outer edge of their party. "If you see or hear anything, tell me. Don't run off."

Frozen leaves crunched under Tamara's feet as she dropped back to walk with Call. "So," she said softly, "how come you thought that wristband belonged to your father?"

Call looked at the others, trying to decide if he was outside the range of their hearing. "Because it came from him."

"He sent it to you?"

Call shook his head. "Not exactly. I . . . found it."

"Found it?" Tamara sounded highly suspicious.

"I know you think he's crazy —"

"He threw a knife at you!"

"He threw it *to* me," said Call. "And then he sent this wristband to the Magisterium. I think he's trying to tell them — to warn them about something."

"Like what?"

"Something about me," Call said.

"You mean you're in danger?"

Tamara sounded alarmed, but Call didn't reply. He didn't know how to tell her more without telling her everything. What if there really was something wrong with him? If Tamara found out, would she keep his secret, no matter how bad it was?

He wanted to trust her. She'd already told him more about the wristband than he'd figured out in months of staring at it.

"What are you guys talking about?" Aaron asked, falling back to join them.

Tamara immediately clammed up, her eyes darting between

Aaron and Call. Call could tell that she wasn't going to tell Aaron anything unless he said it was okay. It sparked a strangely warm feeling in his stomach. He'd never really had friends who'd kept his secrets before.

It was enough to decide him. "We're talking about this," he said, pulling the wristband out of his pocket and handing it over to Aaron, who examined it while Call explained the whole story — his conversation with his father, the warning that Call didn't know what he was, the letter Alastair had sent Rufus, the message with the wristband: *Bind his magic.*

"Bind your magic?" Aaron's voice rose. Tamara shushed him. Aaron returned his voice to a harsh whisper. "Why would he ask Rufus to do that? That's crazy!"

"I don't know," Call whispered back, looking up ahead anxiously. Alex and the other kids didn't seem to be paying any attention to them as they made their way up a low rise of hill, snaked through with big tree roots, calling Drew's name. "I don't understand any of it."

"Well, clearly the wristband was supposed to be a message to Rufus," Tamara said. "It means something. I just don't know what."

"Maybe if we knew whose it was," said Aaron. He handed the wristband to Call, who tied it onto his arm, above his own wristband and under his sleeve.

"Someone who didn't graduate. Someone who left the Magisterium when he or she was sixteen or seventeen — or someone who died here." Tamara looked at it again, frowning at the small medals with symbols on them. "I don't know exactly what these mean. Excellence in something, but what? If we knew, that would tell us something. And I don't know what this black stone means either. I've never seen one before."

"Let's ask Alex," Aaron said.

"No way," said Call, shaking his head and looking warily at the others trooping through the snow in the dark. "What if there *is* something wrong with me and he can figure it out just from looking at this wristband?"

"There's nothing wrong with you," Aaron said sturdily. But Aaron was the kind of person who had faith in people and believed stuff like that.

"Alex!" Tamara said loudly. "Alex, can we ask you something?"

"Tamara, no," Call hissed, but the older student had already fallen back to walk alongside them.

"What's up?" he asked, blue eyes inquisitive. "You guys all right?"

"I was just wondering if we could see your wristband," Tamara said, with a quelling look in Call's direction. Call relented.

"Huh. Sure," Alex agreed, unsnapping the band and handing it over. It had three stripes of metal on it, ending with bronze. It was also studded with gems: red and orange, blue and indigo and scarlet.

"What are these for?" Tamara asked innocently, though Call had a feeling she probably knew the answer.

"The completion of different tasks." Alex sounded matter-of-fact, not like he was bragging. "This one is for using fire successfully to dispel an elemental. This one is for using air to create an illusion."

"What would it mean if you had a black one?" Aaron asked.

Alex's eyes widened. He opened his mouth to answer at the same moment Jasper yelled, "Look!"

A bright light glowed out from the ridge of the hill opposite theirs. As they stared, a scream split the night, high and terrible.

"Stay here!" Alex barked, and started to run, half slipping down the side of the hill they were on, heading toward the light. Suddenly, the night was full of noise. Call could hear other groups shouting and calling to one another.

Something slid through the sky above them — something scaly and snakelike — but Alex wasn't looking up.

"Alex!" Tamara yelled, but the older boy didn't hear her — he had reached the other hill and was starting to scramble up it. The scaly shadow was over his head, swooping and dipping.

The kids were all shouting for Alex now, trying to warn him — all of them except for Call. He started to run, ignoring the twisting burn in his leg as he slid and nearly fell down the hillside. He heard Tamara scream his name, and Jasper yell, "We're supposed to stay *here*," but Call didn't slow. He was going to be the apprentice that Aaron thought he was, the one who there was nothing wrong with. He was going to do the kind of things that got you mysterious heroic achievements on your wristband. He was going to throw himself right into the fray.

He tripped over a loose stone, fell, and rolled to the bottom of the hill, banging his elbow hard on a tree root. *Okay,* he thought, *not the best start.*

Staggering to his feet, he started to climb again — he could see things more clearly now, in the light that poured down from the hilltop. It was a clear knifelike light that threw every pebble and hole into sharp relief. The rise grew steeper as Call reached the top; he fell to his knees and clambered the last few feet, rolling onto the flat surface of the hilltop.

Something brushed past him then, something huge, something that brought a rush of air that sprayed dirt into his eyes. He choked and staggered to his feet.

"Help!" he heard a weak voice call. "Please, help me!"

Call looked around. The bright light was gone; there was only starlight and moonlight to illuminate the hilltop. It was covered with a tangle of roots and bushes. "Who's there?" he said.

He heard what sounded like a hiccuping sob. "Call?"

Call started to blunder toward the voice, pushing through the undergrowth.

From behind him, people were shouting his name. He kicked aside some rocks and half slid down a small incline. He found himself inside a shadowy depression in the ground, lined with thorny bushes. A huddled figure lay at the opposite side.

"Drew?" Call called out.

The slight boy struggled to turn around. Call could see that one of his feet was jammed in what looked like a gopher hole. It was twisted at an ugly, painful-looking angle.

From behind him, two softly glowing orbs lit up the night. Call glanced back and realized they were floating over from the hill where the other students were standing. He could barely see the others from where he was, and he wasn't sure they could see him at all.

"Call?" The tears shining on Drew's face were bright in the moonlight. Call scooted closer.

"Are you stuck?" he asked.

"Of — of course," Drew whispered. "I try to run away, and this is as far as I get. It's h-humiliating."

His teeth were chattering. He was wearing only a thin T-shirt and jeans. Call couldn't believe he'd planned to run away from the Magisterium dressed like that.

"Help me," Drew said through chattering teeth. "Help me get free. I have to keep running."

"But I don't get it. What's wrong? Where are you going to go?"

"I don't know." Drew's face twisted. "You have no idea what

Master Lemuel's like. He — he figured out that sometimes when I'm under a lot of stress, I do better. Like a lot better. I know it's weird, but it's always been the way I am. I do better on a testing day than I ever do in normal practice. So he figured out that he could make me better by keeping me under stress all the time. I barely . . . barely ever sleep. He only lets me eat sometimes and I never know when that's going to be. He keeps scaring me, calling up illusions of monsters and elementals while I'm alone in the dark and I . . . I want to get better. I want to be a better mage, but I just . . ." He looked away and swallowed, his throat bobbing up and down. "I can't."

Call looked at him more closely. It was true that Drew didn't look like the boy Call had met on the bus to the Magisterium. He was thinner. A lot thinner. You could see how his jeans hung loose, secured by a belt that was pulled all the way through to the last hole. His nails were bitten down and there were dark shadows under his eyes.

"Okay," Call said. "But you're not going to be able to run anywhere on this." He leaned forward and put his hand on Drew's ankle. It felt hot to the touch.

Drew yelped. "That hurts!"

Call eyed the ankle where it poked out below the hem of Drew's jeans. It looked swollen and dark. "I think you might have broken a bone."

"Y-you do?" Drew sounded panicked.

Call reached down inside himself, through himself, into the ground he was kneeling on. *Earth wants to bind.* He felt it give way under his touch, making a space where magic could spill in, the way water rose to fill up a hole scraped in the sand of a beach.

Call drew the magic through himself, into his hand, letting it flow into Drew. Drew gave a gasp.

Call pulled away. "Sorry —"

"No." Drew looked at him wonderingly. "It's hurting less. It's working."

Call had never done magic like that before. Healing had been something Master Rufus talked about, but they'd never practiced. But he'd managed it. Maybe there really was nothing wrong with him.

"Drew! Call!" It was Alex, followed by a shining globe of light that lit the ends of his hair like a halo. He skidded down the slope of the incline, nearly knocking into them. His face was pale in the moonlight.

Call moved away. "Drew's stuck. I think his ankle's broken."

Alex bent over the younger boy and touched the earth that was trapping his leg in place. Call felt stupid for not having thought of the same thing as the ground crumbled away and Alex locked his arms under Drew's shoulders, pulling him free. Drew yelled aloud in pain.

"Didn't you hear me? His ankle's *broken* —" Call started.

"Call. There's no time." Alex knelt down to lift Drew in his arms. "We have to get out of here."

"W-what?" Drew seemed almost too stunned to function. "What's going on?"

Alex was scanning the area anxiously. Call suddenly remembered all the warnings about what lurked in the woods outside the caverns of the school.

"The Chaos-ridden," Call said. "They're here."

CHAPTER SIXTEEN

A LOW HOWL CUT through the night. Alex started up the incline, gesturing impatiently for Call to follow. Call scrambled after him, his leg aching.

When they reached the top, Call saw Aaron and Tamara coming over the crest of the hill, Celia, Jasper, and Rafe right behind. They were panting, alert.

"Drew!" Tamara gasped, staring at the limp figure in Alex's arms.

"Chaos-ridden animals," Aaron said, coming to a stop in front of Call and Alex. "They're coming up over the far side of the hill —"

"What kind?" Alex asked urgently.

"Wolves," said Jasper, pointing.

Still holding Drew in his arms, Alex turned and stared in horror. Moonlight showed dark shapes slipping from the woods, advancing toward them. Five wolves, long and lean, with fur the color of a stormy sky. Their snouts scented the air, their coruscating eyes wild and strange.

Alex bent down and laid Drew carefully on the ground. "Listen to me," he shouted to the other students, who were milling fearfully. "Make a circle around us while I heal Drew. They have a sense for the weak, the wounded. They'll attack."

"We only have to hold off the Chaos-ridden until the Masters get here," Tamara said, charging in front of Alex.

"Right, hold them off, *that's* simple," Jasper spat out, but he fell into formation with the others, making a circle of their bodies, with their backs to Alex and Drew. Call found himself standing shoulder to shoulder with Celia and Jasper. Celia's teeth were chattering.

The Chaos-ridden wolves appeared, low and feral, spilling up over the ridge like shadows. They were huge, much bigger than any wolves Call had ever imagined. Ropes of drool hung from their open jaws. Their eyes burned and spun, sparking that feeling inside Call's head again, the itchy-burning-thirsty one. *Chaos*, he thought to himself. *Chaos wants to devour.*

As terrifying as they were, though, the more Call looked at them, the more he thought their eyes were beautiful, like the inside of a kaleidoscope, a thousand different colors all at once. He couldn't tear his gaze away.

"Call!" Tamara's voice cut through his thoughts — Call jolted back into his body, realizing suddenly that he had stepped out of the formation and was several feet ahead of the rest of the group. He hadn't moved away from the wolves. He'd moved *toward* them.

A hand grabbed at his wrist — Tamara, looking terrified but determined. "Would you STOP?" she demanded, and started trying to drag him back toward the others.

Everything after that happened very fast. Tamara tugged Call back; Call resisted. His weak leg went out from under him and he fell, his elbows jamming painfully into the stony ground. Tamara drew her hand back and made a gesture like she was throwing a baseball. A circle of fire shot from her palm, toward a wolf that was suddenly very close.

The fire exploded along its fur and the wolf howled, baring a mouth full of sharp teeth. But it kept coming — in fact, its fur was now standing on end as if it had been electrified. Its red tongue lolled from its mouth as it stalked closer and closer. It was only feet away from Call, and he struggled to get his legs under him, Tamara reaching down to slide her hands under his arms, trying to haul him up. The Chaos-ridden couldn't be chased off like a wyvern. They didn't care about anything but teeth and blood and madness.

"Tamara! Call! Get back here!" Aaron shouted. He sounded scared. The Chaos-ridden wolves were stalking closer, surrounding Call and Tamara, the knot of apprentices forgotten. Alex was in their midst, holding the unconscious Drew. Alex looked frozen, his eyes and mouth wide.

Call staggered to his feet, shoving Tamara behind him. He locked his gaze with the wolf closest to him. The wolf's eyes still spun, red and gold, the color of fire.

This is it, Call thought. His mind seemed to have slowed down. He felt like he was moving underwater.

My father was right. All along, he was right. We're going to die here.

He wasn't angry . . . but he wasn't scared, either. Tamara was struggling, trying to pull him backward. But he couldn't move. Wouldn't move. The oddest feeling was pulsing through him, like a gathering knot under his ribs. He could feel the strange wristband on his arm throb.

"Tamara," he breathed. "Go back."

"No!" She yanked at the back of his shirt. Call stumbled —
and the wolf sprang.

Someone — maybe Celia, maybe Jasper — screamed. The
wolf leaped through the air, terrible and beautiful, its coat shedding sparks. Call began to raise his hands.

A shadow passed across Call's vision — someone skidding to
a stop between him and the wolf, someone with light hair, someone who planted his feet and thrust out both his arms as if he
could hold the wolf back with his hands. *Alex*, Call thought at
first, dizzily, and then, with a cold sense of shock: *Aaron*.

"No!" he called, jerking forward, but Tamara would not let
him go. "Aaron, *no!*"

The other apprentices were shouting, too, calling to Aaron.
Alex had left Drew's side and was pushing his way toward them.

Aaron didn't move. His feet were planted so firmly in the
ground, it was as if they had taken root there. His hands were up,
palms out, and from the centers of his palms spilled something
like smoke — it was blacker than black, dense and sinuous, and
Call knew, without knowing how, that it was the darkest substance in the world.

With a howl, the wolf contorted its body, twisting aside so
that it landed awkwardly on the ground, only feet from Tamara
and Call. Its fur stood up all over, its eyes pinwheeling madly.
The other wolves howled and whimpered, adding their voices to
the madness of the night.

"Aaron, what are you doing?" Tamara said so quietly that
Call wasn't sure Aaron heard her. "*Are* you doing that?"

But Aaron didn't seem to hear. Darkness poured from his
hands; his hair and shirt were stuck to his body with sweat. The
darkness swirled faster, velvety tendrils of it wrapping around
the Chaos-ridden pack. The wind picked up, making the trees

shudder. The ground shook. The wolves tried to back up, to run, but they were fenced in by darkness — darkness that had become a solid thing, a contracting prison.

Call's heart was hammering sickly. He felt a sudden pulsing terror at the idea of being trapped inside that darkness, of the nothingness closing in, erasing him, consuming him.

Devouring him.

"Aaron!" he shouted, but the wind was thrashing through the trees now, obliterating sound. "Aaron, *stop*!"

Call could see the glittering, panicked eyes of the Chaos-ridden wolves. For a moment, they turned toward him, sparks in the darkness. Then the blackness closed around them, and they were gone.

Aaron dropped to his knees as if he'd been shot. He knelt, panting, one hand over his stomach, as the wind dropped away and the ground settled. The apprentices were utterly silent, staring. Alex's lips were moving, but no words were coming out. Call looked for the wolves, but there were now only roiling masses of darkness dissipating like smoke where they'd been.

"Aaron." Tamara broke away from Call and ran over to Aaron, bending down to put a hand on his shoulder. "Oh, my God, Aaron, Aaron —"

The other apprentices had begun to whisper. "What's going on?" Rafe said, his voice plaintive. "What happened?"

Tamara was patting Aaron's back, making soothing noises. Call knew he should join her, but he felt frozen. He couldn't stop remembering the way Aaron had looked right before the darkness devoured the wolf, the way he'd seemed to be summoning up something, calling something — and *that* was what had come.

He thought of the Cinquain.

Fire wants to burn, water wants to flow, air wants to rise, earth wants to bind. But chaos, chaos wants to devour.

Call looked back at the confusion of students. In the distance, behind them, he could see darting lights — the glowing orbs of the Masters running toward them. He could hear the sound of their voices. Drew had an odd expression on his face, stoic and a little lost, as though hope had gone out of him. There were tears on his cheeks. Celia locked eyes with Call, looking from him to Aaron, as if asking Call: *Is he all right?*

Aaron had his face buried in his hands. The pose unlocked Call's feet; he stumbled the short distance over to his friend and dropped down on his knees beside him.

"Are you okay?" he asked.

Aaron lifted his face and nodded slowly, still looking stunned.

Tamara met Call's gaze over Aaron's head. Her hair had come out of its braids and was tumbling down her shoulders. He didn't think he'd ever seen her look so messy. "You don't understand," she said to Call in a hushed voice. "Aaron's what they've been looking for. He's the . . ."

"I'm still here, you know," Aaron said in a strained voice.

"Makar," Tamara finished in a dead whisper.

"I'm *not*," Aaron protested. "I can't be. I don't know anything about chaos. I don't have any affinity —"

"Aaron, child." A gentle voice cut through Aaron's speech — Call looked up and saw, to his surprise, that it was Master Rufus. The other Masters were there as well, their orbs like fireflies as they darted among the students, checking them for injuries, soothing their fright. Master North had lifted Drew from the ground and was holding him in his arms, the boy's head to his chest.

"I didn't mean to —" Aaron started. He looked miserable. "The wolf was there, and then it *wasn't*."

"You've done nothing wrong. It would have attacked you if you had not acted." Master Rufus reached down and gently pulled Aaron to his feet. Call and Tamara stepped back. "You saved lives, Aaron Stewart."

Aaron drew in a ragged breath. He seemed to be trying to pull himself together. "They're all staring at me — all the other students," he said under his breath.

Call turned to look, but his gaze was suddenly blocked by the appearance of two Masters. Master Tanaka and a woman he'd seen once before with a group of Gold Year students, but whose name he didn't know.

"They are staring at you because you are the Makar," the female mage said, her eyes on Aaron. "Because you can wield the power of chaos."

Aaron didn't say anything. He looked as though he'd been unexpectedly slapped in the face.

"We have been waiting for you, Aaron," said Master Tanaka. "You have no idea how long."

Aaron was tensing up, looking ready to bolt. *Leave him alone,* Call wanted to say. *Can't you see you're freaking him out?* Aaron had been right: Everyone was staring at them now — the other kids, huddled together, their Masters. Even Lemuel and Milagros looked away from their apprentices long enough to stare at Aaron. Only Rockmaple was gone — returned to the Magisterium to care for Drew, Call assumed.

Rufus laid a protective hand on Aaron's shoulder. "Haru," he said, nodding at Master Tanaka. "And, Sarita. Thank you for your kind words."

He didn't sound particularly grateful.

"Congratulations," said Master Tanaka. "To have a Makar as an apprentice . . . every Master's dream." He sounded pretty bitter, and Call wondered if he was mad about that whole choosing-first thing back at the Trial. "He must come with us. The Masters must speak to him. . . ."

"No!" Tamara said, and then clapped her hand over her mouth, as if surprised at her own outburst. "I just mean . . ."

"It has been a stressful day for the students, especially Aaron," Rufus said to the two Masters. "These apprentices, most of them Iron Years, were just attacked by a pack of Chaos-ridden wolves. Can the boy go back to his own bed?"

The woman he'd called Sarita shook her head. "We can't have an uncontrolled chaos mage wandering around without any understanding of his own powers." She did actually sound regretful. "The area has been thoroughly swept, Rufus. Whatever happened with this pack of wolves, it was an anomaly. The greatest danger to Aaron right now, and to all the other students, is Aaron."

She held out her hand.

Aaron looked up at Rufus, waiting for permission. Rufus nodded, looking tired. "Go with them," he said. Then he stepped back. Master Tanaka made a beckoning gesture, and Aaron walked over to him. With both of the Masters flanking him, he walked toward the Magisterium, stopping only once to look back at Call and Tamara.

Call couldn't help but think he looked very small.

CHAPTER SEVENTEEN

A S SOON AS Aaron disappeared, the rest of the Masters began herding the remaining apprentices into rows of lines, with the Iron Years at the center and the older students toward the outside. Tamara and Call stood a little distance away, watching everyone else rush around. Call wondered if she was feeling the same way he was — the idea of ever finding the Makar everyone was looking for had seemed like a distant, impossible thing, and now Aaron, their friend Aaron, was the one. Call looked back toward where the wolves had been before Aaron had sent them spinning into the void, but the only sign of them was the prints of their huge paws in the snow. The marks still glowed with a faint, discrete light, as if each print had been made with fire and still kept some of that fire deep inside it.

While Call stared, something small darted between the trees like a shifting shadow. He scowled, trying to see better, but there were no more movements. Whatever it was had either gone or never been there. He shuddered, remembering the huge *something* he had felt brush by him while was running to Drew. Recent events had made him hyperaware of every stray breeze. Maybe he was imagining things.

Master Milagros detached herself from the group of apprentices, now herded into something approximating order, and walked over to Tamara and Call, her expression kind. "We need to start back now. It's unlikely that there are more Chaos-ridden out there, but we can't be sure. It's best if we hurry."

Tamara nodded, looking more subdued than Call could remember seeing her, and began trudging through the snow. Joining the other Iron Year apprentices at the group's center, they began the trek back to the Magisterium. The Masters had taken up posts around the very outside of the group, their glowing orbs casting shards of light through the dawn. Celia, Gwenda, and Jasper were walking along with Rafe and Kai. Jasper had placed his fur-lined coat over Drew when he was lying on the ground, an uncharacteristically nice gesture on his part, and one that had left him shivering in the icy morning air.

"Did Drew say why he left?" Celia asked Call. "You were down there with him before Alex got there. What did he say to you?"

Call shook his head. He wasn't sure if it was a secret.

"You can tell us," said Celia. "We won't laugh at him or be jerks."

Gwenda glanced at Jasper and raised her eyebrows. "Most of us won't, anyway."

Jasper cut his eyes toward Tamara, but she didn't say a thing.

Even though Jasper was almost always a jerk, in that moment, remembering what good friends Tamara and Jasper had been at the Iron Trial, Call felt bad for him. He thought of the time he'd seen Jasper in the Library, straining to make a flame spark, and the way Jasper had snapped at him to leave. Call wondered if Jasper had thought of running away like Drew had.

He remembered Jasper's words: *Only cowards leave the Magisterium.* Then he stopped feeling bad.

"He told me that Master Lemuel was too hard on him," Call said. "That he performed better under stress, so Lemuel was always trying to scare him into being better."

"Master Lemuel does that kind of thing to all of us — jumping out from behind walls, shouting things, and doing middle-of-the-night training," Rafe said. "He isn't trying to be mean. He's trying to prepare us."

"Right," said Call, thinking of Drew's bitten nails and haunted eyes. "Drew ran away for no reason. I mean, who wouldn't want to be chased through the snow by packs of Chaos-ridden wolves if they got the chance?"

"Maybe you didn't know how bad it was, Rafe," said Tamara, looking troubled. "Since Master Lemuel isn't that way with you."

"Drew's *lying*," Rafe insisted.

"He said that Master Lemuel wouldn't let him eat," Call told them. "And he does look skinnier."

"What?" Rafe demanded. "That didn't happen. You saw him in the Refectory with the rest of us. And anyway, Drew never told me any of this. He would have said something."

Call shrugged. "Maybe he didn't think you'd believe him. It looks like he was right."

"I wouldn't — I don't —" Rafe glanced around at the others, but they looked away uncomfortably.

"Master Lemuel isn't nice," Gwenda said. "Maybe Drew didn't think he had any choice but running away."

"That's not how Masters are supposed to act," Celia said. "He should have told Master North. Or someone."

"Maybe he thinks that *is* how Masters are supposed to act," Call said. "Considering no one's ever exactly explained to us how they *are* supposed to act."

No one had anything to say to that. For a while, they walked in silence, boots crunching through the snow. Out of the corner of Call's eye, he kept noticing the small shadow keeping pace with them, slipping from tree to tree. He almost pointed it out to Tamara, except that she hadn't said a word since the Masters had taken Aaron back to the Magisterium. She seemed lost in her own thoughts.

What was it? It didn't look large enough to be threatening. Maybe it was a small elemental like Warren, one that was nervous to reveal itself. Maybe it *was* Warren, too scared to apologize. Whatever it was, Call couldn't seem to get the thought of it out of his head. He let himself fall back, until he was walking behind the rest of the group. The others were tired and distracted enough that, a few moments later, he was able to move toward the trees without anyone noticing.

The woods were hushed, the golden light of the rising sun making the snow bright.

"Who's there?" Call called softly.

A furry snout peeked out from one of the trees. Something fuzzy and pointy-eared bobbed up, peering at Call with the eyes of the Chaos-ridden.

A wolf pup.

The creature whined a little and slunk back, out of sight. Call's heart thudded in his chest. He took a half step forward, wincing when his boot snapped a twig. The wolf pup hadn't moved far. Call could see it as he got closer, huddled against the tree, its pale brown fur ruffled by the morning breeze. It scented the air with a wet black nose.

It didn't look menacing. It looked like a dog. A puppy, really.

"It's okay," Call said, trying to make his voice soothing. "Come on out. Nobody's going to hurt you."

The wolf's small, fuzzy tail began to wag. It wobbled toward Call across the dead leaves and snow on not completely steady feet.

"Hey, little wolf," Call said, dropping his voice. He'd always wanted a dog, wanted one desperately, but his father had never let him have any pets. Unable to help himself, Call reached out and petted the wolf's head, his fingers sinking into its ruff. It wagged its tail faster, and whined.

"Call!" Someone — Celia, he thought — called from up ahead. "What are you doing? Where did you go?"

Call's arms moved without his volition, as if he were a puppet on strings, reaching out to grab the wolf and tuck it inside his jacket. It whuffled and hung on, digging small claws into his shirt as he zipped the jacket up over it. He looked down at himself — you couldn't really tell anything was off, he told himself. He looked as if he had a small potbelly, as if he'd been at the lichen.

"Call!" Celia called again.

Call hesitated. He was absolutely, totally sure that bringing a Chaos-ridden animal into the Magisterium was an expellable offense. Maybe even a magic-binding one. It was an insane thing to do.

Then the wolf pup craned up and licked the bottom of his chin. He remembered the wolves disappearing into the darkness that Aaron had conjured. Had one of them been this puppy's mother? Was this wolf now motherless . . . just like Call?

He took a deep breath and, zipping the jacket up the rest of the way, limped after the others.

"Where were you?" Tamara asked him. She had snapped out of her stunned state and now looked annoyed. "We were starting to worry."

"I got my foot stuck on a root," Call said.

"Next time yell or something." Tamara seemed too tired and distracted to consider his story closely. Jasper, looking back at him, had an odd expression on his face.

"We were just talking about Aaron," Rafe said. "About how weird it is that he didn't know he could use chaos magic. I would have never figured him for being a Makar."

"It must be scary," Kai said. "Using the kind of magic the Enemy of Death uses. I mean, that can't feel good, right?"

"It's just *power*," said Jasper in a superior tone. "It's not chaos magic that makes the Enemy the monster he is. He became that way because he was corrupted by Master Joseph and went totally crazy."

"What do you mean he was corrupted by Joseph? Was that his Master?" Rafe asked, sounding worried, like maybe he thought Master Lemuel being awful could make him into a villain, too.

"Oh, just tell the story, Jasper," said Tamara wearily.

"Okay," Jasper said, sounding grateful that she was speaking to him. "For those of you who don't know anything, which is embarrassing, by the way, the Enemy of Death's real name is Constantine Madden."

"Nice start," Celia said. "Not everyone's a legacy, Jasper."

Underneath Call's jacket, the wolf squirmed. Call crossed his arms over his chest and hoped no one noticed his coat was moving.

"You okay?" Celia asked him. "You look a little —"

"I'm *fine*," Call insisted.

Jasper went on. "Constantine had a twin brother named Jericho, and, like all mages who are good enough in the Trial, they came to the Magisterium when they were twelve. Back in those days, there was a lot more focus on experiments. Master Joseph, Jericho's Master, was super into chaos magic. But to do all the experiments he hoped to try, he needed a Makar to access the void. He couldn't do it himself."

Jasper's voice dropped low and creepy. "Imagine how happy he was when Constantine turned out to be a Makar. Jericho didn't need much convincing to agree to be his brother's counterweight, and the other Masters didn't need much convincing to let Master Joseph work with the two brothers outside of their regular teaching. He was an expert on chaos magic, even though he couldn't perform any, and Constantine had a lot to learn. . . ."

"This doesn't sound good," Call said, trying to ignore that underneath his jacket, the wolf pup was chewing on one of his buttons, which tickled like crazy.

"Yeah, it's not," Tamara put in. "Jasper, it's not a ghost story. You don't have to tell it that way."

"I'm not telling it any way but the way it happened. Constantine and Master Joseph got more and more obsessed with what could be done with the void. They took out bits of the void and put them inside animals, making them Chaos-ridden, like those wolves up there. They looked like regular animals from a distance, but they were more aggressive and their brains were all scrambled up. Pure chaos in your brain will make you crazy. The void — it's like everything and nothing all at once. No one can keep that in their head for long without going insane. Certainly not a chipmunk."

"There are Chaos-ridden chipmunks?" Rafe asked.

Jasper didn't answer. He was on a roll. "Maybe that's why Constantine did what he did. Maybe the void made him crazy. We don't really know. We just know he tried an experiment that nobody had ever tried before. It was too difficult. It almost killed him, and it destroyed his counterweight."

"You mean his brother," said Call. His voice went a little weird at the end of the sentence, but the wolf had picked that moment to stop biting and start licking his chest. He was also pretty sure it was drooling on him.

"Yeah. He died on the floor of the experiment room. They say his ghost —"

"Shut up, Jasper," said Tamara. She had her arm around another Iron Year girl, whose lip was wobbling.

"Well, anyway, Jericho was killed. And maybe you'd think that would have stopped Constantine, but it only made him worse. He became obsessed with finding a way to bring back his brother. To use chaos magic to bring back the dead."

Celia nodded. "Necromancy. That's completely forbidden."

"He couldn't do it. But he did manage to push chaos magic into living humans, which made the first Chaos-ridden. Seemed to drive out their souls so that they didn't know who they were anymore. They obeyed him mindlessly. It wasn't what he wanted and maybe he hadn't meant to do it, but he didn't stop his experiments then either. Finally, the other Masters discovered what he was doing. They were trying to figure out some way to strip him of his magic, but they didn't know Master Joseph was still loyal to him. Master Joseph got him out — he blasted through one of the walls of the Magisterium and took Constantine with him. A lot of people say the blast nearly killed them both and that Constantine was horribly scarred. He wears a silver mask now, to cover up the scars. The surviving Chaos-ridden animals he'd created fled through the explosion, too, which is why there are so many of them in the woods around here."

"So what you're saying is that the Enemy of Death is the way he is because of the Magisterium," Call said.

"No," Jasper said. "That's not what I —"

The Mission Gate came into sight, distracting Call with the promise that if he made it back to his room, it would be a million times easier to hide the wolf. At least it would be easier to hide it from all the people who weren't his roommates. He'd get the wolf some water and food and then — and then he'd figure it out from there.

The gates were open. They passed under the words *Knowledge and Action Are One and the Same* and into the caverns of the Magisterium, where a gust of warm air hit Call in the face, presenting him with another problem. Outside, he'd been freezing. In here, as they trudged along toward their rooms, with his jacket zipped to his chin, he was rapidly overheating.

"So what did Constantine want?" asked Rafe.

"What?" Jasper sounded distracted.

"In your story. You said 'it wasn't what he wanted.' The Chaos-ridden. Why not?"

"Because he wanted his brother back," Call said. He couldn't believe Rafe was being so dense. "Not some . . . zombie."

"They're not like zombies," Jasper said. "They don't eat people, the Chaos-ridden. They just don't have memories or personality. They're . . . blank."

They were nearly at the Iron Years' rooms now, and there were braziers spaced out along the corridors, full of fiery glowing stones. Having a huge furry bundle stuffed down his front was making Call's temperature soar. Also, the wolf was breathing hotly on his neck. In fact, he thought it might be asleep.

"How do you know so much about the Enemy of Death?" Rafe asked, a flinty edge to his voice.

Call didn't hear Jasper's reply because Tamara was hissing in his ear. "Are you okay?" she demanded. "You're turning kind of purple."

"I'm fine."

She gave him the once-over. "Is there something stuffed down your shirt?"

"My scarf," he replied, hoping she wouldn't remember he hadn't been wearing one.

She narrowed her brows. "Why would you do that?"

He shrugged. "I was cold."

"Call —"

But they had reached their rooms. With enormous gratitude, Call tapped the door with his wristband, letting himself and Tamara in. She was in the middle of waving good-bye to the others, when he slammed the door behind them and staggered toward his bedroom.

"Call!" Tamara said. "Don't you think we should — I don't know, talk? About Aaron?"

"Later," Call gasped, half falling into his bedroom and kicking the door shut. He collapsed onto his back, just as the wolf popped its head out of the collar of his jacket and looked around.

Freed, it seemed wildly excited to bound around his room, nails loud on the stone. Call prayed Tamara wouldn't hear as the wolf sniffed its way under Call's bed, around his wardrobe, and on top of the pajamas he'd tossed on the floor when he'd been woken up earlier.

"You need a bath," he told the wolf. It paused its rolling, legs in the air, and wagged its tail, tongue lolling from a corner of its mouth. As he looked down at its strange, shifting eyes, he remembered Jasper's words.

They don't have memories, or personality. They're . . . blank.

But the wolf had plenty of personality. Which meant that Jasper didn't understand as much about what it meant to be Chaos-ridden as he thought he did. Maybe that was how they were when the Enemy made them, maybe they even stayed blank throughout their lives, but the wolf pup had been born with chaos inside of it. It had grown up that way. It wasn't what they thought it was.

His father's words came back to him, making him shiver in a way that had nothing to do with the cold.

You don't know what you are.

Pushing that thought away, Call climbed into bed, kicked off his boots, and pressed his face against the pillow. The wolf jumped up next to him, smelling like pine needles and freshly turned earth. For a moment, Call wondered if the wolf was going to bite him. But then it settled next to him, circling twice before throwing its little body down against his stomach. With the warm weight of the Chaos-ridden wolf next to him, Call dropped immediately into sleep.

CHAPTER EIGHTEEN

CALL DREAMED THAT he was trapped under the weight of an enormous fuzzy pillow. He woke up groggily, waving his arms, and almost thwacked the wolf pup, who was curled on his chest and staring at him with huge, entreating, fire-colored eyes.

The full, crashing realization of what he had done hit Call, and he rolled out from under the wolf so fast that he slid off the bed and hit the floor. The pain of smacking his knees on the cold stone shocked him completely awake. He found he was kneeling, staring directly into the eyes of the wolf pup, who had crawled to the edge of the bed and was gazing at him.

"Mruf," the wolf pup said.

"Shhhh," Call hissed. His heart was racing. What had he done? Had he actually smuggled a Chaos-ridden animal into the Magisterium? He might as well have taken off all his clothes, covered himself in lichen, and run through the caves yelling, *EXPEL ME! BIND MY MAGIC! SEND ME HOME!*

The pup whimpered. Its eyes were spinning like pinwheels, fixed on Call. Its tongue darted out and then vanished again.

"Oh, man," Call muttered. "You're hungry, aren't you? Okay. Let me get you something to eat. Stay there. Yeah. Right there."

He stood up and blinked at the windup clock on the night-stand. Eleven in the morning and the alarm hadn't gone off yet. Weird. He opened his bedroom door quietly — and was instantly faced with Tamara, already in her uniform, eating breakfast at their common table. It was a spread of deliciously normal-looking food: toast and butter, sausages, bacon, scrambled eggs, and orange juice.

"Is Aaron back?" Call asked, carefully shutting the bedroom door behind him and leaning against it in what he hoped was a nonchalant pose.

Tamara swallowed a mouthful of toast and shook her head. "No. Celia came by before and said classes were canceled for today. I don't know what's going on."

"I guess I'd better change," Call said, reaching out to grab a sausage off the table.

Tamara stared at him. "Are you okay? You're acting kind of strange."

"I'm fine." Call grabbed another sausage. "Back in a minute."

He darted into his bedroom, where the wolf pup was lying on a pile of clothes, waving its paws in the air. It bounded to its feet as soon as it saw Call, and jogged over. Call held his breath as he offered it a sausage. The wolf inhaled the food, gulping it down in a single bite. He gave it the second sausage, watching with a sinking feeling in the pit of his stomach as that disappeared just as fast. Licking its muzzle, the wolf waited expectantly.

"Uh," said Call, "I don't have any more. Just wait and I'll get you something else."

Throwing on a fresh uniform should have taken seconds, but not with the wolf bounding all over the room. Revitalized by sausages, it stole Call's boot and dragged it under the bed by the laces, chewing on the leather. Then, once he'd gotten his boot back, it grabbed hold of the hem of his pants and played tug-of-war.

"*Stop*," Call begged, pulling, but that only seemed to make the wolf more gleeful. He bounded in front of Call, eager to play.

"I'll be right back," Call promised. "Just be quiet. And then I'll sneak you out for a walk."

The wolf cocked its head and went back to rolling on its back. Call took that moment to leave the room, shutting the door quickly behind him.

"Ah, good," Master Rufus said, turning away from his perusal of the far wall to face Call. "You're ready. We have to go to a meeting."

Call nearly jumped out of his skin at the sight of him. Tamara, brushing toast crumbs off her uniform, looked at Call oddly.

"But I didn't get to eat breakfast," Call protested, looking over at the remaining food. If he could just smuggle a few more fistfuls of sausage into his bedroom somehow, he could get enough to tide the wolf over until he got back from whatever this meeting was. At his other school, they were mostly hour-long lectures about how bad things could happen to you if you did bad stuff, or what was wrong about bullying, or, at least once, the horrors of bedbugs. He didn't think this was going to be like that, but he hoped it would be over fast. He was pretty sure the wolf would need to go for a walk really, really soon. Otherwise — well, Call was better off not even contemplating that.

"You ate two sausages before," Tamara said unhelpfully. "It's not like you're starving."

"Did you indeed," said Master Rufus drily. "In that case, come along, Callum. There will be some members of the

Assembly of Mages in attendance. We don't want to be late, since I am sure you can guess what it will be about."

Call narrowed his eyes. "Where's Aaron?" he asked, but Master Rufus didn't answer, just led them out into the hallway where they joined the stream of people flooding through the caverns. Call didn't think he'd ever seen so many people in the halls of the school. Master Rufus fell in behind a group of older kids and their Masters, who were heading in a southerly direction.

"Do you know where we're going?" Call asked Tamara.

She shook her head. She looked more serious than she'd been in weeks. Call remembered her the night before, grabbing his arms and trying to drag him away from the Chaos-ridden wolf. She'd risked her life for his. He'd never had a friend like her before. Never had friends like her *or* Aaron. Now that he had them, he didn't know quite what to do with them.

They found themselves in a circular auditorium with stone benches rising up on all sides from a round stage. Along the far back, Call saw a group of men and women in olive green uniforms and guessed they were the Assembly members Master Rufus had been talking about. Rufus led them to a place down in front and there, finally, they saw Aaron.

He was in the front row, sitting next to Master North, just far enough away so that Call couldn't talk to him without shouting. He could really see only the back of Aaron's head, his feathery blond hair sticking up. He looked like he always did.

One of the Makaris. A Makar. It seemed like such an ominous title. Call thought of the way shadows had seemed to wrap around the wolf pack the night before and how horrified Aaron had looked after it was all over.

Chaos wants to devour.

It didn't seem like the kind of power someone like Aaron, whom everybody liked and who liked everybody, ought to have. It should belong to someone like Jasper, who would probably be super into bossing around the darkness and stuffing weird animals full of chaos magic.

Master Rufus got to his feet and ascended to the stage, moving to the center to stand at the podium. "Students of the Magisterium and members of the Assembly," he said. His dark eyes swept the room. Call felt as if his gaze lingered on Call and Tamara for a moment before it moved on. "You all know our history. There have been Magisteriums since the time of our founder, Phillippus Paracelsus. They exist to teach young mages to control their powers and to foster a community of learning, magic, and peace, as well as creating a force with which to defend our world.

"You all know the story of the Enemy of Death. Many of you lost family members in the Great Battle or in the Cold Massacre. You all know of the Treaty as well — the agreement between the Assembly and Constantine Madden, which ensures that if we do not attack him or his forces, he will not attack us.

"Many of you," Master Rufus added, his dark eyes sweeping the room, "also believe that the Treaty is wrong."

Murmuring began in the audience. Tamara's gaze snapped toward where the Assembly members sat, her expression anxious, and Call realized suddenly that two of the Assembly members were Tamara's parents. He'd seen them before at the Iron Trial. Now they sat ramrod straight, their expressions stony as they regarded Rufus. Call could *feel* the disapproval rolling off them in waves.

"The Treaty means that we must trust the Enemy of Death — trust that he will not attack us, that he will not use this hiatus from battle to build up his forces. But the Enemy cannot be trusted."

There was a hum of noise among the Assembly members. Tamara's mother had her hand on her husband's arm; he was trying to rise to his feet. Tamara looked frozen.

Master Rufus raised his voice. "We cannot trust the Enemy. I say this as one who knew Constantine Madden when he was a student at the Magisterium. We have turned a blind eye to the increase in attacks by elementals — one last night, barely a few feet from the Magisterium's own doors — and to the attacks on our supply lines and safe houses. We have turned this blind eye not because we believe in Constantine Madden's promises, but because the Enemy is a Makar — one of the few among our kind ever born to control the magic of the void. On the field of battle, his Chaos-ridden defeated the only other Makar of our time. We have always known that without a Makar, we are vulnerable to the Enemy, and since the death of Verity Torres, we have been waiting for another to be born."

A lot of the other students were sitting forward now. It was clear that while some of them had heard what had happened the previous night outside the gates, or knew because they had been there, a lot of them were just starting to guess at what Rufus was about to say. Call could see a bunch of Silver Year students leaning over toward Alex, one of them tugging on his sleeve, mouthing, *Do you know what this is about?* He shook his head at them. The Assembly members, meanwhile, were buzzing among themselves. Tamara's father was sitting back down, but his expression was thunderous.

"I am happy to announce," Rufus said, "that we have discovered the existence of a Makar, here at the Magisterium. Aaron Stewart, will you please rise?"

Aaron stood. He was dressed in his black uniform, and the skin under his eyes looked bruised with exhaustion. Call wondered if they'd let him sleep at all. He thought about how small Aaron had seemed the night before, being led away from the hill. He looked slight now, even though he was one of the taller kids in Iron Year.

There were several audible gasps in the audience and a lot of whispering. After looking around nervously for a moment, Aaron started to sit back down, but Master North shook his head and made a gesture indicating that Aaron was to remain standing.

Tamara had her hands in fists in her lap and was looking worriedly between Master Rufus and her parents, silent and thin-lipped. Call had never been so glad not to be the center of attention. It was like all the people in the room were devouring Aaron with their eyes. Only Tamara seemed distracted, probably worried that her family looked about ready to run up onstage and beat Master Rufus with a stalactite.

One of the Assembly members had come down from the top bench. He led Aaron up onto the stage. When Aaron spotted Tamara and Call, he grinned a little, raising his eyebrows as if to say *This is crazy*.

Call felt the corners of his mouth lift in response.

Master Rufus left the stage, going to sit beside Master North in the space Aaron left. Master North leaned over and whispered something to Master Rufus. Rufus nodded. Of all the people in the room, Master North seemed to be the only one who didn't look at all surprised by Master Rufus's speech.

"The Assembly of Mages would like to formally acknowledge Aaron Stewart as having an affinity with chaos magic. He is our Makar!" The Assembly member smiled, but Call could tell his smile was strained. Probably he was biting back whatever he wanted to say to Master Rufus; none of them seemed to have liked his speech. Applause broke out at his words, though, led by Tamara and Call, who stamped their feet and whistled like they were at a hockey game. The applause went on until the Assembly member gestured them to silence.

"Now," he said, "it is to be hoped that all of you understand the importance of the Makaris. Aaron has a responsibility to the larger world. He alone can undo the damage that the self-styled Enemy of Death has wrought, free the land from the threat of Chaos-ridden animals, and protect us from the shadows. He must make certain that the Treaty continues to be upheld so that peace can prevail." At this, the Assembly member allowed himself a dark look in Master Rufus's direction.

Aaron swallowed visibly. "Thank you, sir. I'll do my best."

"But no difficult path is walked alone," the Assembly member went on, looking out at the rest of them. "It's going to be the responsibility of all of your fellow students to look out for you, to support you, and to defend you. It can be a heavy burden to be a Makar, but he won't have to bear it alone, will he?" On the final two words, the Assembly member's voice rose.

The audience applauded again, this time for themselves, as a promise. Call clapped as hard as he could.

Reaching into one of the pockets of his uniform, the Assembly member took out a dark stone, holding it before Aaron. "We've been hanging on to this for more than a decade, and it is my great honor to be the one to give it to you. You will recognize this as an affinity stone, one you earn when you gain Mastery of an element. Yours is black onyx, for the void."

Call leaned forward to get a better look, and his heart began to thud dully. Because there, cupped in the Assembly member's palm, was a stone that was the twin of the one in the wristband his father had sent to Master Rufus. Which meant that the wristband had once belonged to a Makar. There had been only two born in his father's lifetime, only two possible Makaris that the wristband might have belonged to — Verity Torres or Constantine Madden.

He stopped clapping. His hands fell into his lap.

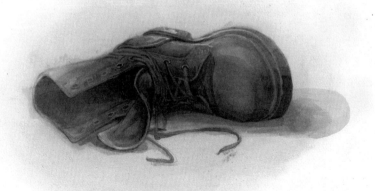

CHAPTER NINETEEN

AFTER THE CEREMONY, Aaron was swept quickly away by the Assembly. Master Rufus rose again to announce that they were going to have the day off. Everyone seemed even more excited about this than they were about Aaron being a Makar. The students immediately scattered, most heading for the Gallery, leaving Call and Tamara to walk back alone toward their rooms, along twisting caverns lit by glowing crystals.

Tamara chatted excitedly most of the way back, clearly relieved that her parents hadn't gotten into a visible disagreement with Master Rufus, not seeming to notice at first that Call was responding mostly with grunts and noncommittal noises. She clearly believed that having Aaron be the Makar was going to be amazing for all three of them. She said they shouldn't worry about politics, they should think of how they were going to get loads of special treatment and all the best missions. She was halfway through telling Call how she was going to get to fire-walk a volcano someday when she finally broke off and put her hands on her hips. "Why are you being such a lump?" she demanded.

Call was stung. "Lump?"

"Anyone would think you weren't happy for Aaron. You're not jealous, are you?"

She was so wrong that Call could do nothing for a minute but splutter. "Yeah, I want everybody standing there eyeballing me like — like —"

"Tamara?"

Jasper was waiting by their door, looking miserable.

Tamara drew herself up. Call was always impressed by the way she managed to make herself seem about six feet tall, when in reality she was shorter than him. "What do you want, Jasper?"

She sounded frustrated at being stopped from further interrogating Call. For the first time ever, Call thought Jasper might be good for something.

"Can I talk to you for a second?" he asked. He looked so miserable that Call actually felt bad for him. "I've got a bunch of extra lessons and . . . I could really use your help."

"Not mine?" Call asked, thinking of the night in the Library.

Jasper ignored Call. "Please, Tamara. I know I was a jerk, but I want to be friends again."

"You weren't a jerk to me," she said. "Tell Call you're sorry and I'll think about it."

"Sorry," Jasper said, looking down.

"Whatever," said Call. It wasn't a real apology — and Tamara didn't even know about the time Jasper had screamed Call out of the Library — so he didn't think he had to accept it. But he figured that if Tamara went with Jasper, it would buy him some time to deal with the wolf. Time he desperately needed. "You should help him, Tamara. He needs lots, and lots, and *lots* of help." He locked eyes with Jasper.

Tamara sighed. "Okay, fine, Jasper. But you have to be civil to my friends, not just me. No more little snide comments."

"But what about him!" Jasper objected. "He makes snide comments all the time."

Tamara looked from Call to Jasper. She sighed. "How about if you both stop making snide comments."

"Never!" Call said.

Tamara rolled her eyes and followed Jasper down the hallway, promising Call she'd see him at dinner.

Which left Call all alone in his room with a squirming, Chaos-ridden puppy. Lifting the wolf and tucking it back into his coat, despite a few yipping protests, Call made for the Mission Gate, going as fast as he could without his leg giving him trouble. He was afraid the door to the outside of the cave would be locked, but it turned out to be easy to open from the inside. The doors of the metal gate were closed, but Call didn't need to go that far. Hoping no one could see, Call let the wolf out of his jacket. It slunk around, looking at the metal nervously and sniffing the air before finally peeing on a frozen clump of weeds.

Call gave him a few more moments before he swept the wolf back up under his coat.

"Come on," he told the pup. "We've got to get back before anyone sees us. And before someone throws away the leftovers from breakfast."

Back through the halls he went, hunching over when he passed other apprentices so they wouldn't notice the shifting shape under his coat. He barely made it back to the room before the wolf leaped free. Then it made itself at home by knocking over the trash and eating the remains of Tamara's breakfast out of it.

Finally, Call managed to corral the wolf back into his room, where he brought it a bowl of water, two raw eggs, and a single cold sausage that had been left out on the counter. The wolf gobbled the food down, shells and all. Then they played a game of tug-of-war with one of the blankets from the bed.

Just as Call yanked the blanket free and the wolf pounced again, Call heard the outer door open. Someone came into their common room. He paused, trying to figure out if Tamara had once again realized Jasper was a jerk and had come back early, or if Aaron had returned. In that silence, he heard the distinct sound of something being thrown against a wall. The wolf hopped off the bed and slunk under it, whining softly.

Call padded to his door. Opening it, he saw Aaron sitting on the couch, taking off one of his boots. The other boot was on the far side of the room. There was a dirt mark on the wall where it had hit.

"Um, are you okay?" Call asked.

Aaron looked surprised to see him. "I didn't think either of you were here."

Call cleared his throat. He felt weirdly awkward. He wondered if Aaron would stay here with them now that he was the Makar or would be taken to some kind of fancy private hero-who-has-to-save-the-world digs. "Well, Tamara went off with Jasper somewhere. I guess they're friends again."

"Whatever," said Aaron, without much interest. It was the sort of thing that normally he would have wanted to talk about. There were other things Call wanted to talk to Aaron about, too, like the wolf, and Tamara's parents' weird behavior, and the black stone in Aaron's wristband, and what that meant about the band Call's father had sent Rufus, but Call wasn't sure how to start. Or if he should.

"So," he said, "you must be really excited about all this . . . chaos magic stuff."

"Sure," Aaron replied. "I'm thrilled."

Call knew sarcasm when he heard it. For a moment, he couldn't quite believe it was coming from Aaron. But there Aaron was, staring at his boot, his jaw set. He was definitely upset.

"Do you want me to leave you alone so you can throw your other boot?" Call asked.

Aaron took a deep breath. "Sorry," he said, rubbing a hand over his face. "I just don't know if I want to be a Makar."

Call was so surprised that for a moment he couldn't think of anything to say. "Why not?" he finally blurted out. Aaron was perfect for the role. He was exactly what everyone thought a hero should be like — nice, brave, and into doing hero stuff like running straight at a Chaos-ridden wolf pack instead of running away like a normal, sane person.

"You don't understand," said Aaron. "Everyone is acting like this is great news, but it's not great for me. The last Makar died at age fifteen, and, fine, she pushed back the war and made the Treaty happen, but she still died. And she died horribly."

Which went with everything Call's father had ever said about the mages.

"You're not going to die," Call told Aaron firmly. "Verity Torres died in a battle, a big battle. You're at the Magisterium. The Masters won't let you die."

"You don't know that," said Aaron.

That's why your mother died. Because of magic, said Call's dad's voice in his head.

"Okay, fine. Then you should run away," Call suggested abruptly.

Aaron's head snapped up. That had gotten his attention. "I'm not going to run away!"

"Well, you *could*," Call said.

"No, I couldn't." Aaron's green eyes were blazing; he looked really angry now. "I don't have anywhere to go."

"What do you mean?" Call asked, but in the back of his head, he knew, or guessed: Aaron never talked about his family, never said anything about his home life. . . .

"Don't you notice *anything*?" Aaron demanded. "Didn't you wonder where my parents were at the Trial? I don't have any. My mom's dead, my dad ran off. I have no idea where he is. I haven't seen him since I was two. I come from a foster home. More than one. They'd get bored with keeping me, or the checks from the government wouldn't be enough, and they'd push me on to the next home. I met the girl who told me about the Magisterium in my last foster home. She was someone I could talk to — until her brother graduated from here and took her away. At least you've always had your dad. Being at the Magisterium is the best thing that's ever happened to me. I don't want to leave."

"I'm sorry," Call mumbled. "I didn't know."

"After she told me about the Magisterium, coming here became my dream," Aaron said. "My *only* chance. I knew I'd have to pay the Magisterium back for all the good things it's done for me," he added quietly. "I just didn't think it would be so soon."

"That's a horrible thing to think," Call said. "You don't owe anybody your whole life."

"Sure I do," said Aaron, and Call knew he would never be able to convince Aaron it wasn't true. He thought of Aaron up there on the podium, with everyone applauding, getting told he was everyone's only chance. For someone as nice as Aaron, there was no way he was going to push that off on somebody else, even if he could. That was what made him a hero. They had him right where they wanted him.

And since Call was his friend — whether Aaron wanted him to be or not — he was going to make sure they didn't make him do anything stupid.

"And it's not just me," Aaron said tiredly. "I'm a chaos magician. I'll need a counterweight. A *human* counterweight. Who's going to volunteer for that?"

"It's an honor," Call said. "To be the counterweight for a Makar." He knew that much, at least. It had been part of Tamara's excited babbling.

"The last human counterweight died when the Makar died in battle," Aaron said. "And we all know what happened before that. That's how the Enemy of Death killed his brother. I can't see anyone lining up for it."

"I will," said Call.

Aaron abruptly stopped talking, his face cycling through expressions. At first he looked incredulous, as though he suspected Call of saying it as a joke or just to be contrary. Then when he realized Call was serious, he looked horrified.

"You can't!" Aaron said. "Didn't you hear anything I just told you? You could *die*."

"Well, don't kill me," Call said. "How about our goal is not to die? Both of us. Together. Not dying."

Aaron didn't say anything for a long moment and Call wondered if he was trying to think of a way to tell Call that he appreciated the offer but he had someone better in mind. It was an honor, like Tamara had said. Aaron didn't have to take Call. Call wasn't anything special.

He was about to open his mouth and say all that when Aaron looked up. His eyes were suspiciously shiny, and for a second, Call thought that maybe Aaron hadn't always been the popular guy who was good at everything. Maybe, back in the foster home, he'd been lonely and angry and sad, like Call.

"Okay," Aaron said. "If you still want to. When it's time, I mean."

Before Call could say anything else, the door banged open and Tamara came in. Her face lit up when she saw Aaron. She ran over and gave him a hug that nearly knocked him off the couch.

"Did you see Master Rufus's face?" she said. "He's so proud of you! And the whole Assembly came out, even my parents. All of them cheering. For you! That was *amazing*."

"It was pretty amazing," Aaron said, finally starting to really smile.

She hit him with a pillow. "Don't go getting a swelled head," she told him.

Call met Aaron's eyes over the pillow, and they grinned at each other. "No chance of that around here," he said.

At that moment, from Call's bedroom, the Chaos-ridden wolf began to bark.

CHAPTER TWENTY

TAMARA JUMPED UP and looked around the room like she was expecting something to leap out at her from the shadows.

Aaron's expression turned wary, but he stayed seated. "Call," he said. "Is that coming from your room?"

"Uh, maybe?" said Call, trying desperately to think of some explanation for the sound. "It's my . . . ringtone?"

Tamara frowned. "Phones don't work down here, Callum. And you already said you didn't have one."

Aaron's eyebrows shot up. "Do you have a *dog* in there?"

Something crashed to the floor and the barking increased, along with a sound like nails scrabbling over stone.

"What's going on?" Tamara demanded, walking to Call's door and yanking it open. Then she screamed, throwing herself back against the wall. Oblivious, the wolf bounded past her out into the common room.

"Is that a —" Aaron stood up, his hand unconsciously going to the band at his wrist, the one with the black void stone in it.

Call thought of the dark curling around the wolves the night before, taking them into nothingness.

He ran as quickly as he could to block the pup with his body, his arms held out wide. "I can explain," he said desperately. "He's not bad! He's just like a regular dog!"

"That thing is a *monster*," Tamara said, grabbing up one of the knives from the table. "Call, don't you dare tell me you brought it here on *purpose*."

"It was lost — and whimpering out in the cold," Call said.

"Good!" Tamara screamed. "God, Call, you don't think, you don't ever think! Those things, they're vicious — they kill people!"

"He's not vicious," Call said, sinking to his knees and seizing the pup by the ruff. "Calm down, boy," he said with as much firmness as he could summon, bending so he could look into the wolf's face. "These are our friends."

The pup stopped barking, staring up at Call with kaleidoscopic eyes. Then it licked his face.

He turned to Tamara. "See? He's not evil. He was just excited from being cooped up in my room."

"Get out of my way." Tamara brandished her knife.

"Tamara, wait," Aaron said, coming closer. "Admit it — it is weird that it's not attacking Call."

"He's just a baby," Call said. "And scared."

Tamara snorted.

Call picked up the wolf and turned it on its back, rocking it like a baby. The wolf squirmed. "See. Look at his big eyes."

"You could get kicked out of school for having him," Tamara said. "We could *all* get kicked out of school."

"Not Aaron," Call said, and Aaron winced.

"Call," he said. "You can't keep him. You *can't*."

Call held the wolf more tightly. "Well, I'm gonna."

"You can't," said Tamara. "Even if we let him live, we have to take him outside the Magisterium and leave him. He can't be in here."

"Then you might as well kill him," said Call. "Because he won't survive out there. And I won't let you take him." He swallowed. "So if you want him out, tell on me. Go ahead."

Aaron took a deep breath. "Okay, so what's his name?"

"Havoc," said Call immediately.

Tamara lowered her hand to her side, slowly. "Havoc?"

Call felt himself blush. "It's from a play my father liked. 'Cry havoc, and let slip the dogs of war.' He's definitely, I don't know, one of the dogs of war."

Havoc took the opportunity to burp.

Tamara sighed, something in her face softening. She reached out her other hand, the one without a knife, to stroke the pup's fur. "So . . . what does he eat?"

It turned out that Aaron had a bunch of bacon in the back of the cold storage, which he was willing to donate to feed Havoc. And Tamara, once she'd been drooled on and watched a Chaos-ridden wolf roll onto its back so she could pet its stomach, announced that they should all fill their pockets with anything vaguely meaty that they could get out of the Refectory, including eyeless fish.

"We need to talk about the wristband, though," she said as she tossed a wadded-up ball of paper to Havoc, trying to get him to fetch. He took the paper under the table and began instead to tear off small pieces with his tiny teeth. "The one Call's father sent him."

Call nodded. In all the uproar about Aaron and Havoc, he'd managed to push the realization of what the onyx stone meant to the back of his mind.

"It couldn't have belonged to Verity Torres, right?" he asked.

"She was fifteen when she died," Tamara said, shaking her head. "But she left school the year before, so her wristband would be Bronze Year, not Silver."

"But if it's not hers —" Aaron said, swallowing, not able to say the words.

"Then it's Constantine Madden's," said Tamara, with tight practicality. "It would make sense."

Call flashed hot and cold all over. It was exactly what he'd been thinking, but now that Tamara had said it out loud, he didn't want to believe it. "Why would my father have the wristband of the Enemy of Death? *How* would he have it?"

"How old is your father?"

"He's thirty-five," Call said, wondering what that had to do with anything.

"Basically the same age as Constantine Madden. They would have been at school together. And the Enemy could have left his wristband behind when he escaped from the Magisterium." Tamara pushed herself to her feet and started to pace. "He rejected everything about school. He wouldn't have wanted it. Maybe your father picked it up, or found it somehow. Maybe they even — knew each other."

"There's no way. He would have told me," Call replied, knowing even as he said it that it wasn't true. Alastair never talked about the Magisterium except vaguely and to describe how sinister it was.

"Rufus said *he* knew the Enemy. And that bracelet was supposed to be a message to Rufus," said Aaron. "It had to mean something to your father and to Rufus. It would make more sense if they both knew him."

"But what was the message?" Call demanded.

"Well, it was about you," Tamara said. "*Bind his magic.* Right?"

"So they'd send me home! So I'd be safe!"

"Maybe," said Tamara. "Or maybe it was about keeping other people safe *from* you."

Call's heart gave a sick thump inside his chest.

"Tamara," said Aaron. "You'd better explain what you mean."

"I'm sorry, Call," she said, and she really did look sorry. "But the Enemy invented the Chaos-ridden here, at the Magisterium. And I've never heard of a Chaos-ridden animal being friendly to anyone or anything but another Chaos-ridden." Aaron started to protest, but Tamara held up her hand. "Remember what Celia said that first night on the bus? About how there's a rumor that some of the Chaos-ridden have normal eyes? And if someone was born Chaos-ridden, then maybe that person wouldn't be blank inside. Maybe they'd seem normal. Like Havoc."

"Call isn't one of the Chaos-ridden!" Aaron said loudly. "That stuff Celia was saying, about Chaos-ridden creatures that look normal — there's no proof that's even real. And besides, if Call was Chaos-ridden, he'd know. Or I'd know. I'm one of the Makaris, so I should know, right? He's not. He's just not."

Havoc bounded over to Call, seeming to sense that something was wrong. He whined a little, eyes pinwheeling.

Alastair's words echoed in Call's mind.

Call, you must listen to me. You don't know what you are.

"Okay, then what am I?" he asked, leaning against the wolf, pressing his face into the soft fur.

But he could see in his friends' faces that they didn't know.

↑ ≈ △ ○ @

As the weeks wore on, they had no new answers, but it was easy for Call to let the questions slip from his mind so he could concentrate on his studies. With Aaron not just training to be a mage but also training to be a Makar, Master Rufus had to split his time. While they mostly trained together, Call and Tamara were often on their own, researching magic in the libraries, looking up histories of the Second Mage War and looking at drawings of the battles or photographs of the people in them, chasing around the various small elementals that populated the Magisterium, for practice, and finally learning how to pilot a boat through the caverns. Sometimes, when Master Rufus needed to take Aaron somewhere or do something that would last the whole day, Call and Tamara would join up with another Master.

The excitement of Aaron being a Makar had been slightly overshadowed by the news that Master Lemuel was being forced to leave the Magisterium. Drew's accusations had been heard by the Assembly, and they determined that Master Lemuel could no longer be trusted with students, despite his steadfast denials and Rafe's speaking up on his behalf. His apprentices were split up among the other Masters, landing Drew with Master Milagros, Rafe with Master Rockmaple, and Laurel with Master Tanaka.

Drew got out of the Infirmary a week after the news about Master Lemuel broke. At dinner, he'd gone around the other tables, apologizing to all the apprentices. He apologized several times to Aaron, Tamara, and Call. Call thought of asking what Drew had been trying to tell him in the hallway that night, but Drew was seldom alone and Call didn't know quite how to phrase the question.

Is there something wrong with me?

Is there something dangerous about me?

How could you possibly know what I don't?

Sometimes, Call felt desperate enough to want to write to his father and ask him about the wristband. But then he'd have to confess that he'd hidden Alastair's letter from Rufus, and besides, he hadn't heard anything from his dad except another care package of gummi candies and a new wool coat, arriving at Christmas. It had a card with it, signed *Love, Dad.* Nothing else. Feeling hollow, Call stuck the card away in his drawer with the other letters.

Fortunately, Call had something else that occupied a lot of his time: Havoc. Feeding a growing Chaos-ridden wolf and keeping him hidden took single-minded dedication and a lot of assistance from Tamara and Aaron. It also required overlooking Jasper's telling Call that he smelled like hot dogs day after day as he snuck food out of the Refectory in his pockets. Plus, there was the matter of sneaking out through the Mission Gate for regular walks. But as winter turned to spring, it was clear to Call that Aaron and even Tamara had come to think of Havoc as their dog, too, and he would often come back from the Gallery to find Tamara curled up on the couch, reading, with the wolf resting on top of her feet like a blanket.

CHAPTER TWENTY-ONE

F INALLY, THE WEATHER became warm enough
for them to start having their classes outside almost daily.
One bright afternoon, Call and Tamara were sent to the edge of
the woods to study with Master Milagros's class while Rufus
took Aaron for special training.

They didn't go far from the Magisterium gates, but enough
greenery had sprung up to block most of the cave entrance from
view. The warm air smelled of the rosemary, valerian, and deadly
nightshade that grew on the grounds, and there was a rapidly
growing pile of light jackets and coats on the ground as the
apprentices dashed around in the sunlight, playing catch with
balls of fire, using air to control the way they moved.

Call and Tamara joined in with enthusiasm. It was fun,
focusing on lifting a flaming orb, then rocketing it between
hands. Call strained to get it close enough to his palms so that it
almost touched but didn't quite. Gwenda had burned herself
once and was now being extra careful; her ball of fire hovered

more than moved. Although Call and Tamara had come late, the exercise was enough like ones Master Rufus had made them practice — particularly the sand exercises, which were forever burned into their minds — that they were able to get the hang of it quickly.

"Very good," Master Milagros said, walking between them. She'd taken off her shoes and sloughed off her black uniform shirt, revealing a T-shirt with a rainbow on the front. "Now I want you to create *two* balls. Split your focus."

Call and Tamara nodded. Splitting their focus was second nature, but some of the others were struggling. Celia managed it, as did Gwenda, but one of Jasper's orbs popped, singeing his hair.

Call snickered, earning a dark look.

Soon, though, everyone was tossing two and then three balls of fire into the air, not quite juggling but something that might have approximated a slow-motion version of it. After a few minutes of that, Master Milagros stopped them again.

"Please choose a partner," she said. "The apprentice without a partner will practice with me. We're going to toss our ball to our partner and catch the ball our partner tosses to us. So extinguish all balls in your hands but one. Ready?"

Celia tapped Call's sleeve shyly. "Practice with me?" she asked. Tamara sighed and went to practice with Gwenda, leaving Jasper to partner with Master Milagros, since Drew had complained of a sore throat and stayed in his room. Back and forth the fire went, searing through the lazy springtime air.

"You're really good at this!" Celia said, beaming, as Call made the fire do a loop-the-loop before dropping it just above her hands. Celia was the sort of friendly person who handed out compliments easily, but it was still nice to hear — even if Tamara was rolling her eyes behind Celia's back.

"All right!" Master Milagros clapped her hands to get everyone's attention. She looked a little disgruntled — there was a burn in her sleeve where Jasper must have thrown a fireball too close. "Now that you all are used to using air and fire together, let's add something even more difficult. Come this way."

Master Milagros led them down the hill to a stream that bubbled over rocks. Four thick oak logs bobbed in the water, clearly magicked to stay in place, since the current flowed around them. She pointed to the logs. "You will climb onto one of those," she said. "I want you to use water and earth to balance yourself there, while keeping at least three fire orbs in the air."

There was a murmur of protest, and Master Milagros smiled. "I'm sure you can do it," she said, shooing the students toward a log. As Call moved forward, she put a hand on his shoulder. "Call, I'm sorry, but I think you better stay here. With your leg, I don't think it's safe for you to do this exercise," she said quietly. "I've been thinking about a version that could suit you better. Let me get the others started and I'll tell you about it."

Jasper, passing by on his way to the stream, looked over his shoulder and smirked.

Call felt a dull red fury bubble up in his stomach. Suddenly, he was back in gym class in sixth grade, sitting on the bleachers while everyone else climbed ropes, or dribbled basketballs, or bounced up and down on the mats.

"I can do it," he told her.

Master Milagros stepped toward the bank of the stream, her bare feet sinking in the mud. She smiled. "I know, Call, but the exercise is going to be very difficult for all the apprentices and it would be even harder for you. I think it's more than you're ready for."

So Call watched as the other apprentices waded or clumsily

levitated to their logs, wobbling as Master Milagros released the magic that had been holding the wood in place. He could see the strain on their faces as they tried to move the log against the current, stay standing, and levitate a ball of fire. Celia fell almost immediately, hitting the stream, soaking her uniform — and laughing all the while. It was a hot day and Call bet splashing in the water felt pretty good.

Jasper, surprisingly, seemed good at the exercise. He managed to lever himself up on his log and stay standing as he conjured his first ball of fire. He tossed it between his hands, smirking at Call, making Call think of what he'd said in the Refectory.

If you could ever learn to levitate yourself, maybe you wouldn't slow down your teammates so much, limping along after them.

Call was a better mage than Jasper; he knew he was. And he couldn't stand that Jasper thought otherwise.

Giggling, Celia pulled herself back up onto her log, but her feet were wet, and she slipped off again almost immediately. She plunged back into the water and Call, seized by an impulse he couldn't control, dashed forward and hopped up onto the abandoned log. After all, he'd skateboarded before — badly, he admitted. But he'd done that and he could do this.

"Call!" cried Master Milagros, but he was already halfway across the stream. It was much harder than it had looked from shore. The log rolled under his feet, and he had to throw his hands out, bracing himself with earth magic, to keep his balance.

Celia surfaced in front of him, tossing back her wet hair. Seeing Call, she gasped. Call was so startled that his magic deserted him. The log rolled forward, Celia dove for the the bank with a little shriek, and Call's bad leg went out from under him. He pitched forward and landed in the water.

The stream was black, icy cold, and deeper than he'd imagined. Call twisted around, trying to swim for the surface, but his foot was wedged between two stones. He kicked desperately, but his bad leg wasn't strong enough to free the good one. Pain shot up his side as he tried to pull himself free, and he screamed — silently, underwater, bubbles escaping his lips.

Suddenly, there was a hand circling his upper arm, pulling him up. There was more pain as his foot pulled free from the streambed, and then he was out of the water, gasping. The person who'd grabbed him was splashing through the stream, and Call could hear the other apprentices yelling and calling out as he was tossed onto the bank, coughing and spitting water.

He looked up and saw angry brown eyes and dripping-wet black hair.

"Jasper?" Call said in disbelief, then coughed again, bringing up a mouthful of water. He was about to turn aside and spit it out, when Tamara suddenly appeared, dropping down next to him on her knees.

"Call? Call, are you okay?"

Call swallowed the water, hoping it didn't have tadpoles in it. "Fine," he croaked.

"Why did you have to show off like that?" Tamara asked angrily. "Why are boys always so dumb? After Master Milagros specifically told you not to! If it hadn't been for Jasper —"

"He'd be fish food," Jasper said, squeezing water out of a corner of his uniform.

"Well, I wouldn't go quite that far," said Master Milagros. "But, Call, that was very, very foolish."

Call looked down at himself. One of his pants legs was torn, his shoe was missing, and blood trickled down his ankle. At least it was his good leg, he thought, so no one could see the twisted-up mess his other one was. "I know," he said.

Master Milagros sighed. "Can you stand?"

Call tried to rise to his feet. Instantly, Tamara was next to him, offering an arm to lean on. He took it, straightened — and yelped as pain shot through him. His right leg felt as if someone had shoved a knife into his ankle: a hot, sickening pain.

Master Milagros bent down and touched cool fingers to Call's ankle. "Not broken, but a bad sprain," she said after a moment. She sighed again. "Class is over for the afternoon. Call, let's get you to the Infirmary."

↑ ≈ △ ○ @

The Infirmary turned out to be a large, high-ceilinged room entirely free of stalagmites, stalactites, or anything that bubbled, dripped, or smoked. There were long lines of beds, made up with white sheets, arranged as though the Masters expected a large quantity of wounded children might be brought there any minute. At the moment, there was nobody but Call.

The mage in charge was a tall red-haired woman who had a snake curled around her shoulders. Its pattern changed as it moved, turning from leopard spots to tiger stripes to wobbly pink dots. "Put him over there," the woman said, pointing grandly as the apprentices carried Call in on a stretcher made of branches, which Master Milagros had created. If Call's leg hadn't hurt so much, it would have been interesting to watch her use earth magic to snap the branches together and bind them with long, flexible roots.

Master Milagros supervised as they deposited Call on a bed. "Thank you, students," she said as Tamara hovered anxiously. "Now let's go and let Master Amaranth get to work."

Call propped himself up on his elbows, ignoring the shooting pain in his leg. "Tamara —"

"What?" She turned around, dark eyes wide. Everyone was looking at them. Call tried to communicate with her with his eyes. *Look after Havoc. Make sure he gets enough food.*

"He's going cross-eyed," Tamara said to Master Amaranth worriedly. "It must be the pain. Can't you do anything?"

"Not with all of you here. Shoo! Shoo!" Amaranth waved a hand, and the apprentices hurried out with Master Milagros, Tamara pausing in the doorway to shoot another worried look at Call.

Call flopped back onto the bed, his mind on Havoc, as Master Amaranth cut away his uniform, showing purple bruising down the expanse of his leg. His *good* leg. For a moment, panic rose in his chest, making him feel as though he was choking. What if he'd managed to make it so that he couldn't walk at all?

The Master must have seen some of the fear in his expression because she smiled, taking a roll of moss out of a glass jar. "You're going to be fine, Callum Hunt. I've fixed worse injuries than this."

"So it's not as bad as it looks?" Call ventured.

"Oh, no," she told him. "It's just as bad as it looks. But I'm very, very good at my job."

Somewhat comforted and deciding he'd be better off not asking any more questions, Call let her cover his leg in bright green moss and then pack the whole thing with mud. Finally, she gave him a drink of some milky liquid that took away most of the pain and made him feel a bit like he was floating up toward the ceiling of the cave, as though the wyvern breath had hit him after all.

Feeling very foolish, Call slipped off to sleep.

↑ ≈ △ ○ @

"*Call*," a girl whispered, very close to his ear, making his hair move and tickle his neck. "Call, wake up."

Then another voice. A boy's voice this time. "Maybe we should come back. I mean — doesn't sleep help healing or something?"

"Yeah, but it doesn't help *us*," the first voice said again, louder this time, and grumpier. Tamara. Call opened his eyes.

Tamara and Aaron were there, Tamara seated beside him on the bed, gently shaking his shoulder. Aaron held up a drooling, panting, tail-wagging Havoc. He had a makeshift rope leash around his neck.

"I was going to walk him," Aaron said. "But since there's no one but you in the Infirmary, we thought we'd bring him for a visit first."

"We brought you some dinner from the Refectory, too," Tamara said, pointing at a napkin-covered plate on the night-stand. "How are you doing?"

Call moved his leg experimentally, within the mud cast. It didn't really hurt anymore. "I feel like a moron."

"It wasn't your fault," Aaron said at the same time that Tamara said, "Well, you should."

They looked at each other, and then at Call.

"Sorry, Call, but it wasn't your *best* idea," Tamara said. "And you totally stole Celia's log. Not that she won't liiiiiike you anyway."

"What? She doesn't," Call protested, horrified.

"Does, too." Tamara grinned. "You could hit her on the head with a log and she'd still be all *Call, you're so good at this magic stuff.*" She looked over at Aaron, who had an expression on his face that told Call he agreed with Tamara and thought it was hilarious.

"Anyway," Tamara said, "we just don't want you to get crushed under a log. We need you."

"That's right," Aaron agreed. "You're my counterweight, remember?"

"Only because he volunteered first," Tamara said. "You should have held auditions." Call had been worried that Tamara might be jealous when she found out Aaron had picked Call as his counterweight, but mostly she just seemed to think that, as much as she liked Call, Aaron could probably have aimed higher. "I bet Alex Strike is still available. He's cute, too."

"Whatever," said Aaron, rolling his eyes. "I didn't want Alex. I wanted Call."

"I know," Tamara said. "He'll be good at it," she added unexpectedly, and Call flashed them a grateful smile. Even flat on his back with his leg wrapped in mud, it felt good to have friends.

"And here I was worried you were going to forget about Havoc," Call said.

"No chance of that," said Aaron cheerfully. "He ate Tamara's boots."

"My favorite boots." Tamara swatted lightly at Havoc, who dodged away, scooted toward the door, and looked pitifully back at Call in the bed. A small whine rose from his throat.

"I think he wants to go for his walk now," Call said.

"I'll take him." Aaron jogged over to the door and looped the free end of the rope around his wrist. "No one's in the corridors right now because it's dinnertime. I'll be right back."

"If you get caught, we'll pretend we don't know you!" Tamara called good-naturedly as the door swung shut behind him. She reached for the plate on Call's nightstand and yanked off the napkin. "Yummy lichen," she said, balancing the plate on Call's stomach. "Your favorite kind."

Call picked up a dried vegetable chip and bit into it thoughtfully. "I wonder if we're going to all be so used to lichen that when we get back home, we won't want pizza or ice cream. I'll wind up in the woods, eating moss."

"Everyone in your town will think you're crazy."

"Everyone in my town already thinks I'm crazy."

Tamara pulled one of her braids around and fingered the end of it thoughtfully. "Are you going to be okay going home for the summer?"

Call looked up from his lichen. "What do you mean?"

"Your father," she said. "He hates the Magisterium so much, but you — you don't. At least I don't think you do. And you're going to come back next year. Isn't that exactly what he didn't want?"

Call didn't say anything.

"You are coming back next year, aren't you?" She leaned forward, worried. "Call?"

"I want to," he burst out. "I want to, but I'm afraid he won't let me. And maybe there's a reason he won't — but I don't want to know it. If there's something wrong with me, I want Alastair to keep it to himself."

"There's nothing wrong with you except that you broke your leg," said Tamara, but she still looked anxious.

"And I'm a show-off," Call said, trying to lighten the mood.

Tamara threw a piece of lichen at him and they talked for a while about how everyone was reacting to Aaron's new celebrity status — including Aaron. Tamara was concerned about him, but Call assured her Aaron could handle it.

Then Tamara started to tell him about how excited her parents were to have her in the same group with the Makar, which was good, because she wanted them to be proud of her, and bad, because it meant they were even more concerned than usual that she behave in an exemplary manner at all times. And their idea of exemplary didn't always match up with hers.

"Now that there's a Makar, what does it mean for the Treaty?" Call asked, thinking of Rufus's speech and the way the Assembly members had reacted to it at the meeting.

"Nothing right now," Tamara said. "No one would want to move against the Enemy of Death while Aaron is so young — well, almost nobody. But once the Enemy hears about him, if he hasn't already, who knows what he'll do."

After a few minutes of talking, Tamara glanced at her watch. "Aaron's been gone a long time," she said. "If he's out there any longer, dinner will be over, and he'll get caught coming back through the corridors. Maybe I should go check on him."

"Right," said Call. "I'll go with you."

"Is that a good idea?" Tamara raised an eyebrow, looking at his leg. It did seem pretty bad, wrapped up in moss and sealed with mud. Call wiggled his toes experimentally. Nothing hurt.

Call swung his legs over the side of the bed, sending splintering cracks through his mud-moss cast. "I can't sit here any longer. I'm going stir-crazy. And my leg itches. I want to get some air."

"Okay, but we're going to have to go slow. And if anything hurts, you've got to rest and then go right back."

Call nodded. He pulled himself to his feet using the bedpost. As soon as he was standing, the cast broke completely in half and fell away, leaving his calf bare under his sliced-up pants leg.

"That's a good look for you," said Tamara, heading for the door. Call quickly yanked on his socks and boots, which had been shoved under his bed. He tucked the individual pieces of his pants into his socks so they wouldn't be flapping around, and picked up Miri, sliding her through his belt. Then he followed Tamara out into the hall.

The corridors were quiet, as the students were all in the Refectory. Call and Tamara tried to make as little noise as possible as they made their way to the Mission Gate. Call felt wobbly. Both his legs hurt a little, although he wasn't going to tell Tamara that. He thought he must look pretty bizarre, with his pants cut open from the knee down and his hair sticking up all over the place, but fortunately, there was no one to see him. They found the Mission Gate and slipped silently out into the darkness.

The night was warm and clear, the moon out, outlining the trees and the paths around the Magisterium. "Aaron!" Tamara called in a low voice. "Aaron, where are you?"

Call turned around, scanning the woods. There was something a little creepy about them, the shadows thick between the trees, the branches rattling in the wind. "Havoc!" he called.

There was a silence, and then Havoc burst out from between the trees, coruscating eyes whirling like fireworks. He dashed up to Call and Tamara, his makeshift rope-leash dragging on the ground behind him. Call heard Tamara give a little gasp.

"Where's Aaron?" she asked.

Havoc whimpered and reared up, pawing at the air. He was practically vibrating all over, his fur standing up, his ears swiveling wildly. He whined and danced toward Call, pushing his cold nose into Call's hand.

"Havoc." Call dug his fingers into the wolf's ruff, trying to get him to calm down. "Are you all right, boy?"

Havoc whined again and danced away, wriggling out of Call's grasp. He jogged toward the forest, then paused and looked over his shoulder at them.

"He wants us to follow," said Call.

"Do you think Aaron is hurt?" Tamara asked, looking around wildly. "Could an elemental have attacked him?"

"Come on," Call said, starting across the dark ground, ignoring the twinge in his legs.

Havoc, assured that they were behind him, raced off like a shot, darting between trees like a brown blur in the moonlight.

As fast as they could go, Tamara and Call followed.

CHAPTER TWENTY-TWO

CALL'S LEGS HURT. He was used to one of them aching, but both of them together was a new sensation. He didn't know how to balance his weight and, although he'd picked up a stick as he walked through the forest and was using it when he felt like he was going to fall, nothing helped the way his muscles burned.

Havoc was leading the way, with Tamara well ahead of Call, looking back regularly to make sure that he was still behind her and occasionally slowing impatiently. Call wasn't sure how far they'd gone — time was starting to blur with the rising pain — but the farther from the Magisterium they got, the more alarmed Call became.

It wasn't like he didn't trust Havoc to lead them to Aaron. No, what worried him was how Aaron could have come so far — and why. Had some enormous creature like a wyvern flown off with him in its claws? Had Aaron gotten lost in the woods?

No, not lost. Havoc would have led him out. So what had happened?

They crested a hill, and the trees began to thin all the way down to a highway that snaked through the forest. On the other side, another hill rose to block out the horizon.

Havoc barked once and started down. Tamara turned and jogged to Call.

"You've got to go back," she said. "You're hurting and we have no idea how much farther away Aaron could be. You should head to the Magisterium and tell Master Rufus what happened. He can bring the others."

"I'm not going back," Call said. "Aaron's my best friend and I'm not leaving him if he's in danger."

Tamara put her hand on one hip. "*I'm* his best friend."

Call wasn't sure how the whole best-friend thing worked. "Fine, then I'm his best friend who isn't a girl."

Tamara shook her head. "Havoc is his best friend who isn't a girl."

"Well, I'm still not leaving," Call said, shoving his stick in the dirt. "I'm not leaving him, and I'm not leaving you. Besides, it makes sense for you to go back, not me."

Tamara looked at him, her eyebrow quirked. "Why?"

Call said what they'd probably both been thinking but neither had wanted to say out loud. "Because we're going to get in a lot of trouble for this. We should have gone to Master Rufus the second Havoc showed up without Aaron —"

"We didn't have time," Tamara argued. "And we would have had to tell them about Havoc —"

"We *are* going to have to tell them about Havoc. There's no other way to explain what happened. We're going to get in trouble, Tamara; it just depends how much. For having a Chaos-ridden animal, for not running for the Masters the second something happened to the Makar, for everything. Big trouble. And if it's going to land on one of us, it should be me."

Tamara was silent. Call couldn't read her expression in the shadows.

"You're the one who has parents who care if you stay at the Magisterium and who care how you do here," he said, feeling weary. "Not me. You're the one who scored high in the Trial, not me. You're the one who wanted help sticking to the rules and not cutting corners — well, this is me helping. You belong here. I don't. It matters to you if you get in trouble. It doesn't matter to me. I don't matter."

"That's not true," Tamara said.

"What isn't?" Call realized he'd made quite a speech and wasn't sure which part she was objecting to.

"I'm not that person. Maybe I wanted to be, but I'm not. My parents raised me to get things done, no matter what. They don't care about rules, just appearances. This whole time I've been telling myself that I'm going to be different from my parents, different from my sister, be the one who stuck to the straight and narrow. But I think I had it all wrong, Call. I don't care about rules or appearances. I don't want to be the person who just gets things done. I want to do the right thing. I don't care if we have to lie or cheat or cut corners or break rules to do it."

He stared at her, dazzled. "Seriously?"

"Yes," Tamara told him.

"That is so cool," Call said.

Tamara started laughing.

"What is it?"

"Nothing. You just always surprise me." She tugged at his sleeve. "Come on, then."

They went down the hill quickly, Call stumbling a few times and fetching up hard against his walking stick, once nearly impaling himself. When they reached the highway, they found Havoc waiting by the side of the road, panting anxiously as a truck rumbled by. Call found himself staring after it. It was strange to be near cars after so long.

Tamara took a deep breath. "Okay, no one's coming, so — let's go."

She darted across the highway, Havoc at her heels. Call bit his lip hard and went after them, every running step sending jolts of pain up his leg and through his side. By the time he reached the far side of the road, he was soaked with sweat — not from running, but from pain. His eyes stung.

"Call . . ." Tamara put her hand out, and the earth stirred under their feet. A moment later, a thin jet of water sprang up, as if she'd knocked over a fire hydrant. Call put his hands in the water and splashed his face as Tamara cupped her palms and drank. It was good to stand still, just for a moment, until his legs stopped shaking.

Call offered Havoc some of the water, but Havoc was pacing back and forth, looking between them and what appeared to be a dirt road in the distance. Call dried his face on his sleeve and set off after the wolf.

He and Tamara walked in silence. She had dropped back to match her pace to his — and also, he imagined, because she was probably getting tired, too. He could tell she was as anxious as he was; she was chewing on the end of one of her braids, which she did only when she was really panicked.

"Aaron will be okay," he told her as they joined up with the dirt road and started along it. Hedges rose on either side. "He's a Makar."

"So was Verity Torres and they never found her head," said Tamara, apparently not a believer in the whole staying-positive thing.

They went on a little farther, until the road narrowed to a

path. Call was breathing hard and trying to pretend he wasn't, hot pain shooting up his legs with every step. It was like walking on broken glass, except the glass seemed to be inside him, stabbing from his nerves into his skin.

"I hate to say this," Tamara told him, "but I don't think we can stay out in the open like this. If there's an elemental up ahead, it will spot us. We're going to have to stick to the woods."

The ground would be more uneven there. She didn't say it, but she had to know Call would go slower and it would be harder for him, that he was more likely to trip and fall, especially in the dark. He took a shaky breath and nodded. She was right — being out in the open would be too dangerous. It didn't matter if the going was harder. He'd said he wasn't leaving her or Aaron, and he'd stick to his word.

Step by painful step, his hand going to brace against the trunks of trees, they followed Havoc as he led them on a path parallel to the dirt road. Finally, in the distance, Call spotted a building.

It was massive and looked abandoned, the windows boarded up and the black carpet of an empty parking lot spread out in front of it. A sign towered over the nearby trees, picturing a huge unlit bowling ball and three pins. MOUNTAIN BOWLING, it said. It looked like the sign hadn't been lit in years.

"Are you seeing what I'm seeing?" Call asked, wondering if the pain was making him delusional. But why would he dream up something like that?

"Yeah," Tamara said. "An old bowling alley. There must be a town not too far from here. But how could Aaron be there? And don't say something like 'working on his score' or 'maybe he's in a bowling league' or something like that. Be serious."

Call leaned against the rough bark of a nearby tree and resisted the urge to sit down. He was afraid he wouldn't be able to get up again. "I'm serious. It might be hard to tell in the dark, but I have my most super-serious face on." He'd wanted the words to come out light, but his voice sounded tense.

They crept closer, Call straining to see if light spilled out from beneath any of the doors or the boards over the windows. They made their way around to the back of the building. It was even darker there, the bowling alley blocking the streetlamps along the distant road. There were Dumpsters back there, looking dusty and empty in the faint moonlight.

"I don't know . . ." Call began, but Havoc jumped, pawing at the wall and whimpering. Call craned his neck back and looked up. There was a window above their heads, almost completely boarded over, but Call thought he could see a little bit of light between the boards.

"Here." Tamara pushed at one of the Dumpsters, inching it toward the wall. She clambered on top of it, then reached down to help Call up after her. He dropped his walking stick and scrambled over the side, hoisting himself entirely with his arm strength, his boots bumping the metal, making an echoing noise. "Shhh," Tamara whispered. "Look."

There was definitely light coming from between the boards. They were held to the wall by very large, very sturdy-looking nails. Tamara looked at them dubiously.

"Metal is earth magic —" she began.

Call slid Miri from his belt. The blade seemed to hum in his hand as he worked the tip under one of the nails and pulled. The wood parted like paper, and the nail rattled down onto the lid of the Dumpster.

"Cool," Tamara whispered.

Havoc leaped onto the trash bin as Call cut the rest of the nails free and threw the wood aside, revealing the smashed remains of a window. The glass panes were missing, along with the muntins. Beyond the window, he could see a dimly lit corridor not far below. Havoc wiggled through the gap, dropped the few inches to the hallway floor, and turned around, looking expectantly at Tamara and Call.

Call slid Miri back into his belt. "Here we go," he said, and climbed through the window. The fall was slight, but still jarred his legs; he was wincing as Tamara joined him, landing noiselessly despite her boots.

They stared around them. It looked nothing like the inside of a bowling alley. They were in a hallway whose floor and walls were made of blackened wood, as though there'd been a fire. Call couldn't explain exactly how, but he *felt* the presence of magic. The air of the place seemed heavy with it.

The wolf set off down the corridor, scenting the air. Call followed him, his heart thudding with dread. Whatever he'd imagined when they first set off after Havoc from the Mission Gate, he'd never imagined they'd wind up in a place like this. Master Rufus was going to kill them when they got back. He was going to hang them up by their toes and make them do sand exercises until their brains bled out their noses. And that was if they managed to save Aaron from whatever had him; if they didn't, Master Rufus was going to do much worse than that.

Call and Tamara stayed dead silent as they passed by a room with its door slightly ajar, but Call couldn't help peeking inside. For a moment, he thought he was looking at mannequins, some standing upright and others leaning against the walls, but then he realized two things — one, that their eyes were all closed, which would have been very strange for mannequins, and two, that their chests rose and fell as they breathed.

Call froze, terrified. What was he looking at? What were they?

Tamara turned and gave him a questioning look. He gestured toward the room and saw the look of horror cross her face as she followed his gesture. Her hand flew to her mouth. Then, slowly, she inched away from the door, signaling for Call to do the same.

"Chaos-ridden," she whispered to him when they were far enough away that she'd stopped shaking.

Call wasn't sure how she could tell without seeing their eyes, but decided he didn't want to know badly enough to ask. He was already so freaked out that he felt as though any movement was going to make him jump out of his skin. The last thing he needed was more terrifying information.

If the Chaos-ridden were here, it meant this had to be some outpost of the Enemy. All those stories that Call had heard, the ones that had seemed to be about something that happened long ago, the ones he hadn't worried about, now flooded his head.

The Enemy had taken Aaron. Because Aaron was a Makar. They'd been idiots to let him go outside the Magisterium alone. Of course the Enemy would have found out about him and would want him destroyed. He was probably going to kill Aaron, if he hadn't already. Call's mouth felt as dry as paper and he struggled to concentrate on their surroundings through his panic.

The corridor's ceiling was getting higher as they made their way farther into the building. Along the walls, the blackened wood became regular wood paneling, with a strange wallpaper above it — a pattern of vines that, if he looked carefully at, Call swore he could see insects moving inside. Shuddering, he tried to ignore everything but being quiet as he kept going.

They passed several closed rooms before Havoc went up to a set of double doors and whined, then turned back to Call and Tamara expectantly.

"Shhh," Call told him softly and the wolf quieted, pawing once at the floor.

The doors were huge, made of a dark, solid wood that bore a pattern of scorch marks, as if they had been licked by fire. Tamara put her hand on the knob, turned it, and peeked inside. Then she eased it closed and spun back to Call with wide eyes. He didn't think he'd ever seen her look so stunned, even by the Chaos-ridden.

"Aaron," she whispered, but she didn't look elated like he would have expected, didn't look happy at all. She looked like she was going to throw up.

Call pushed past her to look.

"Call —" Tamara hissed warningly. "Don't — there's someone else there."

But Call was already leaning in, his eye pressed to the crack in the door.

The room on the other side was huge, soaring up to massive, broad rafters that crisscrossed the ceiling. The walls were lined with empty cages, stacked on top of one another like crates. Cages made of iron. Their narrow bars were stained with something dark.

From one of the rafters dangled Aaron. His uniform was torn and his face scratched and bloody, but he looked mostly unharmed. He was hanging upside down, a heavy chain attached to a manacle on one of his ankles, rising to a pulley bolted to the celing. He was struggling weakly, sending the chains swinging from side to side.

Standing just below Aaron was a boy — small, skinny, and familiar — looking up and grinning a nasty grin.

Call felt his stomach drop. It was *Drew* looking up at Aaron in his chains and grinning. He had a length of chain wrapped around one wrist. He was using it to lower Aaron toward a massive glass container filled with a roiling, roaring darkness. As Call stared at the darkness, it seemed to shift and change shape. An orange eye peered out from the shadows, shot through with pulsing green veins.

"You know what's in the container, don't you, Aaron?" said Drew, his features twisted up into a sadistic smile. "It's a friend of yours. A chaos elemental. And it wants to suck you dry."

CHAPTER TWENTY-THREE

TAMARA, WHO HAD bent down beside Call, made a choked sound.

"Drew," Aaron panted, in obvious pain. He reached out for the manacle around his ankle, then fell back as the chaos elemental lifted a shadowy tentacle. It took clearer form as the tentacle drew closer to Aaron, until it was almost solid, brushing his skin. He jerked and cried out in agony. "Drew, let me go —"

"What, you can't get yourself free, Makar?" Drew sneered, jerking on the chain so that Aaron rose a few feet out of reach of the chaos elemental. "I thought you were supposed to be powerful. Special. But you're not really special, are you? Not special at all."

"I never said I was," said Aaron in a choked voice.

"Do you know what it was like to have to pretend I was bad at magic? That I was a fool? To listen to Master Lemuel bemoan choosing me? I was better trained than all of you, but I couldn't show it or Lemuel would have guessed who'd really trained me. I had to listen to the Masters tell their stupid version of history and pretend I agreed, even though I knew that if it hadn't been for the mages and the Assembly, the Enemy would have given us the means to live forever. Do you know what it was like to learn that the Makar was some stupid kid from nowhere who would never do anything about his powers except what the mages told him to do?"

"So you're going to kill me," Aaron said. "Because of all that? Because I'm a Makar?"

Drew just laughed. Call turned away and saw that Tamara was shaking, her fingers wound tightly together. "We have to get in there," he whispered to her. "We have to do something."

She rose to her feet, her wristband glittering in the shadows. "The rafters. If we climb up there, we can haul Aaron out of the range of that thing."

Panic flooded him. Because the plan was a good one, but when he imagined the climb and trying to balance his weight as he inched across the beam, he knew he couldn't do it. He'd slip. He'd fall. During the whole painful journey through the forest with his legs stiff and aching, he'd told himself that he was going to help save Aaron. Now, when he was right in front of Aaron — Aaron in danger, Aaron needing saving — he was useless. The crush of despair was so awful that he considered not saying anything, just trying to climb and hoping for the best.

But remembering the fear on Celia's face when she surfaced from the river, only to see Call lose control of the log and send it hurling toward her, decided him. If he made things worse by pretending he could help, he was only putting Aaron in more danger.

"I can't," Call said.

"What?" Tamara asked, then glanced at his leg and looked embarrassed. "Oh. Right. Well, just stay here with Havoc. I'll be right back. It's probably better with one person anyway. Sneakier."

At least he'd managed to seem capable for a while, Call thought. At least Tamara thought of him as a person who could do things and was surprised when he couldn't. It was cold comfort, but it was something.

Then, suddenly, Call realized what he *could* do. "I'll distract him."

"What? No!" Tamara said, shaking her head for emphasis. "It's too dangerous. He's got a chaos elemental."

"Havoc will be with me. And freeing Aaron won't work otherwise." Call looked her in the eye and hoped she could see that he wasn't going to back down. "Trust me."

Tamara nodded once. Then, with a quick smile at him, she slid through the door, the tread of her boots so soft that after two steps, he could no longer make them out over Drew's giggles and the growl of the chaos elemental. He counted to ten — *one one thousand, two one thousand, three one thousand* — and then flung open the door as wide as it would go.

"Hey, Drew," Call said, plastering on a grin. "This sure doesn't look like pony school to me."

Drew jerked back so hard in surprise that he hauled on the chain, yanking Aaron several feet up. Aaron yelled out in pain, making Havoc growl.

"*Call?*" said Drew in disbelief, and Call flashed back to that night in the ditch outside the Magisterium, Drew shivering and shouting out for Call, his ankle snapped. Behind him, Call could see Tamara starting to climb the far wall, using the stacked cages as a sort of ladder, jamming her boots in between the bars, moving as silently as a cat. "What are you doing here?"

"Seriously? What am *I* doing here?" Call demanded. "What are *you* doing here? Besides trying to feed one of your fellow students to a chaos elemental. I mean, seriously, what did Aaron do to you? Beat you on a test? Take the last piece of lichen at dinner?"

"Shut up, Call."

"Do you really think you won't get caught?"

"I haven't gotten caught yet." Drew seemed to be recovering from his surprise. He gave Call a nasty smile.

"Was it all just an act — all that stuff about Master Lemuel, all those times you pretended to be a regular student? Have you been a spy for the Enemy all along?" Call wasn't just playing for time now; he was curious. Drew looked the same — tangly brown hair, skinny, big blue eyes, freckles — but there was something behind his eyes Call hadn't seen before, something ugly and dark.

"The Masters are so stupid," said Drew. "Always worrying about what the Enemy was doing outside the Magisterium, worrying about the Treaty. Never thinking there could be a spy right among them. Even when I escaped the Magisterium to send the Enemy a message, what did they do?" He opened his blue eyes wide, and for a moment, Call caught a glimpse of the boy on the bus, sounding nervous about going to magic school. "'Oh, Master Lemuel is so mean. He *scares* me.' And they fired him!" Drew laughed, the innocent mask slipping away again, showing the coldness underneath.

Havoc growled at that, sliding between Drew and Call. "What were you bringing the Enemy a message about?" Call demanded. To his relief, Tamara was almost at the rafters. "Was it about Aaron?"

"The Makar," said Drew. "All these years, the mages have waited for a Makar, but they're not the only ones. We were

260

waiting, too." He jerked on the chain holding Aaron, who made a noise of pain, but Call didn't look up. He couldn't. He kept staring at Drew, as if he could make Drew pay attention to nothing but him.

"We?" Call said. "Because I just see one crazy person here. You."

Drew ignored his dig. He even ignored Havoc. "You can't think I'm in charge of this place," he said. "Don't be stupid, Call. I bet you saw the Chaos-ridden, the elementals. I bet you can feel it. You *know* who's running this show."

Call swallowed. "The Enemy," he said.

"The Enemy . . . isn't what you think." Drew rattled the chain idly. "We could be friends, Call. I've been keeping an eye on you. We could be on the same side."

"We really couldn't. Aaron's my friend. And the Enemy wants him dead, doesn't he? He doesn't want another Makar to challenge him."

"It's so much fun. You don't know anything. You think Aaron's your friend. You think everything they told you in the Magisterium is true. It's not. They told Aaron they'd keep him safe, but they didn't. They couldn't." He jerked on the chain holding Aaron, and Call winced, waiting for Aaron's cry of pain.

It didn't come. Call looked up. Aaron was no longer dangling. Tamara had pulled him up to the rafter and was kneeling over him, her fingers feverishly working to undo the chain around his ankle.

"No!" Drew yanked on the chain once more in a rage, but Tamara had broken it at her end. Drew let go as the chain came falling down.

"Look, we're going to just leave now," said Call. "I'm going to back out of here and —"

"You're not leaving!" Drew shouted, racing forward to press his hand against the glass container.

It was like he'd slid a key into a lock and opened a door, but way more violent. The container shattered, glass blowing in all directions. Call threw his hands up to cover his face, as glass shards, like a rain of tiny needles, pierced his forearms. Wind seemed to be blowing through the room. Havoc was whimpering, and somewhere, Tamara and Aaron were yelling.

Slowly, Call opened his eyes.

The chaos elemental surged up in front of him, filling his view with shadows. Its darkness churned with half-formed faces and toothy mouths. Seven clawed arms reached out for him at once, some scaled, some hairy, and some as pale as dead flesh.

Call gagged and staggered back a step. His hand slapped blindly at his side — his fingers closing around Miri's hilt, and he drew the blade from its sheath, swinging it out in front of him in a big, curving arc.

Miri sank into *something* — something that gave under the blade like rotten fruit. Howls poured from the chaos monster's many mouths. There was a long gash down one of its arms, darkness pouring out of the wound to swirl in the air like smoke from a fire. Another arm tried to grab him, but Call dropped to the ground and it succeeded only in grazing his shoulder. Where it had touched, though, his arm went instantly numb, and Miri dropped from his fingers.

Call struggled up onto his elbow, trying to reach across his body with his good hand, scrabbling for Miri. But he was out of time. The elemental lunged, rolling toward him across the floor like an oil slick, a huge, toadlike tongue slithering out, right for Call —

With a howl, Havoc threw himself into the air, landing directly atop the back of the elemental. His teeth sank into its slick surface, his claws piercing the roiling darkness. The monster spasmed, rearing back. Heads exploded out all over its body, arms shooting out to grab for Havoc, but the wolf held on, riding the monster.

Seeing his chance, Call scrambled to his feet, grabbing Miri with his good hand. He lunged forward and sank the knife into what he thought was the elemental's side.

The blade came away covered in dripping black, halfway between smoke and oil. The chaos elemental roared and thrashed, hurling Havoc off. The wolf flew and hit the floor on the far side of the room, near a pair of doors. He whimpered once, and then was still.

"Havoc!" Call shouted, darting toward his wolf. He was halfway there, when he heard a growling behind him. He whirled on the chaos elemental. Rage was pouring through him — if the creature had hurt Havoc, he would cut it up into a thousand gross, oily pieces. He stalked forward, Miri flashing in his hand.

The chaos elemental shrank back, darkness puddling around it, as though no longer so eager to fight.

"Go on, you coward," screamed Drew, kicking at it. "Grab him! Do it, you big stupid lump —"

The chaos elemental sprang — but not at Call. Twisting around, it lunged at Drew. Drew screamed once, and then the elemental was on him, rolling over him like a wave. Call stood frozen, Miri in his hand. He thought of the icy pain that had shot through him at just a touch of the chaos creature's substance. And now that substance was sinking down over Drew, who was jerking and twisting in its grip, his eyes rolling back to the whites.

"Call!" The voice yanked Call out of his shock — it was Tamara, yelling down to him from the rafters. She was on her knees, and Aaron was beside her. The manacle and chains were a twisted pile: Aaron was free, though his wrists were braceleted with blood where he had clearly been tied up, probably when they had dragged him from the Magisterium, and Call bet his ankles were in even worse shape. "Call, get *out* of there!"

"I can't!" Call pointed with Miri. The chaos elemental, and Drew, were between him and the door.

"Go that way," Tamara said, pointing to the doors behind him. "Look for anything — a window, anything. We'll meet you outside."

Call nodded once, lifting Havoc. *Please*, he thought. *Please*. The body in his arms was warm, and as he pressed the wolf against his chest, he could feel the steady beat of Havoc's heart. The extra weight hurt his legs, but he didn't care.

He's going to be okay, he told himself firmly. *Now move.*

Looking back, he saw that Tamara and Aaron were shinnying down from the rafters, close to the other door. But as he looked up, the chaos elemental rose from where it was hunched over Drew. Several mouths opened and a whiplike purple tongue lashed out to taste the air with its forked tip. Then it started to move toward Call.

Call yelled and jumped back. Havoc jerked in his arms, barked, and leaped to the ground. He ran toward the doors at the far end of the room, Call right behind him. They crashed through the doors together, nearly knocking them off their hinges.

Havoc came to a skidding stop. Call nearly fell over him, and barely righted himself.

He stared around the room — it looked a lot like the laboratory of Dr. Frankenstein. Beakers of odd-colored liquids bubbled all around, massive machinery hung from the ceiling, wheeling and turning, and the walls were lined with cages full of elementals of various sizes, quite a few of them glowing brightly.

Then Call heard it behind him — a thick, bubbling growl. The chaos elemental had followed them into the room and was sailing after them, a massive, dark cloud covered in claws and teeth. Call jerked into an uneven run again, sending beakers of liquid crashing to the floor as he hurtled toward what looked like a display of old weapons on one of the walls. If he went for the elemental with that hefty-looking axe, maybe —

"Stop!" A man in hooded black robes strode from behind a huge bookcase. His face was shrouded in darkness, and he swung a massive staff topped with onyx. Havoc, on seeing him, let out a whimper and dove under one of the nearest tables.

Call froze. The stranger swept past him without a glance and raised his staff. "Enough!" he cried in a deep voice, and pointed the onyx end of the staff toward the elemental.

Darkness exploded from the tip, shooting across the room toward the beast, striking it squarely. The darkness swelled and grew, wrapping the elemental, swallowing it into nothingness. It gave a last horrible, bubbling cry and vanished.

The man turned toward Call and slowly drew back the hood of his robes. His face was half hidden by a silver mask that covered his eyes and nose. Below it, Call could see the jut of a chin, a neck slashed with white scars.

The scars were new, but the mask was familiar. Call had seen it before in pictures. Had heard it described. A mask worn to cover the scars of an explosion that had almost killed the wearer. A mask worn to terrify.

A mask worn by the Enemy of Death.

"Callum Hunt," said the Enemy. "I was hoping it would be you."

Whatever Call had expected the Enemy to say, it wasn't that. He opened his mouth, but only a whisper came out. "You're Constantine Madden," he said. "The Enemy of Death."

The Enemy moved toward him, a swirl of black and silver. "Stand up," he said. "Let me look at you."

Slowly, Call pulled himself to his feet and stood facing the Enemy of Death. The room was almost silent. Even Havoc's whimpers seemed faint and far away.

"Look at you," said the Enemy. There was an odd sort of pleasure in his voice. "It's a pity about the leg, of course, but that won't matter in the end. I suppose Alastair preferred to leave you as you were than dabble in healing magic. He always was stubborn. And now it's too late. Did you ever think of that, Callum? That perhaps if Alastair Hunt had been a little less stubborn, you might have been able to walk properly?"

Call hadn't thought of it. But now the thought lodged like a cold piece of ice in his throat, choking off his words. He took a step away, until his back hit one of the long tables full of jars and beakers. He froze.

"But your eyes . . ." And now the Enemy sounded gloating, though Call couldn't figure out what about his eyes might be worth gloating over. He felt dizzy with confusion. "They say eyes are the windows of the soul. I asked Drew quite a lot of questions about you, but I never thought to ask about your eyes." He frowned, the scarred skin tightening beneath the mask. "Drew," he said. "Where *is* the boy?" He raised his voice. "Drew!"

There was silence. Call wondered what would happen if he reached behind himself, grabbed one of the beakers or jars, and threw it at the Enemy — could he buy himself time? Could he run?

"*Drew!*" said the mage again, and now there was something else in his voice — something like alarm. He strode past Call impatiently, stalking through the double doors into the wooden chamber beyond.

There was a long moment of utter silence. Call looked around desperately, trying to see if there were any other doors, any other ways out of this room besides the way he'd come in. There weren't. There were only bookshelves piled with dusty tomes, tables loaded with alchemical materials, and, high up the walls, small fire elementals set into hammered copper niches lighting the room with their glow. The elementals stared down at Call with their blank black eyes as he heard the noise from the other room — a long, keening cry of grief and despair.

"DREW!"

Havoc wailed. Call picked up one of the glass beakers and staggered to the double doors. Pain was shooting through his leg, up into his body, like razor blades stabbing through his veins. He wanted to fall over; he wanted to lie on the ground and let unconsciousness take him. He grabbed for the arch of the doorway and stared.

The Enemy was on his knees, Drew lying half across his lap, limp and unresponsive. His skin had already begun to turn a cold blue color. He was never going to wake up again.

Call's heart gave a dull thud of horror. He couldn't seem to wrench his gaze away from the Enemy hunched over Drew's body, his staff lying discarded on the floor beside him. His scarred hands raked through Drew's hair, again and again. "My son," he whispered. "My poor son."

His son? Call thought. *Drew is the Enemy of Death's son?*

Suddenly, the Enemy's head jerked up. Even through the mask, Call could sense the glare of his eyes: They were bent on Call, and they were black with laserlike fury. *"You,"* he hissed. "You did this. You unleashed the elemental that killed my child."

Call swallowed and backed up, but the Enemy was already rising, seizing his staff. He swung it toward Call, and Call stumbled, the beaker flying out of his hand to shatter on the floor. He went down on one knee, his bent leg screaming in pain. "I didn't —" he began. "It was an accident —"

"Get up," snarled the Enemy. "Get up, Callum Hunt, and face me."

Slowly, Call rose to his feet and faced the silver-masked man across the room. Call was shaking all over, shaking from the pain in his legs and from the tension in his body, from fear and adrenaline and the thwarted desire to run. The Enemy's face was set in a furious expression, his eyes glittering with rage and grief.

Call wanted to open his mouth, wanted to say something in his own defense, but there was nothing. Drew lay unmoving, still and vacant-eyed among the smashed remains of the glass container — he was dead, and it was Call's fault. He couldn't explain himself, couldn't defend himself. He was facing the Enemy of Death, who had slain whole armies. He would hardly hesitate at one single boy.

Call's hand slipped from Miri's hilt. There was only one thing left to do.

Taking a deep breath, he got ready to die.

He hoped that Tamara and Aaron had made it past the Chaos-ridden, out the window, and back on the path toward the Magisterium.

He hoped that, since Havoc was Chaos-ridden, the Enemy wouldn't be too hard on him for not being an evil zombie dog.

He hoped his dad wouldn't be too mad at him for going to the Magisterium and getting killed, just the way he had always been warned he would.

He hoped Master Rufus wouldn't give his spot to Jasper.

The mage was close enough that Call could feel the heat of his breathing, could see the twist of his narrow mouth, the glint of his eyes, and the tremors that ran through his whole body.

"If you're going to kill me," Call said, "go ahead. Do it."

The mage raised his staff — and flung it aside. He dropped to his knees, his head bent, his whole posture one of supplication, as if he were begging Call for mercy. "Master, my Master," he rasped. "Forgive me. I did not see."

Call stared in confusion. What did he mean?

"This is a test. A test of my loyalty and commitment." The Enemy took a ragged breath. It was clear that he was barely controlling himself through sheer force of will. "If you, my Master, decreed that Drew must die, then his death must be to a greater purpose." The words seemed sliced out of his throat, as if it pained him to speak them. "Now I, too, have a personal stake in our quest. My Master is wise. As always, he is wise."

"What?" Call said, his voice trembling. "I don't understand. Your Master? Aren't you the Enemy of Death?"

To Call's utter shock, the mage raised his hands and drew off the silver mask, baring the face beneath it. It was a scarred face, an old, lined, weathered face. It was a strangely familiar face, but it was not the face of Constantine Madden.

"No, Callum Hunt. I am not the Enemy of Death," he said. "You are."

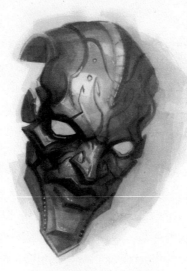

CHAPTER TWENTY-FOUR

W-WHAT?" CALL GAPED. "Who are you? Why are you telling me this?"

"Because it is the truth," said the mage, holding the silver mask in his hand. "You are Constantine Madden. And if you look at me closely, you will know my name as well."

The mage was still kneeling at Call's feet, his mouth beginning to twist into a bitter smile.

He's insane, Call thought. *He has to be. What he's saying doesn't make any sense.*

But the familiarity of his face — Call had seen him before, at least in photographs.

"You're Master Joseph," Call said. "You taught the Enemy of Death."

"I taught *you*," said Master Joseph. "May I rise, Master?"

Call said nothing. *I'm trapped*, he thought. *I'm trapped in here with an insane mage and a dead body.*

Apparently taking this as permission, Master Joseph stood with some effort. "Drew said that your memories were gone, but

I couldn't believe it. I thought that when you saw me, when I told you the truth about yourself, you might recall something. No matter. You may not remember, but I assure you, *Callum Hunt*, the spark of life within you — the *soul*, if you will — all that animates the shell of your body belongs to Constantine Madden. The real Callum Hunt died as a mewling baby."

"This is crazy," Call said. "Things like that, they don't happen. You can't just swap souls."

"True, I cannot," said the mage. "But *you* can. If you will permit me, Master?"

He held out his hand. After a moment, Call realized that he was asking for permission to take Call's hand in his.

Call knew he shouldn't touch Master Joseph. Much of magic was communicated through touch: touching elements, drawing their power through you. But even though what Master Joseph was saying was insane, there was something in it that pulled at Call, something his mind couldn't let go of.

Slowly, he held out his hand, and Master Joseph took it, wrapping his wide, scarred fingers around Call's smaller ones.

"*See,*" he whispered, and an electric jolt went through Call. His vision whitened, and all of a sudden, it was like he was seeing scenes projected onto a massive screen in front of him.

He saw two armies facing off against each other on a vast plain. It was a mage war — explosions of fire, arrows of ice, and gusts of gale-force wind hurtled among the fighters. Call saw familiar faces: a much younger Master Rufus, a teenage Master Lemuel, Tamara's mother and father, and, riding a fire elemental at the head of them all, Verity Torres. Chaos magic spilled darkly from her outstretched hands as she hurtled across the field.

Master Joseph rose up, a heavy object in his hand. It glittered the color of copper — it looked like a copper claw, fingers outstretched like talons. He gathered a burst of wind magic and sent it sailing through the air. It buried itself in Verity's throat.

She fell backward, blood ribboning through the air, and the fire elemental she had been riding howled and reared back. A bolt of lightning shot from its claws — it struck Master Joseph and he fell, his silver mask dislodging to show his face beneath.

"It's not Constantine!" cried a hoarse voice. Alastair Hunt's voice. "It's Master Joseph!"

The scene shifted. Master Joseph stood in a room made of scarlet marble. He was shouting at a group of cowering mages. "Where is he? I demand that you tell me what happened to him!"

The heavy tread of feet came from the open door. The mages broke apart, creating an aisle down which marched four of the Chaos-ridden, carrying a body between them. The body of a young man with blond hair, a huge wound in his chest, his clothes soaked in blood. They set the body down at Joseph's feet.

Master Joseph crumpled, taking the body of the young man in his arms. "Master," he hissed. "Oh, my Master, death's enemy . . ."

The boy's eyes opened. They were gray — Call had never seen Constantine Madden's eyes before, never thought to ask what color they were. They were the same gray as Call's. Gray and empty as a winter sky. His scarred face was slack, emotionless.

Master Joseph gasped. "What is this?" he demanded, turning to the other mages with fury on his face. "His body lives, if barely, but his soul — where is his soul?"

The scene shifted again. Call was standing in a cave carved of ice. The walls were white, shifting in color where shadows touched them. The floor was scattered with bodies: mages lying crumpled, some with their eyes open, some in pools of frozen blood.

Call knew where he was. The Cold Massacre. He closed his eyes, but it made no difference — he could still see, since the images were inside his mind. He watched Master Joseph pick his way among the murdered, stopping here and there to turn over a body and stare at its face. After a few moments, Call realized what he was doing. He was examining the dead children, not touching the adults. At last, he stopped and stared, and Call saw what he was looking at. Not a body at all, but a set of words, carved into the ice.

KILL THE CHILD

Again, the scenes shifted, and now they were fluttering by fast, like leaves in a breeze: Master Joseph in one town or city after another, searching, always searching, examining the birth records in a hospital, property records, any possible lead . . .

Master Joseph standing on the concrete of a playground, watching a group of boys threatening a smaller boy. Suddenly, the ground underfoot shook and trembled, a huge crack splitting the playground nearly in half. As the bullies ran off, the smaller boy on the ground levered himself up, gazing around with a bewildered look. Call recognized himself. Skinny, dark-haired, with gray eyes just like Constantine's, his bad leg twisted beneath him.

He felt Master Joseph begin to smile. . . .

Call came back to reality with a shock, as if he had slammed into his body from a great height. He staggered back, yanking his hand out of Master Joseph's. "No," he choked. "No, I don't understand. . . ."

"Oh, I think you do," said the mage. "I think you understand very well, Callum Hunt."

"Stop that," Call said. "Stop calling me Callum Hunt like that — it's creepy. My name is Call."

"No, it's not," said Master Joseph. "That's the name that belongs to that body, that shell you wear. A name that you will discard when you are ready, just as you will discard that body and enter Constantine's."

Call threw up his hands. "I can't do that! And do you know why? Because Constantine Madden is *still around*. I really, really don't understand how I can be this person that's out leading armies and raising chaos elementals and making giant wolves with freaky eyes when that person already exists and is SOMEBODY ELSE!" Call was shouting, but his voice sounded pleading, even to his own ears. He just wanted all this to stop. He couldn't help hearing the horrible echo of his father's words again and again.

Call, you must listen to me. You don't know what you are.

"Still around?" Master Joseph said with a bitter smile. "Oh, the Assembly and the Magisterium believe that Constantine is still actively engaged with the world, because that is what we wished them to believe. But who has seen him? Who has spoken to him since the Cold Massacre?"

"People have seen him . . ." Call began. "He's met with the Assembly! He signed the Treaty."

"Masked," said Master Joseph, holding up the silver mask he had been wearing when Call had first seen him. "I impersonated him at the battle with Verity Torres; I knew I could do it again. The Enemy has remained hidden since the Cold Massacre, and when he absolutely had to show himself, I went in his place. But Constantine himself? He was mortally wounded twelve years ago, in the cave where Sarah Hunt and so many others died. But as he felt the life ebbing from him, he used what he had already learned — the method of moving one soul to another body — to save himself. Just like he was able to take a piece of chaos and place it inside the Chaos-ridden, he took his own soul and placed it inside the optimal vessel at hand. You."

"But I was never at the Cold Massacre. I was born in a hospital. My leg —"

"A lie told to you by Alastair Hunt. Your leg was shattered when Sarah Hunt dropped you onto the ice," said Master Joseph. "She knew what had happened. The soul of her child had been forced out, and the soul of Constantine Madden took its place. Her child had become the Enemy."

Call heard a roaring in his ears. "My mother wouldn't —"

"Your *mother*?" sneered Master Joseph. "Sarah Hunt was only the mother of the shell that contains you. Even she knew it. She didn't have the strength to do it herself, but she left a message. A message for those who would come upon the battlefield after she was dead."

"The words in the ice," Call whispered. He felt dizzy and sick.

"*Kill the child*," said Master Joseph, with a cruel satisfaction. "She scratched it into the ice with the tip of that knife you carry. It was her last act in this world."

Call felt as if he were about to throw up. He reached behind him for the edge of a table and leaned back against it, breathing hard.

"The soul of Callum Hunt is dead," said Joseph. "Forced from your body, that soul shriveled up and died. Constantine Madden's soul has taken root and grown, newborn and intact. Since then, his followers have labored to make it seem like he wasn't gone from the world, so that you would be safe. Protected. So that you would have time to mature. So that you would live."

Call wants to live. That was what Call had, jokingly, added to the Cinquain in his mind; now it didn't seem like a joke. Now, in horror, he wondered just how true it was. Had he wanted to live so much that he'd stolen another person's life? Could that have really been him?

"I don't remember anything about being Constantine Madden," Call whispered. "I've only ever been me —"

"Constantine always knew he could die," said Joseph. "It was his greatest fear, death. He tried again and again to bring back his brother, but he could never recover his brother's soul, all that made Jericho who he was. He resolved to do whatever it took to remain alive. All this time, we have waited, Call, for you to be old enough. And here you are, nearly ready. Soon, the war will begin again in earnest . . . and this time we are sure to win."

Master Joseph's eyes were shining with something that seemed a lot like madness.

"I don't see why you think I'd ever be on your side," Call said. "You took Aaron —"

"Yes," said Joseph, "but we wanted *you*."

"So you went through all that effort, the kidnapping, just to get me here to — what? To tell me all this? Why not tell me before? Why not grab me before I even ever went to the Magisterium?"

"Because we thought you *knew*," Master Joseph ground out. "I thought you were lying low on purpose — allowing your mind and body to grow so that you might once again become the formidable foe to the Assembly that you were before. I did not approach you because I assumed that if you wished to be approached, you would have contacted me."

Call laughed bitterly. "So you didn't come near me because you didn't want to blow my cover, and all that time, I didn't even know I had a cover? That's freaking hilarious."

"I see nothing amusing about it." Master Joseph didn't change expression. "It is fortunate that my son — that Drew was able to ascertain that you had no idea who you really are, or you might have inadvertently given yourself away."

Call stared at Master Joseph. "Are you going to kill me?" he asked abruptly.

"Kill you? I've been *waiting* for you," Joseph said. "All these many years."

"Well, your whole stupid plan has been for nothing, then," Call said. "I am going to go back and tell Master Rufus who I really am. I am going to tell everyone at the Magisterium that my father was right, and that they should have listened to him. And I'm going to stop you."

Master Joseph smiled, shaking his head. "I think I know you a little better than that, in any guise. You'll go back and you'll finish your Iron Year, and when you return for your Copper Year, we'll talk again."

"No, we won't." Call felt childish and small, the weight of the horror overwhelming him. "I'll tell them —"

"Tell them what you are? They'll bind your magic."

"They won't —"

"They will," said Master Joseph. "If they don't kill you. They'll bind your magic and they'll send you away to a father who knows now, for certain, that he is not your father."

Call swallowed hard. He hadn't thought, until this moment, what Alastair's reaction would be to this revelation. His father, who had begged Rufus to bind his magic . . . just in case.

"You'll lose your friends. Do you really think they'd let you close to their precious Makar, knowing who you are? They will raise Aaron Stewart to be your enemy. That's what they've been looking for all this time. That's what Aaron is. He is not your companion. He is your destruction."

"Aaron's my friend," Call said, in a hopeless sort of voice. He could hear how he sounded, but he couldn't stop it.

"As you say, Call." Master Joseph had the serene look of a man who knew better. "It seems your friend has some choices ahead of him. As do you."

"I choose," said Call. "I choose to go back to the Magisterium and tell them the truth."

Joseph smiled a glittering smile. "Do you?" he said. "It is easy enough to stand here and throw your defiance at me. I would have expected nothing less from Constantine Madden. You were always defiant. But when it comes down to the wire, when the choice must be made, will you really give up everything that matters to you for the sake of an abstract ideal you only partly understand?"

Call shook his head. "But I'd have to give it up anyway. You're not exactly going to let me go back to the Magisterium."

"Of course I am," Master Joseph said.

Call jolted back, slamming his elbow painfully into the wall behind him. "*What?*"

"Oh, my Master," the older mage breathed. "Don't you see —"

He never finished his sentence. With an enormous crash, the roof tore itself apart. Call barely had time to look up before everything overhead seemed to explode in a shower of splintered wood and concrete. He heard Master Joseph's hoarse shout, just before a mountain of rubble poured down between them, obscuring the mage from view. The ground buckled under Call, who fell sideways, throwing out his arm to pin a squirming, panicked Havoc.

Everything shook for another moment, and Call buried his face in the wolf's fur, trying not to choke on the thick, swirling dust. Maybe the world was ending. Maybe Master Joseph's allies had decided to blow the whole place up. He didn't know, and he almost didn't care.

"Call?" Through the ringing in his ears, Call heard the familiar voice. Tamara. He rolled over, one hand still gripped in Havoc's fur, and saw what had ripped the building apart.

The huge sign that read MOUNTAIN BOWLING had plunged through the roof, slicing the building in half like an axe plunging through a concrete block. Aaron was crouching on top of the sign as if he had ridden it down through the air, Tamara behind him. The sign was sparking and hissing where electrical wires had been severed and bent.

Aaron sprang off the sign and ran across the floor to Call, bending down to grab his arm. "Call, come on!"

In disbelief, Call scrambled up, letting Aaron haul him to his feet. Havoc gave a whine and jumped up, planting his front paws on Aaron's waist.

"Aaron!" Tamara yelled. She was pointing behind them. Call spun around and peered down through the clouds of dust and rubble. There was no sign of Master Joseph.

But that didn't mean they were alone. Call turned back to Aaron.

"Chaos-ridden," Call said grimly. The hallway was full of them, marching over the rubble, their gait eerily regular, their roiling eyes burning like fires.

"Come on!" Aaron turned and sprinted toward the sign, jumping up onto it and reaching back to haul Call up after him. The sign was still attached to its base: The main part of it had crashed through the building at an angle, like a spoon that had fallen into a pot and was leaning against the side. Tamara was already running up over the words MOUNTAIN BOWLING, Havoc at her heels. Call started to limp after her, when he realized Aaron wasn't following. He whirled around, sparks springing up from the wires at his feet.

The room below them was rapidly filling with Chaos-ridden, who were methodically making their way over to the sign. Several of them were already climbing onto it. Aaron stood a few feet above them, looking down.

Tamara had already made it far enough up the sign to drop onto the roof. "Come on!" he heard her shout as she realized they hadn't followed her — and that she had no way to get back up onto the sign. "Call! *Aaron!*"

But Aaron wasn't moving. He was balanced on the sign as if it were a surfboard, the expression on his face grim. His hair was white with powdered concrete, his gray uniform torn and bloody. Slowly, he raised his hand, and for the first time, Call saw not just Aaron his friend, but the Makar, the chaos magician, someone who could be as powerful one day as the Enemy of Death.

Someone who would be the Enemy's enemy.

His enemy.

Darkness spread from Aaron's hand like a bolt of black lightning: It shot forward, wrapping the Chaos-ridden in shadowy tendrils. As the darkness touched them, the lights in their eyes went out, and they slid to the ground, limp and unresisting.

That's what they've been looking for all this time. Your destruction. That's what Aaron is.

"Aaron!" Call shouted, sliding down the sign toward him. Aaron didn't turn, didn't even seem to hear him. He stood where he was, black light exploding from his hand, searing a path across the sky. He looked terrifying. "Aaron," Call gasped, and tripped over a knot of torn wires. Excruciating pain shot through his leg as his body twisted and he fell, knocking Aaron to the ground, half pinning the other boy under him. The black light vanished as Aaron's back hit the metal of the sign, his hands jammed between himself and Call.

"Leave me alone!" Aaron shouted. He looked out of his mind, as though maybe he'd even forgotten who Call and Tamara were in his rage. He twisted under Call, trying to get his hands free. "I need to — I need to —"

"You need to *stop*," Call said, grabbing Aaron by the front of his uniform. "Aaron, you can't do this without a counterweight. You'll die."

"It doesn't matter," Aaron said, struggling to get away from Call.

Call wouldn't let him go. "Tamara's waiting. We can't leave her. You have to. Come on. You *have* to."

Slowly, Aaron's breathing calmed, his eyes focusing on Call. Behind him, more Chaos-ridden were creeping toward them, crawling over the bodies of their dead companions, their eyes coruscating in the dark.

"Okay," Call said, easing himself off Aaron, pushing himself to stand upright on his aching leg. "Okay, Aaron." He held out his hand. "Let's go."

Aaron hesitated — then reached his hand up and let Call haul him to his feet. Call let go and turned, started to climb the sign again. This time Aaron followed him. They scrambled high enough to drop down beside Tamara and Havoc on the roof. Call felt the impact of hitting the asphalt tiles through his legs, all the way to his teeth.

Tamara nodded in relief at seeing them, but her face was tight — the Chaos-ridden were still behind them. She spun and was already running for the edge of the sloped roof and another leap — this one onto a Dumpster. Call staggered after her.

Down he went, over the side of the building, his heart drumming half with fear of what was chasing them and half with a fear that no amount of running could escape. His feet slammed down on the metal lid of the Dumpster and he fell to his knees, his legs feeling as though they were made of bags of sand, heavy and numb and not quite solid. He managed to roll his way off the edge and stayed upright by leaning against the metal side, trying to catch his breath.

A second later, he heard Aaron drop down next to him. "You okay?" Aaron asked, and Call felt a wave of relief even in the middle of everything else — Aaron sounded like Aaron again.

There was the sound of clattering metal. Call and Aaron spun to see that Tamara had sent the Dumpster rolling away from the buildings. The Chaos-ridden, with nothing to jump down onto, were milling around at the edge of the roof above.

"I — I'm fine." Call glanced from Aaron to Tamara, both of whom were looking at him with identical expressions of concern. "I can't believe you came back for me," Call added. He felt dizzy and sick and was sure that if he took a single step farther, he was going to fall again. He thought about telling them that they ought to leave him and run, but he didn't want to be left behind.

"Of course we did," Aaron said, frowning. "I mean, you and Tamara came all this way to get me, didn't you? Why wouldn't we do the same thing for you?"

"You matter, Call," Tamara said.

Call wanted to say that saving Aaron was different, except he couldn't quite work out how to explain why. His head was spinning. "Well, it was pretty amazing — what you did with the sign."

Tamara and Aaron glanced at each other quickly.

"That wasn't what we were trying to do," Tamara admitted. "We were trying to get to the top of it to signal the Magisterium. The earth magic got a little out of hand and — well. Uh, it worked out, right? And that's the important thing."

Call nodded. That was the important thing.

"Thanks for what you did up there, too," Aaron said, putting his hand on Call's shoulder and patting it awkwardly. "I was so angry — if you hadn't stopped me using the chaos magic, I don't know what would have —"

"Oh, for goodness sake. Why do boys always have to talk about their feelings all the time? It's so gross," Tamara interrupted. "There are still Chaos-ridden trying to come after us!" She pointed up to where bright, pinwheeling eyes peered down at them from the darkness on the rooftop. "Come on, enough, we've got to get out of here."

She started walking, her long dark braids swinging behind her. Steeling himself for the endless walk back to the Magisterium, Call pushed himself away from the wall and took a single excruciating step before passing out cold. He wasn't even awake long enough to feel his head strike the ground.

CHAPTER TWENTY-FIVE

CALL WOKE UP back in the Infirmary. The crystals on the walls were dim, so he guessed it was probably night. He felt sore all over. Plus, he was sure there was some bad news he was supposed to tell someone, although he couldn't quite remember what. His legs hurt, and there were blankets tangled around him — he was in bed, and he'd hurt himself, but he couldn't remember how. He'd been showing off during that exercise with the log and he'd fallen into the river, causing Jasper — Jasper of all people — to save him. And there was more — Tamara and Aaron and Havoc and a walk through the woods, but maybe that was a dream? It seemed like one now.

Turning on his side, he saw Master Rufus seated in a chair beside the bed, his face half in shadow. For a moment, Call wondered if Master Rufus was asleep, until he saw a smile curl across the mage's mouth.

"Feeling a bit more human?" Master Rufus asked.

Call nodded and struggled to sit up. But as he cast off sleep, all the memories came flooding back, the ones of Master Joseph with his silver mask, Drew being devoured, Aaron hanging from the rafters with manacles cutting into his skin, and Call being told that he had Constantine Madden's soul inside him.

He slumped back down on the cot.

I have to tell Master Rufus, he thought. *I'm not a bad person. I'm going to tell him.*

"Are you up to eating a little?" Master Rufus asked, reaching for a tray. "I brought you tea and soup."

"The tea, maybe." Call took the earthenware mug and let it warm his hands. He sipped tentatively, the comforting taste of peppermint making him feel a little more awake.

Master Rufus set the tray back down and turned to study Call from beneath hooded eyes. Call gripped his mug as if it were a life preserver. "I'm sorry to ask, but I must. Tamara and Aaron told me what they knew of where Aaron was being held, but they both said that you were inside longer and that you'd been in a room they hadn't. What can you tell me about what you saw?"

"Did they tell you about Drew?" Call asked, shuddering at the memory.

Master Rufus nodded. "We researched what we could and discovered that Drew Wallace's name and identity, in fact his entire past, consisted of some very convincing forgeries designed to get him into the Magisterium. We don't know what his real name was or why the Enemy sent him here. If not for you and Tamara, the Enemy would have succeeded in dealing us a terrible blow — and as for Aaron, I shudder to think what they might have done to him."

"So we're not in trouble?"

"For not informing me that Aaron had been kidnapped? For not telling anyone where you went?" Master Rufus's voice deepened to a growl. "So long as you never, ever do anything like that again, I am prepared to overlook how foolishly you both behaved, in light of the fact that you succeeded. It seems silly to quibble over exactly how you and Tamara saved our Makar. What's important is that you did."

"Thanks," Call said, not sure whether he was being scolded or not.

"We sent some mages out to the abandoned bowling alley, but not much remained. Some empty cages and smashed equipment. There was a large room that seemed to be a laboratory. Were you in there?"

Call nodded, swallowing. This was the moment. He opened his mouth to say the words: *Master Joseph was there and he told me I am the Enemy of Death.*

The words wouldn't come. It was as if he were standing on the edge of a cliff, and everything in his body was willing him to throw himself over, but his mind wouldn't let him. If he repeated what Joseph had said, Master Rufus would hate him. They'd all hate him.

And for what? Even if he had been Constantine Madden once, it wasn't like he remembered any of it. He was still Callum, wasn't he? Still the same person. He hadn't become evil. He didn't wish harm to the Magisterium. And what was a soul, anyway? It didn't tell you what to do. He could make his own decisions.

"Yeah, there was a lab with a lot of bubbling stuff and elementals in the niches that lit the whole place. But no one was there." Call swallowed, steeling himself to the lie. His heart sped. "The room was empty."

"Is there anything else?" Master Rufus said, studying Call intently. "Any detail you think might help us? Anything, no matter how small?"

"There were Chaos-ridden," Call said. "A lot of them. And a chaos elemental. It chased me into the lab, but that's when Aaron and Tamara broke through the roof, so —"

"Yes, Tamara and Aaron have already told me of their impressive stunt with the signpost." Master Rufus smiled, but Call could tell he was hiding disappointment. "Thank you, Call. You did very well."

Call nodded. He had never felt so terrible.

"I remember that when you first came to the Magisterium, you asked me several times if you could talk to Alastair," Master Rufus said. "I never *formally* granted your request." He said it with an emphasis that made Call blush. He wondered if finally, now, of all times, he was going to get in trouble for sneaking into Rufus's office. "But I'm granting it now."

He plucked a glass globe off the nightstand and held it out to Call. A small tornado was already spinning inside.

"I believe you know how to use this." He rose to his feet and walked to the far end of the Infirmary, his hands clasped behind his back. It took a moment for Call to realize what he was doing: giving Call privacy.

Call held the clear glass globe in his hand and studied it. It was as if a huge soap bubble had hardened in midair, leaving it solid and clear. He concentrated on thinking about his dad — blocking out thoughts of Master Joseph and Constantine Madden, and just thinking of his father, of the smell of pancakes and pipe tobacco, of his father's hand on his shoulder when he did something right, of his father painstakingly explaining geometry, Call's least favorite subject.

The tornado began to condense and shaped itself into his dad, who was standing in oil-stained jeans and a flannel shirt, his glasses pushed up on his head, a wrench in one hand. *He must be in his garage, working on one of his old cars*, Call thought. His father looked up as if someone had said his name.

"Call?" he inquired.

"Dad," Call said. "It's me."

His father put the wrench down, which made it vanish out of the image. He turned around, as if he were trying to see Call, though it seemed clear he couldn't. "Master Rufus told me what happened. I was so worried. You were in the Infirmary —"

"I still am," Call said, and then added quickly, "but I'm fine. I got a little banged up, but I'm fine." His voice came out weak, even to his own ears. "You shouldn't worry."

"I can't help it," his dad said gruffly. "I am still your father, even if you are away at school." He looked around and then back at Call, as if he could see him. "Master Rufus says you saved the Makar. That's pretty incredible. You did what a whole army couldn't do for Verity Torres."

"Aaron's my friend. I guess we saved him, but it was because of that, not because he's the Makar. And it's not like we knew what we were going up against."

"I'm glad you have friends there, Call." His dad's eyes were serious. "It can be hard — to be friends with someone so powerful."

Call thought of the wristband in the letter from his father, of the thousand unanswered questions he had. *You were friends with Constantine Madden?* he wanted to ask, but he couldn't. Not now, and not with Rufus within earshot.

"Rufus also tells me that one of the other Magisterium students was there," his father continued. "Someone working for the Enemy."

"Drew — yeah." Call shook his head. "We didn't know."

"It's not your fault. Sometimes, people don't show their true faces." His father sighed. "So this student — Drew — was there, but the Enemy wasn't?"

There is no Enemy. You've been fighting a phantom all these years. An illusion Master Joseph wanted you to see. But I can't tell you that, because if the Enemy isn't Constantine Madden, then who is he?

"I don't think we'd have gotten away if he was," Call said. "I guess we were lucky."

"And this Drew — he didn't say anything to you?"

"Like what?"

"Anything about — about you," his father said cautiously. "It's just strange, that the Enemy would leave a captured Makar protected only by a schoolboy."

"There were a lot of Chaos-ridden, too," said Call. "But no, nobody said anything to me. It was just Drew and the Chaos-ridden, and they don't talk much."

"No." His father almost twitched a smile. "They don't, do they?" He sighed again. "I miss you around here, Callum."

"I miss you, too." Call felt his throat narrow.

"I'll see you when school's out," his dad said.

Call nodded, not trusting his voice, and passed a hand over the surface of the globe. The image of his father vanished. He sat and stared at the device. Now that there was nothing in it, he could see a little of his reflection in the glass. Same black hair, same gray eyes, same slightly pointed nose and chin. Everything familiar. He didn't look like Constantine Madden. He looked like Callum Hunt.

"I'll take that," Rufus said, and plucked the globe from his hand. He was smiling. "You should probably stay here for a day or so, to rest your injuries and heal completely. In the meantime, there are two people who've been waiting very patiently to see you."

Master Rufus strode over to the Infirmary door and threw it open.

Tamara and Aaron rushed in.

↑ ≈ △ ○ ⊚

Being in the Infirmary when you'd gotten injured being awesome was totally different from being in the Infirmary for doing something dumb. Classmates kept coming to visit him. Everyone wanted to hear the story over and over again, everyone wanted to hear how scary the Chaos-ridden were and how Call had fought a chaos elemental. Everyone wanted to hear about the sign crashing through the roof and laugh at the part where Call passed out.

Gwenda and Celia brought him candy bars from home. Rafe brought a pack of cards and they played Go Fish on top of his blankets. Call had never realized how many people in the Magisterium knew who he was. Even some of the older students came by, like Tamara's sister, Kimiya, who was super tall and so serious that she scared Call when she told him how glad she was that Tamara had him for a friend, and Alex, who produced a bag of Call's favorite sour gummies and grinningly warned him about how all this hero stuff was making the rest of the school look bad.

Even Jasper visited him, which was extremely awkward. He shuffled in, looking nervous as he tugged on the raggedy cashmere scarf he was wearing over his uniform. "I brought you a sandwich from the Gallery," he said, handing it over to Call. "It's lichen, of course, but it tastes like tuna. I hate tuna."

"Thanks," Call said, turning the sandwich over. It was oddly warm, which made him think it had probably been in Jasper's pocket.

"I just wanted to tell you," Jasper said, "that everyone's talking about what you did, rescuing Aaron, and I wanted you to know, that I also thought that it was a good thing. What you did. And that it's okay. That you got my place with Master Rufus. Because maybe you deserve it. So I'm not mad at you. Anymore."

"Way to make it all about you, Jasper," said Call, who had to admit he was enjoying the moment.

"Right," Jasper said, yanking so furiously on his scarf that a piece of it almost came off. "Good talk. Enjoy the sandwich."

He staggered out, and Call watched him go with amusement. He realized he was glad it seemed that Jasper didn't hate him anymore, although he did throw out the sandwich, just to be safe.

Tamara and Aaron visited as much as they were allowed, throwing themselves on Call's bed like it was a trampoline, eager to fill him in on everything that was going on while he was laid up. Aaron explained how he'd vouched for Havoc with the Masters, claiming that as the Makar, he needed to study a Chaos-ridden creature. They hadn't liked it, but they'd allowed it, and Havoc was going to be a permanent fixture in their rooms from now on. Tamara said that the way they let Aaron get away with stuff was going to go to his head and make him even more annoying than Call. They talked and joked so loudly that Master Amaranth released Call early just to get some peace and quiet. Which was probably a good idea, since Call was getting used to the idea of lying around all day and having people bring him things. Another week and he might have never left.

Five days after coming back from the Enemy's compound, Call returned to his studies. He got into the boat with Aaron and Tamara a little stiffly; his injured leg was almost healed, but it was still hard to move around. Upon their arrival in front of their classroom, Master Rufus was waiting.

"Today, we're going to do something a little different," he said, gesturing down the hall. "We're going to visit the Hall of Graduates."

"We've been there before," Tamara said, before Call could kick her. If Master Rufus wanted to take them on a field trip instead of teaching them boring exercises, then better to go along with it. Also, Master Rufus didn't know they'd been in the Hall of Graduates, since they'd been busy being lost and messing up an assignment at the time.

"Oh, is that so?" Master Rufus said, beginning to walk. "And what did you see there?"

"The handprints of people who've gone to the Magisterium before," Aaron said, following along. "Some of their relatives. Call's mother."

They walked through a door that Master Rufus opened with his wristband, and down a spiral staircase made of white stone. "Anything else?"

"The First Gate," Tamara told him, looking around in confusion. They hadn't gone this way before. "But it wasn't on."

"Ah." Master Rufus passed his wristband in front of the solid wall and watched as it shimmered and disappeared, revealing another room beyond it. Rufus was smiling at their surprise. "Yes, there are some routes through the school you don't know yet."

They stepped into a room that Call remembered passing through when he'd thought they were lost, with long stalactites and steaming mud heating the air. He spun around, wondering if he'd be able to retrace his way to the door that Master Rufus just showed them, but even if he could, he wasn't sure his wristband would open it.

They ducked through another doorway and found themselves inside the Hall of Graduates. One of the archways seemed to be roiling with some substance, something membranous and alive. The carved words *Prima Materia* glowed with an odd light, as though illuminated from within the letters' grooves.

"Uh," Call said. "What's that?"

The small grin on Master Rufus's face transformed into a wide smile. "You all see it? Good. I thought so. That means you're ready to pass through the First Gate, the Gate of Control. After you pass through it, you will be considered a mage in your own right, and I will give you the metal for your wristband that formally confers upon you the status of Copper Year students. How far you go in your studies after this point will be up to you, but I believe that all three of you are some of the best apprentices I have ever had the pleasure to teach. I hope you continue your studies."

Call looked at Tamara and Aaron. They were grinning at each other and at him. Then Aaron put up a tentative hand.

"But I thought — I mean this is great, but aren't we supposed to pass through the gate at the end of the year? When we graduate?"

Master Rufus raised both his bushy eyebrows. "You are apprentices. That means you learn what you're ready to learn and you pass through the gates when you're ready, not after and certainly not before. If you can see the gate, then you're ready. Tamara Rajavi, you first."

She stepped forward, shoulders back, and walked up to the gate with an awed expression on her face, like she couldn't quite believe it was happening. Reaching out, she touched the swirling center and made a sharp sound, pulling back her fingers in amazement. She glanced over at Call and Aaron, and then, still grinning, stepped through, disappearing from view.

"Now you, Aaron Stewart."

"Okay," Aaron said, nodding and looking a little nervous. He wiped his palms against his gray uniform pants, as though they'd become sweaty. Stepping up to the gate, he threw up his arms and hurled himself into whatever was beyond it, like a football player making a touchdown.

Master Rufus shook his head in amusement, but didn't otherwise comment on Aaron's gate-crossing technique. "Callum Hunt, go ahead," he said.

Call swallowed and moved across the room toward the gate. He remembered what Master Rufus had said, back when he'd told Call why he took him on. *Until a mage passes through the First Gate, his or her magic can be bound by one of the Masters. You would be unable to access the elements, unable to use your power.*

If his magic were bound, then Callum couldn't become the Enemy of Death. Couldn't even become *like* him.

That was what his father had asked Master Rufus to do, sending along Constantine Madden's wristband as a warning. Standing there in front of the gate, Call finally admitted it to himself: Tamara had been right when she'd said his father's warning hadn't been about keeping Call safe. It had been about keeping other people safe *from* him.

This was Call's last chance — his final chance. If he walked through the Gate of Control, his magic could no longer be bound. There would no longer be any easy way to make the world safe from him. To make sure he could never turn on Aaron. To make sure he would never become Constantine Madden.

He thought about going back to regular school, where he didn't have any friends, of spending weekends under the grim eye of his father. He thought of never seeing Aaron and Tamara again and of all the adventures they'd have without him. He thought about Havoc in his bedroom back home and how miserable the wolf would be. He thought of Celia and Gwenda and Rafe and even Master Rufus, thought of the Refectory and the Gallery and all the tunnels he'd never get to explore.

Maybe if he told, things wouldn't go like Master Joseph said. Maybe they wouldn't bind his magic. Maybe they'd help him.

Maybe they'd even tell him that the whole soul thing was impossible — that he was only Callum Hunt and there was nothing to be afraid of, because he wasn't going to become a monster in a silver mask.

But maybe wasn't good enough.

Stepping forward, taking a deep breath and ducking his head, Call walked through the Gate of Control. Magic washed over him, pure and powerful.

He could hear Tamara and Aaron on the other side, laughing.

And despite himself, despite the terrible thing he was doing, despite all of it, Call began to grin.

ABOUT THE AUTHORS

Holly Black and **Cassandra Clare** first met over ten years ago at Holly's first-ever book signing. They have since become good friends, bonding over (among other things) their shared love of fantasy — from the sweeping vistas of The Lord of the Rings to the gritty tales of Batman in Gotham City to the classic sword-and-sorcery epics to *Star Wars*. With Magisterium, they decided to team up to write their own story about heroes and villains, good and evil, and being chosen for greatness, whether you like it or not.

Holly is the bestselling author and co-creator of The Spiderwick Chronicles series and won a Newbery Honor for her novel *Doll Bones*. Cassie is the author of bestselling YA series, including The Mortal Instruments and The Infernal Devices. They both live in Western Massachusetts, about ten minutes away from each other. This is their first collaboration, and marks the start of a five-book series.

Authors' Note

Since we met ten years ago – at Holly's first ever book signing – we've become not just good friends but also critique partners. In helping each other work through the knottiest of plot tangles, we often talked about how much fun it would be if the other person could not just talk us through it, but go ahead and write the scene for us. Which led us, inevitably, to talk about co-writing.

When you decide to co-write a project, you want to focus on themes and storylines that fascinate you both equally.

We both grew up loving fantasy – from the sweeping vistas of *Lord of the Rings* to the gritty tales of Batman in Gotham City to the classic sword and sorcery epics to *Star Wars*. Stories about heroes and villains, good and evil, and being chosen for greatness, whether you like it or not.

And over the last decade, fantasy has had a renaissance. From *Harry Potter* to *The Golden Compass* to the resurgence in superhero narratives to the massive popularity of *Game of Thrones*, mainstream readers know and love fantasy.

Which means readers are familiar with the tropes of fantasy. When they open a fantasy novel or go to see a fantasy movie, they expect to find a chosen hero, whose high and lonely destiny is to defeat the villain, whatever the personal sacrifice to himself.

We wanted to tell a story about a protagonist who had all the markers of a hero – tragedy and secrets in his past, magical power. We wanted people to believe they knew what kind of story they were in for.

When Call discovers that the Masters of the Magisterium are searching for a chosen one, a mage with special powers, we wanted readers to assume that chosen one was Call because that's how the story usually goes.

And then we wanted them to be surprised.

As we wrote, we got interested not just in Call's struggles, but in those of his friends – Tamara and Aaron, Jasper and Celia, Havoc and Warren. We came to love those characters. We hope you'll love them too – we hope you'll laugh and gasp as we did – and most of all, we hope you'll be surprised.

Congratulations Aspirant.

You have been selected to apply for the Magisterium. In order to proceed with your magical education you must pass the following examination.

Remember to show your workings.

1)   A dragon and a wyvern set out at 2 P.M. from the same cavern, headed in the same direction. The average speed of the dragon is 30mph slower than twice the speed of the wyvern. In 2 hours, the dragon is 20 miles ahead of the wyvern. Find the flight speed of the dragon, factoring in that the wyvern is bent on revenge.

_____

_____

_____

2)   Lucretia is preparing to plant a crop of deadly night-shade this autumn. She will plant 4 patches of common night-shade with 15 plants in each patch. She estimates that 20% of the field will be planted with a test crop of woody night-shade. How many nightshade plants are there in all? How many woody nightshade plants were there planted? If Lucretia is an earth mage who has crossed three of the gates, how many people can she poison with the deadly nightshade before she is caught and beheaded?

3)   An apprentice mage is travelling in a small boat downstream. The river flows at an average velocity of 1.5mph.
The nearest cavern chamber is 3 miles away. Halfway there,
the current increases, leading to a new average velocity of
2mph. How long will it take him to reach his destination,
assuming that the mage is able to increase his speed by per-
suading the water to do his bidding?

4)   In *A History of the Devoured*: 1308-1854 by Master J.
R. Allegro, the strengths and weaknesses of these unfortu-
nate creatures are described. Outline these in brief, using
clear examples and case studies.

5)   Six water mages enter the void before teatime armed
with twelve emeralds and a handful of lichen. What are the
odds of the mages escaping within the following ten thousand
years?

_____

_____

_____

6)   Jack has one fire orb twice the size of Jane's. Jane has three fire orbs less than Billy. Given that Billy has five medium-sized fire orbs, how many more fire orbs will they need to disperse the rogue elemental that is attacking them?

_____

_____

_____

7)   If you have fourteen lizard elementals tunnelling into an underground cave, what is the probability that an air mage will transform into a sea serpent?

_____

_____

_____

8)   Fire wants to   _____

      Water wants to   _____

      Air wants to rise   _____

      Earth wants to   _____

      Chaos wants to   _____

A Q & A with Holly Black and Cassandra Clare

What first inspired you both to write the *Magisterium* series?

For both of us, it was a love of fantasy. We have always been huge fans of this genre and we wanted to play with people's expectations of the books. They expect the main character to be the hero, the one destined to save them all. With Callum Hunt, it's a bit more complicated than that . . .

Were there any books or films that influenced your writing of *Magisterium*?

Lots and lots! There are such a broad range of books and films that inspired us and fed our imaginations whilst writing *Magisterium*: *Lord of the Rings*, *Harry Potter*, *Percy Jackson*, lots of comic books, anything which features a battle of good versus evil and characters struggling to overcome a darkness within themselves.

Call Hunt is a complex character. There's a lot of anger in him, and he has to face some difficult choices during the book. Unlike most kids, he's not interested in learning magic at the start of the book. How did you come up with the character of Call?

It was precisely his lack of interest in magic that excited us about his character. Kids usually love magic! Who wouldn't want to go to magic school?! But Call isn't like that. His whole life he's been told that the Magisterium is a dark and dangerous place as well as being responsible for his mother's death. We loved exploring Call's journey as he learns more about the school and begins to discover what he can achieve as an apprentice mage.

What's the best advice you can give to aspiring writers?

There is a special mantra we writers use: BICHOK – Butt in chair. Hands on keyboard.

The special trick is to keep writing! Even when you don't feel like it and you just want to hurl your laptop out of the window, just keep writing. Try to have fun with it too – writing can be very frustrating and draining at times, so it's important not to lose the sense of excitement you felt when you first imagined the story coming together and the characters began to form in your mind.

Where do you both do your best thinking?

Holly: I have a secret library in my house which is the perfect place to write. There's something about having a hidden space that really allows you to switch off from all of the other things you have to think about and focus on the story. I think being surrounded by books helps too – it reminds you what all the work and effort is building towards and that it will all be worthwhile in the end.

Cassie: I find it really hard to work at home. I get very easily distracted by reality TV or my cats, so I usually escape to local coffee shops and restaurants for a change of scene.

How do you find being on tour?

Going on tour is always a really fun experience. It's a chance for us to escape from our writing desks and go and meet our fans. We love hearing their reactions to our books: who their favourite characters are, what part they loved best. Writing can be a very solitary experience, so it's wonderful to be reminded that the books are out there reaching people. To see that your stories are exciting readers across the world is really special and makes all those moments where you are despairing over the next line worthwhile!

What are your favourite books?

Cassie: Picking a favourite book is like having a favourite child or family member – impossible! There are so many books I love which have influenced me over the years. To name just a few: *The Hunger Games*, *Twilight*, *Daughter of Smoke and Bone*, the *Alanna* series, everything by John Green. I could go on and on and on.

Holly: So many to choose from! I grew up reading books like *Interview with a Vampire*, *Tales from the Flat Earth*, *The Crystal Cane*, all of Tolkien. When I went to college, I discovered Neil Gaiman and devoured all of his books.

How did you first meet each other and start working together?

We have known each other for a long time. We first met on book tours promoting our earlier books and became friends straight away. This project has been the culmination of years of brainstorming and working together.

The writing process is really interesting as we write alternate chapters and physically hand the laptop to each other once we're done. Working on *Magisterium* has been a fascinating experience – we've learnt so much from working together and it's really useful having another person to bounce ideas off.

What magical powers would you love to have?

Cassie: I would like to be invisible so that I could sneak into movie theaters and spend time in museums after they close.

Holly: I would like the magical power of never needing to sleep and never being tired. But until I get that, I have coffee.

MAGISTERIUM

HOLLY BLACK & CASSANDRA CLARE

team up again for book two in the series.

SEPTEMBER 2015